"Had we not pursed the hydrogen bomb, there is a very real threat we would all be speaking Russian. I have no regrets."

-Edward Teller. Father of the thermonuclear detonation.
Ivy Mike. 1952.

Carl Lakeland

Project AMBER

RELOADED

THE MILESTONE INCIDENT

First Published in Australia by Carl Lakeland 2017

Copyright © Carl Lakeland 2018
Typesetting: Carl Lakeland
Editing and Proof Reading: Trent Maier, Jodie Payne, Anne Parry.
Cover design: Carl Lakeland, and Damonza.com

The right of Carl Lakeland to be identified as Author of the Work has been asserted in accordance with the Copyright, Designs and Patents Act 1988.

ISBN number: 9780987619891 (hardback)

All rights reserved. No part of this publication may be reproduced, stored in a retrieval system, or transmitted, in any form or by any means without the prior written permission of the publisher, nor be otherwise circulated in any form of binding or cover other than that in which it is published and without a similar condition being imposed on the subsequent purchaser.

A catalogue record for this book is available from the National Library of Australia

Table of Contents

ONE

The Circle Opens

CHAPTER ONE

Alice Springs, Central Australia 1996

MY MOTHER HAD SWITCHED OFF everything that used electricity. The fridge. The dishwasher. The radio that she loved so much on Sunday afternoons while she sat in her easy chair and spun Merino wool into long curly skeins. The tall clock that demanded attention at the end of the hall stood proud but no longer ticked. There was no whirring of the Whirlpool from the laundry. There was no scent of freshly baked lamingtons or vanilla slices from the kitchen. There were no songs by Hi-Five from the television in the living room. There was no laughter. There was no happiness. There was nothing. And everything was dark.

After pulling down all the blinds, my mother scurried around the place, and with her hands visibly shaking, she reached with her trembling fingers, clawing at power points and switches. She raced methodically from one switch to another, muttering to herself as though somewhere in her mind there was a method in the things she was doing. But I could see it on her face. Her skin was sweaty. I was just old enough to recognise panic. I was old enough to feel brewing terror that made my skin feel incredibly hot. I remember as my mother scampered around the place; I kept telling myself it was just a game. It was, of course, no game at all. "Quickly, Angelique. We have to hide," my mother said with a voice that crackled and quivered.

My mother's eyes darted here and there. Was she trying to decide the best place in the house for us to hide? We had no basement or attic. There was only one place inside the house which had a lock behind the door — the bathroom. I recall as a child; there were so many times I got into trouble if I stayed in the shower for too long. The door was locked. Nobody could do anything about it. My mother decided to hide in there as soon as she grabbed me tightly by the top of my arm. She pulled me forcefully into the cold darkness behind the shower curtain. In the bathtub, we both quietly sat down facing each other. My mother's facial expression was steady as she appeared to listen for signs of movement from the outside of our house.

"Mum?"

"Shhh. We'll be safe in here," my mother told me while she held her finger up to her lips.

"But Mum, Dad will know we're home. Our car is at the end of the driveway. He'll come looking for us as soon as he gets inside."

"He can't get in. He doesn't have a key. I've changed all the locks. And he'll think we're at Maggie's house."

If my father knew we were at Maggie's house, he'd never go looking there. Maggie's husband was an Alice Springs police officer. And not only that, he was a sergeant, I recall thinking. My father and Theo were always at each other. Theo sometimes brought my drunken father home late at night and dumped him near our front door. My young mind began to put things together. What my mother was trying to achieve was to give my father a decoy. He'd turn up at our house and find he wasn't able to enter. He'd put his ear up to the door and listen for anything inside. My father would then most likely choose to meet with his mates at the pub. Or maybe an afternoon betting on horse races at the TAB. That's how my mother had explained it. She said it to me in plain words and sentences like I was already an adult. Then after she was done, she began to cry.

"Mum, you're scaring me."

My mother pulled me into her chest and wrapped her arms around me. I remember feeling nothing could ever hurt us. Any ten-year-old would be comforted. But I was also cautious. I was also vigilant. Why did Uncle Scotty have to show up and ruin everything?

* * *

As I sat in the cold and darkened bathroom with my mother, who seemed to be thinking of ways to get us out of danger, I reflected briefly on the horrible things that had happened. I remembered the blue, square, object that Uncle Scotty had given her after he arrived so urgently on our front porch. My uncle's tone of voice said he was hopelessly in a mad flap. "You need to get this to Maggie," I heard him say. "I'd do it, but I can't, love. You know I'm on the grid. If I approach Maggie, I'll blow my cover."

I recall as I stood and peered through the living room window, my Uncle Scotty gave my mother something else. It was something that looked like a handkerchief—a piece of cloth with something printed on it. He took it from his pocket and thrust it into my mother's hand. "These are the decryption codes for the computer disk," he said.

"So, what am I supposed to do with them?"

"Alisha. Get them to Maggie. Find a way. She'll know what to do next."

"And Franco? Any ideas where he is right now?"

Scotty immediately answered without a breath. “He’s most likely down the pub gettin’ plastered. Maybe . . . I’m not sure.”

“You can’t be sure? This place is so much better when you’re both away on work. The two of you should’ve stayed at Pine Gap!” My mother sucked back a big gulp of air and paused a beat. “How much time do we have before he shows up?”

“You’ve got as much time as it takes to grab a few things and get out, I reckon. Grab your kit and go. Right-bloody-now.”

After Scotty launched himself from the porch, ran to his car and drove away, my mother slowly closed the front door. She turned and looked down at me. I’ll never forget her face. Her skin was paper white. Her eyes had become glassy like they were full of fear and sadness. I knew she tried her best to hide her true feelings from me. I could see straight through her. I knew what was *really* going on.

“Angelique, we have to pack a bag and get ready to go. Quickly now, kiddo.”

I sprinted into my room, thinking about the things I needed to pack. I slid open my wardrobe door and grabbed my rucksack from the hanger. My mind immediately thought about my camera and photos. They were up on a high shelf. I often wondered why my mother had placed them up so high that it was difficult for me to get to them. My toes almost broke with my weight as I reached up to grab them. I jumped and missed. I jumped and missed again. It was no good. Then, I used the bed as a trampoline. That worked amazingly well, and I had my camera and all my photo albums, all at once.

After ramming my most precious items into my rucksack, I grabbed some of my clothes from my dresser and quickly formed them into a tight ball, shoving them in so hard I swore they were going to burst through the bottom. My mother stepped inside my room as I was finishing up. She brought the objects in that Scotty gave her. She showed them to me. "If anything bad happens, make sure Maggie gets these things." My mother then slipped the blue computer disk and codes into the top pocket of the rucksack. As soon as she was done tightening the straps, she held out her hand to me. "Let's go," she said. "Fuck this place."

We were only five footsteps from my bedroom door when that sound of someone pushing a key into a keyhole, punched through the silence. My mother instantly crouched and pushed me down next to her. She put a finger up to her lips. I knew what it meant. Not a sound. Not a movement. Just like the game we used to play called 'quiet as a mouse.'

As we both crouched, whoever it was at the front door continued to scratch away at the lock. Then, the Mad Man made himself known.

"Alisha!"

My mother looked at me with terror sitting in her red-rimmed eyes. She again pushed her finger up to her lips. When she removed her finger, she tried to give me a comforting smile. But the corners of her mouth refused to cooperate.

"Alisha! Open the bloody door!" My father bashed the door a couple of times.

"Don't say anything," my mother said to me in a whisper so low, it was difficult to hear. But then she physically turned me around and gave me a gentle push toward my bedroom. "Go. Quietly," she whispered.

"Alisha. Open the door. My key won't fit the bloody lock!"

I couldn't be sure how many times my father had yelled out and demanded to be let inside. Each time he yelled out, his voice raised in obvious frustration. His bashing at the door became louder and heavier. Then, there was no sound at all. He was gone. And my mother immediately began shutting things down and switching things off.

* * *

In the darkness of the bathroom from behind the shower curtain, we both waited in the cold silence. I could feel the steady beat of my mother's heart through her chest as she held me tightly in her arms. Sometimes her heartbeat picked up and raced race as soon as she heard sounds from outside. But through it all, it occurred to me; we could've easily used the time to exit through the back door and get far away. It might've worked out better than being boxed in. We could've already arrived at Maggie's house. And after having arrived there, we could've been safe from the rage of my drunken father. Things and events could have been drastically different than they turned out. It was a moment in time that has stayed with me for my entire life. I keep asking myself the same question. Why didn't we go? In that precise moment? Why? All through my twenties. All through my thirties. Even to this very minute, it still causes me heartache. It still causes nightmares and chills me awake. Why can't I go back and change anything? Why?

It was as though my mother had the same thought as me, and at the same time. She let go of me and looked down into my eyes. She seemed so much better without any panic. I was even able to breathe long breaths again. "Time to go, eh kiddo?"

I nodded my happiness, but my moment of joy shattered with the sound of someone scraping at the lock in the back door. My father was back from wherever he'd gone. He was angry. I could hear it in his tone. "Alisha! You've bloody-well changed the back-door lock too? What have you done? Are you doing this to make me angry? Alisha, this is my house too. Let-me-in!"

I shrunk from my father's rage. "Mum!"

My mother pulled me into her arms again. "It's okay kiddo. But I want you to understand something. Whatever happens, run. Run as fast as you can. Take the rucksack and run to Maggie's. Don't look back. Don't worry about me. Just run. Do you hear me? Just run."

I nodded, hoping my mother could feel my answer on her chest.

"That's good. You know what you need to do. That's good." It was as though my mother had said those final words to herself rather than to me. It was after she'd said it, I noticed for the first time how badly she was trembling.

But then, silence ensued once again. We both waited. We both listened out for the slightest of sounds. It was as though my father had finally left. Each moment felt more like hours, and we waited.

SMASH!

I heard a window somewhere near the back of the house, cave in and shatter.

"MUM!"

My mother pulled me in tighter. Much tighter than before.

I heard my father stomping with heavy footsteps around the house. "Alisha! Where are you? Are you home? Angelique?"

My mother immediately got out of the bathtub and went to the window. She used both her hands to push the ages-old window up, but it wouldn't budge. She put her entire weight behind it. It was no good.

"Smash it, Mum. Just smash it."

"No good, kiddo. The glass has got wire inside it."

Then, my father's footsteps stopped at the bathroom door. I could hear him breathing as though he'd pushed his face up close to the door jamb. My mother put her hand over my mouth. She placed her lips right next to my left ear and whispered, "Not a word, kiddo. Shhh."

"C'mon Alisha, I know you're in there. Angelique. I know you're both there. The car's outside, remember? I'm tired, and I need a lie-down. C'mon out and we'll chat a while. Maybe, I'll put a few snags on the barbie. What do ya reckon?"

For some reason, my mother took her hand away from my mouth. Perhaps it was a moment of weakness. Maybe she was about to get up and let my father inside. I couldn't let her do that. I had to stop her. I seized the opportunity, and I shouted, "Just go away and leave us alone!"

"Kiddo! What have you done? Didn't I say not a word?"

"Ya see? I knew you were both at home. Now, c'mon out, the two of ya. This is being silly; don't ya reckon?"

"Go away, Franco. Take the car keys; they're on the kitchen bench. Go away and leave us in peace."

"Peace? Do'ya want peace? I'll show ya fucking peace!" It was like my father's rage came rushing up from wherever he'd put it last. This time, he beat heavily on the door. "Don't make me break this door in, Alisha. I will break it if I need to. Come out! Come out now!"

I screamed as loud as I could. I hoped my high pitch squeal was enough to grab anybody's attention who might be in range. Perhaps the people from next door would hear. Maybe they'd call Theo Mack, and he'd rush down here with his siren blaring and his lights flashing. But even for someone as young as I was at the time, I knew it wasn't likely.

Then it was like a miracle. Suddenly, my father's footsteps walked away. I heard him walk through the kitchen, grabbing at the keys that my mother had told him were on the bench. I heard him a couple of minutes later start the car. The car reversed up the driveway, and my father was gone.

It was like a weight had lifted from my spirits. Even my mother looked happier than she was only a moment ago. We both cautiously exited the bathroom. I ran straight for my bedroom and picked up my rucksack. “Come on Mum; we need to get going to Maggie’s. Let’s go.” I was happy that I could make a suggestion. My mother even laughed a little under her breath. “Oh, I see. You’re making all the calls now, huh?”

“Let’s go, Mum, let’s go.”

We were about to leave.

We were both about to exit our house of horrors, and I couldn’t have cared less if it was for the last time in my young life. I was happy to be away and to be safe. But just as we were at the back door, my mother suddenly stopped her forward momentum. I grabbed her arm and pulled her. “What’s wrong? C’mon Mum. We’re running out of time.”

“No, kiddo. We’ll stay here. Your father already knows where we’re going, and he’ll be waiting for us somewhere.”

I watched in dismay as my mother closed the back door, then grabbed a chair from the dining room. She brought the chair back with her and wedged the chair under the doorknob. “I’ll make a phone call to Theo Mack, and he can sort this out; once and for all.”

I couldn’t believe what I was seeing. We had the chance to get away, and it was gone. Even if it were only to the house next door, even if that were the case, we’d still be away. But now . . . We were again trapped. There was only one thing left for me to do. And that was to get under my bed as far as I could get and hide. I ran there. I ran to my bedroom while my mother picked up the phone. I heard her jiggle the hanger a couple of times. “Hello?” Another jiggle. Another jiggle. “Hello!” I heard my mother draw an annoyed sigh before she banged the handset hard down. “Shit!”

As I lay hidden under my bed, my eyes began to fill with tears. I was now more scared than I can ever remember. I only hoped the chair at the back door was strong enough to keep my father out. Just as I had that thought, the back door exploded into what I thought must be more than a thousand pieces.

I hurried out from under my bed and raced to the back door to where my father was standing in the aperture; a gigantic sledgehammer dangled ominously from his grip. It occurred to me then that this was his solution to the locked bathroom door. I realised much later in life, had my mother and I still been in there; we would've been much more boxed in and vulnerable than we already were. Maybe my father would've killed us both.

As I stood, shocked, seeing my father with his face that told of nothing but hatred and anger, I managed to catch sight of my mother as she suddenly burst past me. "Get out! Get out! Get out!" my mother screamed with words that still chill me after all this time. She tried with all her weight to push my father back through the door. He grabbed my mother and spun her around. He locked his elbow around the base of her throat and squeezed. "Now, none of that," my father said in cold tone. "You don't have to be all pushy. I'll go. But you know what I want don't ya? I want those things my mate Scotty-Blue gave ya. I know you have the disk and codes. Give them to me, and I'm gone, Alisha."

My mother managed some words through her squeezed neck. "Franco . . . What're you talking about?"

"Don't play games with me. Don't-you-fucking-play-games-with-me!"

I picked up my rucksack and threw it at my father with all the strength I had in my body. "Leave my mother ALONE!"

"Angelique . . . run. Run, Angelique. RUN!"

My father laughed at me. He laughed hard, and sardonically like he'd seen something so very funny. He let my mother go. But only for a second. It was like he had all the power. He quickly gathered her up and choked her all over again.

"Angelique! RUN!"

"No Mum. I can't leave you!"

"Just . . . run . . . kiddo!"

My father squeezed his elbow around my mother's throat harder than before. Her face immediately went cherry red. Her eyes bulged, and I saw blood at the corners of her eyelids. She tried to say something, but it never came out. Her body went limp, and after my father let go of her, she slid slowly to the floor. Then, my father turned his attention on me. He reached and grabbed a handful of my hair. I remember the hot pain on my scalp as he picked me up and swung me. I floated only inches above the floor. "You're going in your bloody room, and you're gonna STAY THERE!"

After my father had thrown me through the doorway, I again slid under my bed as far as I could get. My cheeks felt raw and wet as I cried uncontrollably. But my father paused, laughing at me like my sobbing was one of the funniest things he'd ever seen. Before slamming my door closed, he shouted, "And don't come out!"

* * *

While I lay there, I listened as my father stomped around the house. I heard him rummage through drawers then slam them closed. I heard cupboard doors open, and I imagined the contents thrown across the room. I heard clanging of pots and pans. I heard the smashing of glass. I heard my father racing around the house. "Where is it? What have you done with it?"

"I don't know what you're talking about, Franco. You must be out of your mind. Go back to your mates at the pub. Maybe they know where it is what you're looking for."

I was glad I heard my mother's voice, but I was also terribly afraid for her. I heard my father's heavy footsteps rush across the floor. Then, the ugly sound of his fist connecting with flesh.

"NOOO!" I scampered madly from under my bed and ran out of my room. I saw my father standing over my mother. I launched myself onto my father's back, I began beating him as hard as I could.

My mother pleaded with me; her voice so dry. "Angelique. Stop. Please stop. I'm okay."

Before I had the opportunity to do more damage, my father peeled me off his back. He again lifted me by my hair and carried me to my bedroom. He tossed me like a pendulum with such force, I flew through the air and landed heavily on my bed. I grabbed my pillow and buried my face as I cried harder than I'd ever known.

Outside my room, I heard them arguing. The bickering went on and on and on. He wanted whatever he wanted, and she wasn't about to let him have it. Back and forth, they fought. Sometimes it was physical with the awful sounds of fleshy beatings. If I knew my mother, she'd give back just as much as what she was given. Maybe that would make things worse. She screamed at him. He yelled back at her. Hurtful and spiteful. Cruel and cutting. Words and sounds a child should never have to endure.

But suddenly, everything stopped.

I felt an urge rip up through my body. I felt as though there were eyes upon me. There was something outside of my bedroom window; I just knew it. Looking out, I saw an eagle had settled and had found a perch on the back fence. The moment the eagle's eyes made contact with mine, I knew it was not just any eagle, but it had to be *my* eagle. It was Charlotte.

It was at that moment that all my sadness and hurt had melted away. I felt strength take over the weakness in my body. I sprinted from my room and out through the back door. I cut a short distance across the back yard toward where Charlotte was busy, happily preening her feathers as though she was making herself beautiful just for me. I couldn't have been happier than in that moment. It was one of the most delightful times of my life. As I approached Charlotte, it was as though she beckoned me closer, and when I got there, she put her head down and flared out her huge wings in a warm gesture of hello.

I don't know how long I was there in Charlotte's company. It seemed like only minutes. But after Charlotte had lifted her head again, she appeared to become startled. She turned away from me and put her head down. She looked over her shoulder one last time before she launched into the sky; her huge wingspan compressing the air as she lifted herself into the sky.

I stood back and watched Charlotte disappear into the afternoon sun. And after she'd gone, my thoughts returned to the horrors of which I was given just a small amount of respite. Remembering my father's words to 'not come out of my room,' I slowly turned to get back into the house, but instantly, my legs stopped carrying me forward.

"Time to come in, love. It's gonna be tea-time soon," my father said as he stood there on the back veranda, watching me.

But in my mind, a warning sounded, and somehow, I knew not to go to him. As he repeated the same sentence over, I noticed the sledgehammer in my father's grip. I noticed the thick dark coloured blood that dripped in steady drops from the shiny metal. I noticed the red stains on his white singlet. I noticed the blood spatter all over his face and arms. He repeated his words slowly. "Come inside, Angelique. Tea-time."

My legs were like pins that held me into place. Not forward. Not backward. I was frozen still. I felt coldness sweep up and over me, giving me goosebumps on my arms and neck as my father appeared to grow angrier with each passing second. "Get inside you little bitch!"

I moved one foot in front of the other. Then the other in front of that. Slowly, I gained speed, and in the next crucial second, I began sprinting across the back yard toward the gate. As I moved as fast as I could go, I caught sight of my father as he hitched the sledgehammer over his shoulder and launched himself off the veranda. "Get back here!" he screamed. I ran. I ran hard.

At the back gate, I jumped and cleared it with my father only inches behind me. I felt the breeze of his sledgehammer swish past me. I could hear his hard breathing as he struggled to get over. I ran on and paced away. Breathing. Running. Breathing. Running.

Out in the street, I turned and sprinted down the middle of the bitumen. If a car was coming, I could put up my arms and scream. Maybe whoever was driving might stop. As I ran, I saw a shadow on the road. The shadow of an eagle raced on ahead in front of me, and then suddenly, it disappeared. From behind, I heard an eagle screech with an ear-piercing cry and echoed through the suburbs. I stopped and spun around in time to see Charlotte's silhouette in the late afternoon sun. Her outline became backlit from the bright sunlight, as she tumbled and turned over high in the sky. I saw Charlotte as she tucked in her wings and became a bullet, head down, screeching her cry through the air as my father ran almost out of breath, panting, and still trying to shut me down.

With no warning, Charlotte came down from behind him and attached her giant talons around my father's neck. Screeching and squealing, she flared out her wings, and I saw her talons disappear deep into his flesh. Long red ribbons ripped away from my father's neck as Charlotte again took to the skies. My father screamed out then gurgled chillingly in a way I'd never heard before. He placed both his hands over his gaping open wounds but to no avail. The fountains of his blood reached high above him. Then, his body seemed to collapse from under his weight. I knew from that moment; there was no life left in him. The Mad Man was dead.

From a distance, I heard the sounds of sirens. Theo Mack would arrive, but by the time he reached the scene where blood was everywhere, the mandatory police 'guns drawn' approach was of no use. Theo exited his police vehicle exactly as I thought. "Get on the ground!" he shouted; pistol pointed at my lifeless father. When he got close enough, I saw his shoulders droop, and he put his gun away.

As I turned away from what I was seeing, Maggie was there, standing in front of me with her arms held out. "Come with me, love," she said, gathering me up and pulling me into her arms. Maggie smelled of lavender. After that moment, lavender took on a new meaning for me. Whenever I smell lavender, it transports me back to the time I was orphaned and left without my parents. My Angel saved me from the Mad Man, but now, I must somehow live with the memory.

CHAPTER TWO

Melbourne Present Day

OUT ON PORT PHILLIP BAY, the *Spirit of Tasmania* clung to her moorings. From where I stood, I saw people lined up, resembling a trail of ants on a mission, as they'd begun boarding via long gangways. I saw vehicles of all descriptions nose to tail that were all making a line to get going.

HMAS Canberra, with her strange upturned bow, sat in the water, up close and personal, to the Bass Straight Ferry. I assumed *Canberra* had cut her way silently through the heads during the night, while most of Melbourne slept. And berthed behind *Canberra* was the Nimitz-class nuclear-powered super-carrier, the *USS John Steinbeck*. She was a monster of a warship – a city to herself. It wouldn't have surprised me, in the least, if *Steinbeck* had her own weather patterns that followed her wherever she went, and she towered ominously out of the water, dwarfing all other ships in close proximity, making them appear to be nothing more than bath toys.

From the balcony of my apartment in Port Melbourne, I couldn't help but cast a critical eye over the US Flagship. I wasn't as happy to see her as most citizens of Melbourne, and I had valid reasons for my concerns. The Americans were either remaining silent or lying.

I'd spent hours digging and searching, utilising all the sources I had available. Every little possibility of the answer I was looking for, in the end . . . led me nowhere. Then it hit me. After I realised it, I knew it in my heart that I'd found the Americans' Achilles Heel. As I played it around in my head, what I discovered had the potential to wreck relationships. America was a friend and ally to Australia. What could happen to our alliance if I choose to speak my mind?

From my balcony, and looking out over the bay, I tapped the tip of my cigarette on the back of my hand. After lighting up, I hoped the rush of nicotine would help settle my mind. I drew back smoke and held it in my lungs, wishing it had the same effect as something else that wasn't quite legal. My mind thumped hard. It was going to be one hell of a day.

I felt a hand land gently on my shoulder. Those horrible thoughts about *Steinbeck* melted away to the back of my mind as I turned around to meet Jenny's sweet gaze.

"Coffee for the birthday girl?" Jenny smiled, handing me my favourite mug of coffee that smelt so heavenly. Only God knew how much I needed the caffeine. I needed anything to help make this day easier.

"Thanks . . . Another birthday. I forgot. How about that?"

"Oh, I think you remembered, all right. You just choose to ignore."

"You know I don't like birthdays. It's my right to forget. And why you keep insisting I have them is beyond my better understanding."

Jenny laughed, then I watched her eyes regard my smoking habit. "Better enjoy them while you have them. Who knows how many of them you have left?"

"Ouch!" I immediately stubbed out the cigarette.

"Seriously, Angel. The handrail?"

"It needs paint anyway."

I smiled, then I turned to avoid Jenny's scorn. I peered back toward the *Steinbeck*. My mind drifted to that bloody subject all over again.

"How do you think you'll go?" Jenny asked me from behind.

"I really don't know. But I reckon it's no big deal." Yeah. I lied.

"No big deal? You've just turned thirty. You're the youngest journalist in history who's managed to score an interview, one-on-one, with the US Secretary of State. Who else could do that?"

"Sometimes, Jen, I just wish I could get back behind the lens where I used to be."

"Why on earth would you want to do that?" Jenny said while taking a seat on the metal chair and placing her mug noisily down. I wondered if she did that on purpose just to gee me up. Gosh, where's my head? This business with *Steinbeck* is getting to me.

"The tabloid press is no place for you, Angel. They're all a bunch of dogs biting each other to get to a bone."

"Yeah, I know. But I think it'd be nice just to have a break for a while. I miss my camera. And I miss the action down on the streets."

While I gazed once again out at the *Steinbeck,* my thoughts returned to the documents I'd received as an email attachment. The dossier included all the interview questions I was expected to share with Madam Secretary and listed with those questions were her prepared responses. Protocol, I kept thinking. It all amounted to rules, regulations, and the need to keep things tight. But my interview questions were at best described as lacklustre. I knew it was my job to break the protocol. I knew I had to bring up the *Steinbeck* debacle and bloody-well throw it at her!

Nathan Masters. If it wasn't for him, I wouldn't be in this mess right now. Nathan had discovered that *Steinbeck's* arrival was unauthorised. The United States Chief of Naval Operations had informed Australian officials, and The Australian Nuclear Safety Commission—dubbed 'Nuke Patrol'—of the US impending arrival. Things went bad for them after the Americans chose to button their lips and keep quiet about their planned manoeuvres. However, because of their non-disclosure of operations, Nuke Patrol flat out rejected the *Steinbeck*'s entry into Port Phillip Bay. The super-carrier arrived anyway, blatantly ignorant to the instructions of the Australian nuclear watchdog.

Now, I had a choice.

One – Play it safe and go with the interview down to the letter. Two – Take a risk and give air to something that will never go down well. But I'd already decided. I'm all about risk. Safe is for wussbags. But how could I manage it? And was it at all possible? My mind began to twist with trying to find an answer, and then, I was most rudely interrupted from my train of thought with the vibration of my mobile phone in my pocket.

Jenny's eyes were full of words.

"What is it, Jen?"

"Nothing. Go ahead and read your messages."

Messages received.

Nathan: "Angel. Congrats on your birthday. Big 3—0 today, huh? I remember it well."

That made me smile.

Delete. Next message.

Chief: "Congrats Angel. Have a great birthday."

Hmmm.

Delete. Next message.

Melanie: "Hey Angel. Happy Birthday. Hugs."

She'd better have my coffee ready when I get there. Just saying.

Delete. Next message.

Eddie: "Angel. H.B. Enjoy."

I'll be needing your expertise later today, Eddie.

Delete. Next message.

Sender unknown: "Happy birthday Angelique."

I don't know what I must've looked like from the outside. Everything inside me went still. I hadn't used the name 'Angelique' in . . . how long?

I fingered and swiped the screen and then flipped to my contacts. Nothing. The number didn't match anything in my address book either. Was this some kind of sick joke? Was this supposed to rattle me? Get me all out of whack for my interview?

"Something wrong?" Jenny asked.

"Nothing . . ." I quickly tapped out a reply.

Angel: "Who is this?"

Send.

But it seemed like minutes before the message actually left my phone.

Message failed, Retry?

"*What* . . . is going on?"

I heard Jenny leave her seat and she appeared behind me. "Hon? What is it?"

"Somebody sent me a message. I don't know who. It's weird."

"A random prankster?"

"Maybe. But how does this person know my name?"

"You're on the telly. That's not hard."

"My old name. Angelique. It's been twenty years since . . ."

Without looking up from the screen I was about to dial the number but then I held back. What if it was a scam? I shut the phone down and stuck it deep in my pocket.

* * *

I tried to let things slide as I met Jenny in the kitchen. I was protective of her, and probably a little too much. Jenny didn't need the worry, and I guessed for her to be living with a *'celebrity'* must've been at times difficult to cope with. But she was also master at hiding her true feelings if she knew it would be to my detriment. It was as though Jenny was also as protective of me.

Jenny smiled warmly as I approached her. "You might've forgotten your birthday, but I haven't. There's a small package for you on the table," Jenny said as she pointed with suds that dripped from the tips of her fingers.

Still distracted by that strange message, I regarded the package Jenny had left on the dining table. The package was wrapped in silver paper and tied with a red bow. I noticed a birthday card was tucked underneath. "Jenny, you've gone to so much trouble." I unwrapped the package, noticing the scent of my favourite perfume. Obsession. That just made everything even more wonderful. My eyes went to Jenny who was smiling like I'd never seen her smile before. From a very expensive-looking polished timber box, I retrieved a figurine of an eagle which I knew must've been delicately crafted from rock crystal. Holding it up to the light, I suddenly found myself overwhelmed. "Oh, Jen, It's beautiful. How on earth . . . where on earth . . .?"

"I saw it at Federation Square. It's just you, isn't it?"

I held it up and spun it around. The rock crystal figurine also had a gold inclusion running diagonally through the base, stopping at the tip of one flared out wing.

"I don't know what to say." My eyes went all watery as I held the figurine up a final time and looked at it with awe. I placed it on the bookshelf, giving it pride of place, setting it among the other figurines, statuettes, and dioramas of eagles which were set in various poses and postures. "I think I'll call this one Charlotte."

* * *

I burst out of the elevator checking my watch at the same time. 10:42 am. Late again. I juggled my briefcase and dossiers as I cut my way across the newsroom floor. The chatter. The sounds of telephones ringing. The sounds of live and breaking news echoed around from several strategically mounted LCDs above workstations. Normal as ever. I almost made it to my office door unscathed. Unchallenged. The relief at just that. My PA met me as I strode, carrying a cardboard tray with large paper cups containing black and unsweetened coffee. My hand fell on the door handle and I entered my office with Melanie at my heel.

My Desk . . . I must get there.

I pulled my chair out and sat heavily down. Time to breathe. Melanie closed the door quietly behind her and placed my coffee down on my desk. "Wow . . . Angel, ready to do this?"

I could have given Melanie a straight answer. Umm-no. But I decided a quick change of subject would do. “Melanie. Where're my missives for this morning?”

“Nothing yet.”

“Thank goodness. Bloody traffic, Mel. It does my head in.”

“There’s the tram. Why not give it a try?”

“Yes, and get a cold. No thanks.”

I couldn’t help it. My eyes were already on my coffee. The aroma of Colombian legal crop reached my senses. Breathe, and something delightful to enjoy. “Is she in Melbourne yet?”

“Her PR sent a memo. The US Secretary of State will be on time. Are you looking forward to it?”

Melanie giggled.

I sighed. “Yes . . . and no.”

I thumbed through the dossier pages over again. I flipped to the back page, then back to the front. “This interview isn’t how I would’ve preferred it to go. These questions suck big time, Mel. I’ll look like an idiot in front of the US Secretary of State if I stick to this bullshit.” I closed the file and slammed it down.

It was the first time I saw Melanie without her smile. I realised it then how a smile-less face didn’t suit her. I almost wanted to kick my own arse.

“So . . . Chief tells me Madam Secretary has insisted on a delayed telecast. Why am I not surprised? I wonder what kind of feed buffer she’s requested?”

“Chief didn’t tell you?”

“He managed to get side-tracked when we spoke. He said there was going to be a delay. He didn’t tell me how much of a buffer.”

“I’m not sure. Eddie would know more. As a matter of fact, I think I overheard someone saying there’s a twenty second buffer for tonight’s scheduled program.”

“Twenty seconds? bloody hell! This won’t do.”

"It's there for her security, Angel."

"It's there so she can't stuff up. Nothing more. Do you realise, the *Steinbeck* is here without formal authorisation?"

"No. I didn't know. How is it possible?"

"The Americans just muscled their way in. Ignorant to anything. Know what that means?"

Melanie finally sat down. After she sat, she placed a hand to her chin. Now, I was worried. "No Nuke Patrol security measures?"

"There're no nuclear protocols set up," I replied. "But worse than that, Mel. Non-disclosure of operations. They shut up shop. There must be a reason for doing that. I mean, what a risk to take. Are we supposed to let it slide? This is serious. This is the kind of news that has my name on it and I can't break this if there's a twenty second feed delay. No, it won't do. Tonight needs to be live as it happens."

"I'll get Eddie up here pronto," Melanie said as she quickly got out of her chair. "Was there anything else I can get you?"

"That's it for now. Oh, and by the way, I love your outfit. You know you're going to have to tell me where you got those boots."

"Thanks, Angel." Melanie beamed brightly. She was Melanie again. "Don't forget. Makeup and wardrobe at 3:00 pm sharp."

* * *

Just as I thought I was finally getting my head around things, my desk phone suddenly rang, slicing the silence, causing me to startle. I glanced down thinking perhaps I should let it ring out. My voicemail could have this one. But my mind went back to that message again. The phone kept ringing. I put a hand on the handset. Crap, it wasn't going to voicemail.

"Hello, newsroom."

"Angel," Nathan Masters said urgently. Why did he always sound like he was calling from the Moon?

"Oh . . . thank god, Nathan. Why don't you ever reply to my emails in a timely manner? Have you read the interview dossier?"

"Canter," Nathan said. "You're on a desk line. It's Canter."

"Sorry . . . Canter."

"Yeah, I've read the dossier."

"And?"

"At first, I thought—it is, what it is. Nothing anyone can do about it. But then I thought if it were me? I'd be bloody upset right now. So, I reckon you'd be wanting to break the protocol. Am I right?"

"I'm stuffed, Nathan . . ."

"Canter."

"I somehow have to bring up the rejection order on live TV. But Madam Secretary, in all her wisdom, has requested a twenty second buffer on the broadcast."

"Did she request the delay? Or did her PR request it?"

"Does it matter?"

"It matters because if it were her public relations, there'd be room for negotiation."

"And if *she* requested it?"

"Then she'll kick your arse around the studio if you break her protocol. Besides, what we've found out is too hot for you to handle by yourself. If you spill it, your life will never be the same. They'll shred your reputation, and you'll never have another interview opportunity like this again. How about lifting the drama? Spin it a little."

How did I know this would happen?

"You know, Canter . . . I thought you were with me on this. What's happened to you?"

"Just thinking about your safety. You're important to me. The Americans flouting the rejection order is never gonna go down well. If you wanna play, you've picked a dangerous opponent. They can do you serious damage. They'll get you. And I mean literally."

"There's simply no choice in the matter. This is serious. It makes you wonder what the American motive is really about. We can't pretend this never happened. Our public has the right to know."

"Angel. People have been known to simply disappear over finding out too much. Stick with the script . . . and play nice."

"I think about it time and time again. Something in my DNA is telling me *Steinbeck* has a secret agenda. This agenda that needs to be explained. How dare they . . ."

Silence.

"You gonna give me an answer?"

"It wasn't a question."

"Okay. Let's make it one. So, answer me!"

"Yeah, I will. Gimme a sec."

I reclined back in my chair and waited. Then, it occurred to me Nathan knew something he was not about to let go of easily. "You bloody-well know, don't you?"

"About what?"

"Don't give me the shits. You're keeping something from me. What is it?"

"Look. This not for airing on live TV. Throwing mud at the US Secretary of State is asking for trouble. Don't make me beg you. Please."

"Beg? That doesn't look good on you, Nathan."

"It's Canter! So, you've made up your mind? You're going through with it?"

"Yes. We should take this opportunity now that we have it. But I need to know the whole story. So, spill."

Silence. White noise. I waited patiently.

"Jesus," Nathan finally said. "I can't believe this. You're scaring the shit out of me. It seems I don't have a choice, do I?"

"None."

This is getting to be like a bloody tooth extraction. "Canter, your silence is deafening. Please. Time is a luxury, and I don't have any."

"Okay, here's what I can do. I'll pull the video delay with a local area patch-in. But I need to know the LAN address."

"So, you'll fix it for me?"

"Yeah . . . anything for my rock star. But it'll cost you. Make sure your IT guy gets back to you with the LAN details. Without that, there's no live, as it happens, broadcast."

"But *why* is that damn warship here? Can't you give me that?"

"Just bring up the *Steinbeck*. Madam Secretary will either deflect, trip up or shut down. Either way, it isn't gonna be pretty. That's all I can give you right now."

"I'll get on to it. My treat at Busby's this Saturday night." Then I realised Nathan might not show up at all. Even if it was an invitation to a steak dinner at his favourite.

Before I hung up there was the subject of that strange message. Perhaps Nathan might know what to do. "I received a strange text message on my phone this morning. The number it came in on was unknown to me. There was also no matching number in my address book."

"Were you on Wi-Fi or 4G when the message came through?"

"Wi-Fi. I'm sure it was Wi-Fi."

"Did you dial the number?"

"No. But I messaged back. It came up message failed."

"You should've left it alone, Angel. In that case, I'll need your phone. First, manually disable Wi-Fi and Bluetooth and remove the Sim. Wrap the phone and sim card in foil. Tonight before you go to air, leave the phone at your desk in a padded bag. I'll take care of the rest. Maybe there's nothing to worry about, but we'll take precautions."

CHAPTER THREE

Enter Sandman

EDDIE BURST THROUGH THE DOOR AND INTO MY OFFICE, dressed in his usual casual attire, still wearing his studio headset with attached microphone that dangled a little awkwardly from the corner of his mouth. I gestured with an outstretched hand for Eddie to take a seat. He looked oddly anxious as he pulled out a chair and sat down. I met Eddie's gaze as he took his headset off. Then . . . Eddie just stared and said nothing.

"I need you to give me the LAN address for tonight's program," I asked, as Eddie let his head drop and he audibly sighed.

"Why, Angel. Why are you asking this of me?

"We're going to delete the feed delay."

"Yeah. I'm not a dumb-arse. I knew that's what you wanted. It can't be done. It's protocol. If we break prtocol, the studio can be prosecuted and guess what? I'll lose my job. The same goes with you."

"Trust me, Eddie. This needs to happen."

"I don't think you understand. It's just not possible," Eddie went on. With an elbow on my desk, I listened as Eddie went on with his protests. Finally, I raised a hand and Eddie stopped his ranting. As Eddie sat silent and staring at some point in space, I went about doing as suggested by Nathan—prepping my mobile phone exactly as he'd instructed.

"Can I at least ask why we're about to delete the feed delay?" Eddie said, breaking the silence.

"Of course, you can ask."

"Oh, and you're not about to say, are you?"

"The less you know, the better. We'll leave it at that. Besides, you'll be in the know after I go to air."

"Now, you're making me nervous."

"No time for nerves, Eddie. Let's make this happen. Give me the LAN address, please."

Eddie didn't reply. I looked up and regarded him as I placed my mobile phone into a padded bag. "Tick-tock."

Finally, Eddie reached for a Post-it note. "The LAN address is static. I can give you the address now." Eddie scrawled the details and stuck the Post-it on the back of my laptop monitor. "After the remote patch-in, you'll hear a tone in your headset. I'm not even gonna to ask where the remote location is. I reckon you've got that part all sorted out and you're right. The less I know, the better. After you hear the tone, you've got a live as it happens feed. You need to keep me out of this, Angel. I have a mortgage."

"Don't worry. You'll be fine. I promise."

After Eddie repositioned his headset, he gave a sharp nod and left my office as quickly as he arrived. As soon as my office door was closed, I hurried an email back to Nathan containing the LAN address. Almost immediately, I had Nathan's reply.

canter@bya.com
GTG.

* * *

"Fifteen minutes to air, Angel." Eddie said as he opened the door to the Green Room and peered inside. "Your chair is ready when you are."

I *was* ready.

I'd specifically instructed makeup to give me the best damn smoky eyes they'd ever created. Getting into the mood, I left the green room with my favourite high-powered earbuds slammed into my ears. Metallica played loud. Full volume. The way I liked it. I entered the studio from the rear door. I don't know *what* I must've looked like to others. I strutted, giving an extra swish to my hips with enough energy to throw anybody. I moved across the studio floor, dressed to destroy in that executive-styled, figure-hugging black business suit I loved so much. I walked between hot halogen pillar lights with black barn doors that swung out on a wide arch. My black patent leather pumps clicked on the hardwood floor as I strode. Eddie noticed as I walked past him. He ogled and mouthed words in the shape of *'Oh my god,'* and I was happy. I smiled briefly, then put it away. I was convinced, heads would be severed.

Seconds later, I was at my anchor with a background that looked surprisingly realistic – a view, high over the city of Melbourne across the Yarra. I removed my earbuds and with a defiant smile, I gave my hair a huge flick to one side. I stepped up and shook the hand of Madam Secretary. I exchanged a few brief, polite words, then took my seat while straightening my skirt with the palms of my hands. No one knew how I was truly feeling. In reality, my insides were nothing but mush. My lips were parched. My throat was dry. My inner voice was telling me not to do it. Not to go through with it. To get out of the chair and walk away. My true feelings; I hid them the best I could. The time had come. It was too late to back out. It was too late do anything. Let the chips fall where they may. Time to play. Let's do it.

To my left was the second-most powerful person in the world, who was encircled by her entourage of security men and makeup artists. They fussed over her, dusting her cheeks, repositioning her hair and making final adjustments to her audio equipment.

"Five minutes to air, Angel." Eddie snapped a clapperboard in front of me, then he disappeared seeming to be as nervous as how I was feeling deep inside. I took a deep breath and placed a tiny earphone into my left ear.

"One minute to air."

I reached for a glass of water and took a quick sip. I cleared my voice, checked my papers, everything was ready. Another sigh. Another adjustment to my skirt.

"Stand by . . . in five . . . four . . . three . . ."

After two long seconds, the light shone green and lenses zoomed in. I opened the interview in my normal way—the way I'd done so many times. My nervous tension left me as soon as I began. The expected small talk, to begin with. It went off well and without fuss.

I'd memorised the bullshit questions I was supposed to ask. There was no further use for the bunch of papers I had which were attached to an aged and well graffitied clipboard. I chose to disregard them all. There was no further use for the autocue that shone through the studio darkness which scrolled steadily with text. I started to ask Madam Secretary some of the scripted questions, and as predicted, I received her well-rehearsed replies.

The US Secretary of State was looking much too comfortable for my liking. She was smiling with the smugness of a seasoned politician. Then, a low tone sounded in my earpiece. Nathan had patched in. Now, there was no delay in the broadcast. The feed was wrenched off the twenty seconds delay. From this moment, every word said would be transmitted around the world without the possibility of wind back – without the possibility of a censor.

I took my moment and locked my eyes with hers. I hardened my gaze and shoved the politeness to one side. "Madam Secretary, Let's talk about the *USS John Steinbeck*."

And there it was.

As soon as I'd said it, I noticed her eyelid twitch. Not that anyone would notice a split second of discomposure. It was, nonetheless, a small victory. My small victory. I'd rattled the second most powerful person on earth and now, there was no coming back.

The US Secretary of State glanced fleetingly sideways, perhaps for her microphone. Then she leaned in and hardened. The game had begun. "Isn't she wonderful, Angel? Have you had the chance to visit her? I'm sure you'd be impressed. Our flagship is the pinnacle of technology and engineering."

Madam Secretary continued on about *Steinbeck* as though it was the show pony of the United States fleet.

She's hiding, my inner voice told me. She's running and hiding. I had to find a break in her dialog and finally drive this one home.

"Madam Secretary!" I blurted out, and I found myself surprised that I actually *did* stop her monologuing. I was also surprised by the studio crews' shock. Now was the time. Let's do this. "The *USS John Steinbeck*, being a nuclear-powered super-carrier, requires the authorisation from the Australian Nuclear Safety Commission before she can enter our waters. But I have it on good authority that the ANSC, *and* The Australian Federal Government, rejected the *Steinbeck*'s entry into Port Phillip Bay."

"Wind-Back!" I heard someone yell from somewhere in the studio background. Madam Secretary's response to my probe was professional and she held her own. She was uncomfortable. I knew it. But no one would ever guess it. "Are you asking me a question, Angel?"

"I'm asking you why the *Steinbeck* is here? Seeing she was disallowed entry into our waters due to non-disclosure of operations, that says to me that *Steinbeck's* ignorance of the rejection order was a risk the US Navy was willing to take. What, I wonder, could be behind all that risk?"

"Wind-back. Wind-back for god's sake!"

The producers in the studio background went wild. I imagined them attempting to rewind precious seconds in time. I imagined their horror when they found out no feed buffer existed. Even if the producers tried to cut to a commercial, I guessed that wouldn't work either. Nathan had fixed it. Nathan had fixed everything.

I held up a set of documents I'd kept secretly and in safe keeping for this exact moment. "These are your rejection orders issued by the Australian Federal Government and the ANSC, dated four weeks prior to the *Steinbeck*'s arrival. You ignored it. You took the risk that perhaps Australia wouldn't do anything about it. Yet here we both are. Would you care to explain why that is?"

"Wind-Back! Wind-Back, damn it!"

The damage was done. I sat back and waited patiently for my reply. I wondered at the same time what that reply might be.

The US Secretary of State reached for a glass of water and then cleared her voice. She was about to speak. She opened her mouth and it was as though her mind went elsewhere. I noticed she'd snuck a murmur into her coat sleeve. Going live as it happened, I wondered if viewers from around the world caught the same glimpse I'd seen. I almost felt sorry. It didn't matter. People ran back and forth beyond the studio lights. Things got knocked over. There were clatters and bangs. Voices erupted into shouts.

Finally, Madam Secretary's minders sprung from out of the darkness, scooped her up, and immediately whisked her away.

* * *

I arrived at my office at 9:00 am sharp the next day. There was no buzz in the air. Everyone was silent and seated at their workstations. I cut my way across the newsroom floor. LCDs positioned on poles and pillars high above workstations showed the *Steinbeck* out to sea. Breaking news of the scandal scrolled across the lower portions of the screens. Headline title—US WARSHIP SHUNS AUSTRALIAN DO NOT ENTER ORDER.

I made it to my office door. At my desk, I discovered two Post-it notes attached to my laptop monitor. The first note from Nathan said, 'Call me on this number, landline only. Canter.' The second note was from Chief. There were two words. 'My office.' Which were double underlined.

Just as I thought my head would explode, Melanie appeared, coffee in hand. "Good morning, Angel. It's extra strong. I think you'll probably need it today."

"That bad, huh?"

"That depends on which way you look at it. There's already talk about everything that went down."

"No one's saying anything out *there*. It's like a funeral parlour." As soon as I said it, I wondered what my funeral would be like. Then it dawned. They were *all* avoiding me. Maybe everyone was embarrassed to be working here.

"Well, I think they're all in shock," Melanie said, breaking my train of thought. "Chief isn't happy and that's to be expected. Rumour has it he came a cropper with the Prime Minister's office. I recommend you go there now and get that all sorted out."

"Yeah. I expected the blowback. I'll get up there after my coffee."

"Oh, any preferences on your new phone?"

"New phone? What new phone?"

"There was a missive on your desk requesting a new phone. I assumed it was from you."

I noticed the padded bag I'd left was gone. Nathan had already taken it. "Yes, new phone. Anything will do, Melanie. Thanks."

* * *

By the time I got to the elevator and pressed the call button, I thought I could taste my own heart. Getting out of the elevator on the top floor felt as though I was trapped in a sort of slow motion. I walked, measuring my steps, toward the Chief Editor's office. As I approached, I heard him in there, ranting and raving and I knew this was going to be a long day. I stood briefly to take a breath, then I walked on.

I knocked, opened the door and entered. Chief, still on his phone, spun and eyed me, gesturing with a hand for me to take a seat. I sat and crossed my legs, folding my cold, shaking hands in my lap, but at the same time, I'd never show Chief how I was feeling inside. I called upon all my energy to change my outward appearance and remain steadfast.

Chief finished his phone call, placing the mobile phone upside-down on his desk. He reached across and drank from a glass of water. Wiping the corners of his mouth with a tissue, he patted away beads of sweat from his brow. "That was the Director-General of Security. He wants your source. I told him in no uncertain terms—we will *not* divulge our sources. Not even to ASIO. Who knows how this will play out, Angel?" Chief paused long enough to take a deep breath, then continued. "I was going to fire your arse. I was going to put you out on a spike. That was before I took the call from Canberra. It appears there's more to this we don't know about. Or, it's as simple as they're not likely to 'fess up any sensitive info to guys like us. Probably the latter. I feel it."

"Guys like us?"

"C'mon Angel, we'll never be privy to what goes on behind closed doors at ASIO HQ. And because of your blatant public exposition of *Steinbeck* with the US Secretary of State, you've managed to cause an uproar, and there's a monumental shit storm heading our way. The PM's office had this whole situation in hand. What you put out publicly was being handled in Canberra, away from the public domain. Throwing it up and giving it air served no purpose other than to cause an outrage. One—You've managed to cause an untold amount of damage between allies. Two—You've achieved a public upheaval to which now, the entire community of Australia will demand answers. I don't know if there's a way back from this. Maybe there just isn't."

I braced myself for a continued verbal onslaught, but instead, the dressing down melted away and there was something else. Chief sat quietly in his chair and began to rub his hands together as though he didn't quite know how to proceed. He avoided eye contact momentarily while breathing heavily. "The late-night news crew called me at 3:00 am about the Chinooks," Chief went on.

"What Chinooks?" I asked him. "I'm afraid I don't know what you're talking about."

"Angel. A dozen or so Chinooks left the *Steinbeck*'s flight deck and headed inland. North-westerly direction by all reports. Here, have a look for yourself." Chief reached to his laptop and spun it around. A video played that was shot by onlookers from the street at precisely 3.00am. "Any ideas on this?"

"No."

"You live so close to the water, Angel. How is it that you didn't hear anything?"

"How is it that I wasn't contacted about this?"

Chief cleared his throat as though he had no direct answer. "Breaking the story of the Chinooks was expressly cut short by the Australian Secret Intelligence Service."

"Holy crap! ASIS is in this now?"

"Yeah. How about that, huh? Anyway. I don't like it. This entire sorry mess should've been left up to the politicians."

"They'd have botched it. You know they would have."

"Maybe. But we don't get to decide that, do we, Angel."

I leaned in, "Boss, the *Steinbeck* was here for a purpose. That purpose appears to be shrouded in secrecy or the Americans wouldn't have ignored the formal rejection order."

Chief held up his hand. "I know, Angel. We don't know what we're dealing with. Clearly, there's motivation for the Americans to take all that risk. The question is why? And I have an ugly feeling the Chinooks have something to do with it. Something is going on that defies our better understanding. And now it's out? I have no idea *where* this will go.

"So, considering ASIO and the PM were already in the loop, I have to ask, how is it *you* knew about everything?"

"You said it yourself, Boss. And I can't divulge my source."

Chief paused, rolling his eyes. He got up from his chair and went back to the office window. He gazed out anxiously as though expecting to see something out of the ordinary. "I might've known. You're behind removing the feed buffer. You disappoint me, Angel. That's a rule not to be broken. It's against all the laws and procedures we exist by."

"I'm not entirely happy about this, Boss. But I might not have succeeded at all with a twenty second feed delay."

"My oath you wouldn't. That's what the delay is for. I expect the United States won't let this one slide. There'll be blowback. But the PM's office is grateful you've managed to get *Steinbeck,* the fuck out of here. Not so with ASIO. The entire agency is on the warpath. The repercussions are anyone's guess. We'll wait and see what happens. That's all we can do."

"I can chase down some American Chinooks. That's a start."

"Absolutely. Take all the time you need. Get us something, but do it quietly. No heroics this time. By the book. Okay?"

"Sure. By the book. As you say, Boss."

I left Chief's office realising nothing was going to be by the book. Since when has Nathan ever done that?

* * *

The buzz had returned by the time I got back to the newsroom. The US Secretary of State was on breaking news. Crews from all available networks jostled her as they flung questions in her direction. Security men jostled with cameras and people bearing microphones, getting Madam Secretary safely into an awaiting SUV. She made no attempt to comment. The heavy SUV door closed, and with her eyes darkened by sunglasses, she faced directly forward as she and her entourage sped away.

As I continued to cut my way across the floor to my office, hoping to go unnoticed, everyone turned and arose from behind their workstations. An eruption in applause left me standing in my own surprise. It was in that moment, I realised I'd accomplished the impossible. I looked into the eyes of the world's most powerful nation and did something that no other had previously dared. With the super-carrier out to sea, I'd given the Americans something to think about. But also, it was time to get over it. What came out of everything was much darker than I at first understood.

Much more disturbing than ever. I'd have a job to discover the secrecy behind the Chinooks. There was only one who I knew would have answers and he was just a phone call away.

As I sat down at my desk, I again pondered Nathan's Post-it note. I grabbed it from my laptop screen, and using the desk phone as instructed, I dialled the number.

The phoned toned twice and Nathan answered immediately. "Angel."

"Yes, it's me. I need to discuss something. And you'd better tell me what you know this time."

The line went silent. Nathan baulked as though he knew what I was about to ask, but he changed the subject altogether. "I located the source of the message you received on your phone. I apologise in advance for destroying it. It was for your own safety."

"You're changing the subject!"

"This is important, listen to me. The message originated from a location close to Alice Springs Airport."

"That doesn't make sense. Who'd send a message from there?"

"Can you think of anything on your phone that could compromise you?"

"I keep everything on my phone. You know that."

"This isn't a joke. I hope you're calling from a landline. Not an internet connection?"

"Yes. It's my office line."

"Good."

"You're scaring me."

"I apologise. But it is what it is. They hacked your phone. They took your data."

I thought about it. Horrible, the realisation. "No . . . Oh no. All my contacts? All my call history? Everything?"

“Angel, they’re gonna make a meal of you! Didn’t I tell you to leave it alone?”

“The Americans knew I was going to break the story?”

“The CIA knew.”

“SHIT!”

“I had your phone connected to my laptop. I used ROVER protocol to ping the IP originator of the message.”

“And?”

“A CIA hack appeared at the ROVER back door and locked everything down. That’s when I unplugged your phone and cooked it in the microwave. Scratch one mobile phone. And scratch one bloody microwave. Whether they got most or all of your data is impossible to say. But it’s clear with a CIA hack, there’s more to this than we know.”

“I need you to tell me everything, Nathan. I don’t like where this is going.”

Silence again.

“Nathan?”

“It’s Canter! Jesus, Angel!”

“Sorry.”

“Now, we need to be careful.”

“I did what I had to do. Don’t even think about giving me that guilt trip.”

“Yeah. I get it. But we need to think about what to do next.”

“So, what do you suggest?”

“Let’s get up to Alice Springs and look around. I think we should start up there.”

CHAPTER FOUR

Secrets

TWO-THIRTY AM. MY laptop computer awoke from sleep mode and chimed loudly, announcing the arrival of an email. I chose to ignore. I chose sleep. But that lasted only seconds.

"Another email for you. I hate it when you keep your laptop in sleep mode," Jenny said groggily as she nudged me hard in the middle of my back.

"There's no choice. Important things are happening with work. You know that."

I sat up and rubbed my eyes awake. I managed to push my legs to the side and dangled them from the edge of the mattress. The polished floorboards were cold at night. In the darkness, I hoped my slippers were in the right position to make contact with my bare feet.

The laptop chimed again.

"Just leave it, hon," Jenny said as she turned over and pulled up the covers.

"Go back to sleep. I'll handle this. It'll keep chiming until I see what the fuss is about. It'd better be worth it."

Grabbing my robe and flinging it over my shoulders, I cut my way through the darkness. My laptop chimed once more before I lifted the lid and peered into the bright screen. After my eyes adjusted and the screen became clear, I opened the email from Nathan.

* * *

I arrived at Busby's at roughly 4.00 am. I entered through the large rotating door, and I was welcomed by a brightly lit array of bain-maries that had more than enough breakfast offerings. A lone figure of jet-black skin colour worked frantically behind the window to the kitchen. The glass displays with fresh offerings for the coming morning rush were always Busby's priority.

Nathan was seated in his normal booth and most probably tucking into his usual Canadian-style pancakes. I ordered coffee at the counter, then cut across the polished black-and-white tiles, taking a seat opposite him. "This had better be good. I take it this is on the record?" I said at the same time as I grabbed my brand-new smart phone and placed it on the table at exactly the same distance between us. I glared at Nathan. I wasn't happy. I needed a cigarette.

"No." Nathan put his hand out and stopped me from starting the recorder. "This is not on the record. This is between us, and it stays that way."

Most annoyed, I put my phone back into my handbag, secretly activating the recorder as I placed it inside. Risky. But I had a job to do.

"It's pitch black outside. Have you noticed?"

"I wouldn't have got you out so early if this wasn't important. If we're going up to Alice Springs today, you need to know."

"What about?"

I couldn't help it. I reached into my bag and grabbed a cigarette. Of course, I couldn't light up. But smelling the tobacco would have to do.

"About everything," Nathan laughed nervously. "It's your lucky day. I've decided to break my OSA contract and give you something that every journo dreams about."

"Really . . . But I can't use it, seeing what you're about to spill is off the record. How is it the stuff of dreams?"

Nathan didn't answer, only to put his head down with an almost child-like pout. I almost felt sorry for him but I quickly put that aside. "Start by telling me about this OSA."

"*The Official Secrets Act 1989*. I'm about to tell you everything. The things I've seen. The things I've done. You'd better prepare." Nathan rubbed his palms together as if he was cold as he dropped his eyes and scanned the area around us.

Nathan faced me directly. He opened his mouth to say something, then he closed it again. His expression caught me off guard. It seemed as though he had a bout of having second thoughts. He was about to change his mind and say nothing. He pushed his plate to the side, looked away and scanned the area again.

"Nathan?" Now, I was concerned. I'd never seen him seem so uneasy. This wasn't the Nathan I'd known all my life. This was somebody else. "What is it?" I asked. "For god's sake, say something. Anything."

Nathan final spoke, but the words quivered as they came out. I didn't understand them. I didn't know what he was talking about. He shook his head and looked away; once again, scanning the area and slowly checking if anyone was close by.

I put my cigarette away and reached out to him. I was no longer the journo he'd called out so early in the morning. I was his friend. I was the little girl he'd taken from Alice springs and raised on his own. The moment I put my hand on his, Nathan became Nathan again. He was again the steadfast, resolute and committed man I'd grown up with.

"Nathan, did you write it down?"

"If I wrote it down, it would end up being a book."

Busby's was absent of souls. Nathan checked around us again. It was as though he needed to be absolutely sure. Finally, he took a long breath and leaned forward. In a soft whisper, he said, "Jesus. This is major. I hope you're up for it."

I was now concerned for Nathan. I lightly squeezed his hand. "Just start from the beginning."

"Roswell, New Mexico. 1947. That's a good place to start. But it's not the beginning."

I immediately released myself of any worry. I wasn't sure what to make of it. At first, I wanted to laugh. However, Nathan's expression told me it was nothing funny. I knew about the incident in New Mexico. I remembered what I'd heard about what happened at Roswell, which in the end became a cult for millions of souls. I considered what happened at Roswell the stuff of great fiction stories; far away from anything that resembled hard facts. It was either aliens and UFOs or the Project Bluebook version. I pushed back in my chair and folded my arms, wondering if Nathan was all right; or if he was just being Nathan. I almost reached into my bag to turn off the recorder. But that would do more harm than good. Best never let Nathan know I'd switched it on. I'll get rid of the recording later.

"Yeah. I know about the crashed weather balloon. What about it?" My god, I wished I was outside so I could at least smoke and let that wonderful nicotine settle my mind.

"Weather balloon my arse," Nathan said. "Project Bluebook concluded that was the case, but it wasn't. Project Bluebook was a scam. It was an attempt to debunk. But the thing is, it worked.

Project Bluebook instilled doubt and confusion. It caused deflection. Exactly how *they* wanted it to go down."

I thought about what Nathan might say next. I wanted to close my ears. But it came out exactly as I imagined.

"It *was* a crashed spacecraft," Nathan said plainly.

"Okay . . . I'm leaving."

I'd already had enough. I could've used my time more productively elsewhere. I got up from my chair. Nathan grabbed my arm and pulled me back down. "Hear me out. Please. There's more to this than you realise. It's where Milestone begins."

As I sat down, I realised I'd heard the word before. A memory from somewhere. My mind reacted with the recognition but no matter how hard I tried to force the memory, it wouldn't come. As I sat, I asked Nathan about Milestone. I wasn't as prepared to hear Nathan's explanation as I thought.

"Milestone was conceived in 1948 by a secret organisation called The Guardianship of Milestone. A collaboration of former and retired top political officials from a coalition of countries. They work autonomously, deeply shrouded in secrecy using the infrastructure of several intelligence agencies. The Guardianship of Milestone flies so far under the radar, the legitimate intelligence agencies themselves don't even know they're there. The CIA, MI6. Even MOSSAD, FSB and BND. The Guardianship is dark to them all. But they lurk. They operate. They plan and execute. They are, by all standards, invisible and deadly. They have but one objective; the mission called Milestone."

Nathan went silent for a while. He looked around then gestured for me to move in closer. In a whisper, he said, "Milestone is an operation to bring about calamity on Earth. Milestone is an operation to destroy humanity. That's the aim of The Guardianship. That's their mission."

"Okay. Stop."

I tried hard to stem my laughter but I only marginally succeeded. I giggled. "I don't know what to tell you. Do you seriously want me to believe you when you say there's a bunch of guys walking around out there who are planning to . . . what? Blow up the planet?"

But Nathan sat there quietly facing me with an expression that told me he was not amused.

"I'm going outside for a cigarette," I said, still giggling. "Back in a sec. Okay?"

"Sure. Go ahead."

* * *

It took a certain amount of effort to go back inside Busby's. If Nathan wasn't such a dear friend, perhaps I might've got the next tram home. But as I returned to my chair, Nathan eyed me critically as though he knew what I was thinking. The thing was, did I have the stomach to hear more of this trumped-up nonsense that Nathan so clearly believed in.

"I need to know something right here and now, Nathan. I want a yes or no answer."

To my surprise, Nathan nodded his response.

"I need to know why those Chinooks are here. The Chinooks that left *Steinbeck's* hard deck. Do you know why they're here?"

Nathan looked down and shook his head. Why didn't I believe him?

"I suspect the Chinooks have something to do with Milestone."

"How do you know?"

"A hunch. And that's why I'm telling you everything now. I feel like Milestone will begin sooner than we both realise."

I didn't know if I was ready to hear it or not. I forced my mind to be the professional me this time around. I owe Nathan that much at least. I will sit and listen. After that, I will decide what I must do.

"I have the hard proof to back-up what I'm telling you. I know this is hard for you to believe."

"Hard to believe is putting it mildly. What you're suggesting is seriously insane, Nathan. I'm surprised at you."

"Just . . . hear me out."

"Go on. Give it to me. I'm ready. You can start about your thoughts on what actually happened at Roswell. What exactly was it that crashed? And don't even think of telling me it was aliens, because if you do . . ."

"It wasn't aliens," Nathan cut in. "It was worse than that. They were humans."

Nathan immediately retrieved a blue plastic 3.5-inch floppy disk from his back pocket and placed it on the table. I instantly recognised it. "That belonged to my mother. I was supposed to give it to Maggie. I thought I'd lost it."

"It never belonged to your mother. But you're right, it was to go to Maggie. You never knew about it after Maggie took you in. She found it in your backpack."

"I was ten years old but it's one of the things I remember clearly. My mother put it in my backpack. Uncle Scotty gave it to her. I remember how scared my mother was."

"Scotty-Blue was mates with your father," Nathan said. "And he was working with him at Pine Gap. It means he was the one who downloaded the intelligence. Without him, we wouldn't have gotten a head start on Milestone. Perhaps we'd never know. Maybe, we'd all . . ."

"All what? Perish?"

"Maybe. But Scotty-Blue changed that inevitability the moment Maggie found out what was downloaded."

I reached out and picked the disk up from the table. I finally settled into my chair and ran my eyes over it. I spun it around in my hand. "We'll need an old computer to look at this."

"There's no need. I keep the disk just to remind myself where the human race is headed if we don't change it. If we don't intervene. If we don't get there in time."

After hearing those words, I found myself softening a little. I placed the floppy disk back down on the table and pushed back in my chair. "All right. Go for it. Tell me what we have that's on this disk."

It was as though Nathan wasn't Nathan anymore. He was someone else. His face lit up, almost like a child. And as he explained what needed explaining, I found myself starting to believe.

"They *were* humans who crash at Roswell. Humans, not from Earth but somewhere else."

"Human aliens."

"Yeah. If you insist. And they're still here, Angel. It *was* a spacecraft they were testing. A spacecraft meant to be capable of interstellar travel. However, one can only guess why it failed. But out of what was learned by testing the technology, they later used it in the Oxcart Program, at Area 51 in Nevada."

"Oxcart?"

"You and I know it as the SR-71 Blackbird. Oxcart was the CIA version and is still classified to this day."

Nathan leaned forward and took a deep breath. He was about to speak when a young couple entered Busby's and took a seat in a booth to our rear. Nathan gestured for me to lean in closer.

"These other worldly humans are known as Oudarretians. They've been here for centuries, living among us. We didn't know of their existence until 1935."

As soon as Nathan said those words, I couldn't help but draw a correlation between what he mentioned and something else which I considered to be much darker. "The rise of the Nazi Party?"

"Correct." Nathan smiled for the first time in what seemed hours.

"So, something major must've happened during those times."

"Something did happen, Angel. It was the time of new science and new discoveries. The splitting of the uranium atom in 1938 by Otto Hahn. You see, Otto Hahn had an assistant who was close to him at the time. In 1941, Otto Hahn's assistant was captured by the Gestapo and he was never heard from again. He was taken prisoner; we suspect purely because of his black skin colour. But, out of the ground-breaking discovery of nuclear fission, the Manhattan Project was born. As a result, the Americans had what they needed to end the second world war."

"So, what? Are you saying Otto Hahn was an alien?"

"Angel. It wasn't Hahn. It was his assistant. It was the guy with the black skin. The assistant taught the teacher."

"And?"

"They're all black. The Oudarretians. The other-worldly beings. They all have the same skin." Nathan sat back and tapped lightly on the floppy disk. "It's all there, Angel. Everything is on the disk."

I had another foggy memory of the word, Oudarretian. I didn't quite know from where. Just a strange feeling that was enough to tell me that Nathan was truthful in what he was saying.

"That's who you call them? Oudarretians?"

"That's who they're known as. Yes."

"And you're saying if not for these Oudarretians, we might not have had nuclear weapons in the first place?"

"Exactly. During World War II, American intelligence revealed Germany was coming close to a super weapon. If they had the weapon, Hitler would use it. But the fall of Germany in 1945 tells us they didn't get there in time. Who knows what the world would look like today if they did get the bomb and use it? After Germany fell, Truman decided to use nuclear devices on Japan. The rest is what we learn in school."

I thought about it for a while. Something just didn't sit well no matter which way I looked at it. "Why would an advanced race show us the way to our destruction?"

"It's all part of the plan. Otto Hahn's Oudarretian assistant wanted to give the Germans the war, only, it never eventuated because of the unforeseen circumstances. A close call, wouldn't you say?"

CHAPTER FIVE

Terra Duo

I SAT QUIETLY AND thought about what Nathan had told me, taking a few sips of coffee—if only to lubricate my desert-dry lips. I locked eye contact. "Nathan, why now? Why destroy the Earth, if that's the motivation behind this . . . Milestone of yours?"

"I'm getting to that. But first let me explain something." Nathan paused long enough to take a heavy breath and sat back, scanning the area before leaning forward. "Edward Teller. Do you know about him?"

"Vaguely. The name sounds familiar. But I'm not sure."

"Edward Teller was the man responsible for the thermonuclear version of the Manhattan Project. The hydrogen bomb. The explosive yield of Little Boy and Fat Man, which were dropped on Japan, pales into insignificance in comparison to the massive destructive capabilities of a thermonuclear device."

"And your point is?"

"Edward Teller also had many assistants working with him during his early research. My point is this—One of his assistants was black."

"The same person who assisted Otto Hahn?"

"No, not the same person, but the same race."

"So let me guess. Another Oudarretian?"

Nathan smiled. "Now you're seeing the picture." Nathan tapped lightly on the floppy disk again if only to draw my attention to it. I realised for the first time how everything was beginning to fall into place. I wanted . . . Needed to remain sceptical, until I had the evidence to prove the things Nathan had told me were true. But my enquiring mind began to release me of my scepticism. Now I wanted to know more. I leaned forward towards him. I asked him, "These Oudarretians. Tell me about where they come from. Do you know?"

"They're our galactic neighbours. They're from the vicinity of the Perseus Arm in our galaxy. I'm not privy to the exact location. That information isn't on the disk, I suspect because it's classified beyond the reach of all but a few."

I took the disk and eyed it momentarily. "I take it a copy of this has been made?"

"Oh absolutely. All of the information has been downloaded and in the hands of the people who need it. But that doesn't change the inevitability of the things which are going to occur."

The significance of Nathan's words passed over me. My curiosity speared off into another direction. I wanted to know more about these so-called Oudarretians. "Perseus Arm? I can't begin to imagine where that is."

"Pass me your pen and I'll show you."

I immediately rifled around in my handbag. I also realised it was an opportunity to turn off the recorder. At the crucial second, however, I decided to keep it recording. Who knew where this was going to lead? It was my job, and if it screws up my relationship with Nathan, so be it. He'd have a tizzy for a bit. Nothing major. Finally, I found what I was looking for. I retrieved a gold Parker ballpoint that matched my cigarette case. I handed the pen to Nathan. He took a napkin from the holder, unfolded and straightened it out with the palm of his hand and began to sketch.

Nathan drew out long spirals that looked like the shape of a galaxy. I recognised what he was doing.

"Andromeda?" I asked.

"You wish. Andromeda is much too far away. I imagine it's too far away even for the Oudarretians. No, this is our galaxy—the Milky Way."

When Nathan completed the sketch, he placed a dot out on one of the spiral arms. "This here is where we live," he pointed out. "Our solar system on the Orion Arm is here. The Perseus Arm is here, the next spiral arm in parallel. Roughly ten thousand light years away."

I thought about it but it didn't make any sense. "It's not possible. Ten thousand light years equals ten thousand years spent travelling at the speed of light. Even I know that."

"I know. But they're here. What does that tell you?"

"They have technology beyond our known physics?"

"Yeah. It's hard to imagine that Einstein's theories have been shot to shit, huh?"

"And the connection with Milestone?"

"Hang on a sec. It's all relative, Angel. Trust me."

Nathan sat back in his chair. Without making Nathan aware, I managed a sideways glance to my wristwatch and saw it was getting close to five-thirty. I thought about how much more time was needed to get ready for the trip to Alice Springs. Time was getting away. It was going to be a tight squeeze. But I needed to get the full story for my record. "Human, you say?"

"They are indeed."

"And do they look like us? I mean have you . . ."

"Met one? I think we all could've come into contact with them. And they absolutely resemble us. No doubt about it. They're human in every way you can imagine except for their deep black skin."

"So, it would be impossible to tell them apart?"

"It's possible. But it's a process. Not an easy one. Just so happens I knew our conversation would go this way. Believe it or not, I've come prepared. I'll demonstrate to you now."

Nathan eyed me curiously. He had a look in his eyes that for a second scared me. In all the time I'd known him, I'd never seen that expression on him. It almost made me start. He appeared to go away somewhere in his head. Then after a lengthy silence, he dropped his gaze.

"You okay?" I asked.

"I'm okay, Angel. There's much to process. I said to you before—you needed to hear some details. It all relates to this. I've had it in my head for many years. In all those years I tried to find a way to tell you in a way you'd understand. I failed finding the right words. So, I'll tell you how it is, and hope for the best."

"This all sounds serious."

"Serious? Angel. It's very serious. This is the cross I've had to bear for twenty years. You're a very strong personality. I know you can handle it. All I'm saying is . . . Now's a good time to prepare. So, prepare hard. Always know I'm here for you. I always have been. And I always will be."

"Should I be scared?"

"That's hard to answer."

"Nathan!"

"Prepare, Angel. Just . . . go with it. In any case, it's of no consequence now."

Without any further delay, Nathan began by pricking the tip of a finger with his fork and squeezed until he drew a drop of blood. He then smeared the blood from his finger onto his forearm. In that second, everything seemed so surreal. I couldn't think of a single reason why Nathan would do such a thing. My eyes opened wider. I felt the moisture rise to my eyelids and pool there. Nathan took some liquid from a small plastic container which he'd kept in his pocket. He drew some out and lightly smeared it over the patch of blood on his forearm. Under a hand-held UV light, Nathan momentarily made the patch of blood glow a light blue before it faded away.

I blinked, sort of relived it was something that I was already familiar with. Nothing strange there. "Crime scene investigators do that. But what's your point exactly?"

"My point is this. If you did that to an Oudarretian, there'd be no glow. The Oudarretians' skin hosts an enzyme that absorbs white light, ultraviolet and gamma radiation. Their skin has zero light reflectivity. They've evolved this way because their 'home Sun' is closer to the surface of their planet in comparison to ours."

"So, you need cut them and make them bleed. Then hit them with the luminol to find out if they're Oudarretian?"

"There's no other way of knowing."

Nathan sat back and eyed me with the exact expression he had on his face as before. Once again, I became concerned and wondered at the same time where Nathan was going to go next.

"I want you to do the same test."

And then, the relief washed over me. "Oh, haha. I don't have black skin. I don't have an enzyme thing. Why on earth . . .?"

"Please—just do it. There's a reason why I ask. The details I have to tell you will be a lot easier for me to explain after you have the test."

I pricked my skin and bled for Nathan. But there was no blue glow on my skin. None at all. Nathan sat back in his chair and breathed heavily. I watched the colour in his complexion drain. I burned into him. "No! This is complete bullshit, Nathan. I'm not one of them." I stood tall from my chair. I wanted to get away from the place but no matter what I thought, I realised, walking away from Nathan was never going to do any good.

"Angel, please. This is not aimed at anything other than to put you in the right picture."

I put both hands up to my face. I felt like screaming. Nathan got up and grabbed both my hands. I slowly sat back down. "I'm . . . I'm . . . I'm an alien?"

"No, Angel. You're not one of them."

"But I don't understand. What's all this about? My father? He wasn't my father? Is that what you're trying to tell me? My whole life? Was it all a lie? Now you? What am I supposed to think, Nathan? What the *fuck* am I supposed to think?"

The urge to get up and run ripped up through my body and pounded at the back of my forehead. Nathan hadn't let go of my hands. If he had, perhaps I would've left Busby's with great amount of speed. But as Nathan held on tight catching me as I fell; I fell rather hard.

"How?" I finally managed to ask.

"Your mother was taken by the Guardianship."

"My mother . . .? Did they rape her, Nathan?"

"No. It was never like that. Your mother was artificially inseminated."

"And did my father know about this?"

Nathan put his head down and slowly nodded as though he was ashamed to give me any further detail. "Your father was party to the unfortunate scenario. Your father turned and became a member of the Guardianship."

"Shit!"

"I'm sorry."

"And so you bloody-well should be sorry! Why, Nathan? Why did you keep this from me?"

“I . . . I don’t have that answer. Over the years I’ve looked for an opportunity that never came.”

“So, why now. You could’ve kept it, and never said anything at all. Why now?”

“Because, Angel, you’re humanities only hope.”

* * *

After a while of sitting and breathing, I managed to settle. But my mind still twirled after what had been said. But somehow there was a place within me that wanted to know more. Confusion and anger –and maybe a bit of sadness had melted away and my number one emotion rose to the surface to greet me again. Curiosity. “Okay. You may continue with this horrible shit. But I’m still angry with you.”

“You *will* get over it. You’re strong. I’d never consider giving this to you if I knew for a second you couldn’t handle it.”

“You’d be right, Nathan. I’m stronger that you think I am. Start by telling me more about these black skinned people.”

“You sure?”

“Well, they’re *my* people, are they not?”

Nathan chose to ignore my sarcastic remark and continue to scribble on the napkin. He wrote the word Oudarret and held it up. “That’s the name of their home-world. That’s not hard to work out why. But what’s most interesting is this.” Nathan then re-wrote the word. But he wrote it out backward, then held it up.

I looked at it, which took more than a few seconds to sink in. “Terra Duo?” When the realisation hit me, I became genuinely shocked. “Are you kidding me?”

Nathan smiled and nodded. “In Latin, it means what?”

I was about to answer. My voice almost left my lips. I wanted to say, ‘Earth Two,’ as perhaps Nathan might’ve expected, but instead . . . "I need a moment," and I promptly got up and left the table.

As I moved toward the restroom, it felt as though the door shrank further and further away. I pushed the heavy door open and entered, virtually throwing myself at the wash basin. My heartbeat raced, and I could feel the thumping at my chest bone. Sweat broke through and prickled my face. I felt my breath slow to a shallow, asthmatic rhythm. I reached into my handbag for my puffer. I flicked off the lid and gave it a shake, then squirted life back into my lungs.

I must give up the damn smokes . . .

I reached down and turned on the tap, then splashed cool water over my face, stopping momentarily just to breathe again. My hands rested on the sink as I leant forward supporting my weight. I looked down.

Breathe . . . Just breathe . . .

Finally, I was able to stand tall again. My reflection in the mirror showed a woman under stress. Real stress. There was a part of me who wanted to believe Nathan. I felt an overwhelming rip at my logic and common-sense. It wasn't easy to swallow. Then, looking at my reflection in the mirror, I flicked my hair around my left ear and studied it. I placed a hand up to my earlobe and ran my fingers over the empty space. It was as if some small creature had taken a bite from my ear. An ear with an upturned U shape in the place of an earlobe. How I wished I had the chance to wear matching earrings for once. It was no tiny creature—it was a bullet. A near miss. Someone had wanted me dead. Why would anyone want to kill a child only ten years old?

Then the realisation came. Whoever wanted me dead was of no importance. It was all about what was on the disk. If Nathan was right, things would happen. Bad things. Massivley bad things. What did Nathan mean by telling me I was humanities last hope?

I cast my mind back. Nathan had taken me away from Alice Springs. At Maggie's specific request? This brought up a whole new set of questions. Who the hell are you, Nathan Masters? What were you doing in Alice Springs all those years ago?

Now I find Nathan had protected me, and kept me out of harm's way. I thought about the floppy disk and how my mother had slid it into the pocket of my rucksack. The disk Scotty-Blue had given to her with a direct request to get it to Maggie. But why Maggie? Was Nathan right? Was Scotty-Blue trying to leak its contents? What has Maggie got in this? Why leak to her? The owner of a photography shop? It didn't make any sense. And now the scenario that Nathan claims will happen. The fall of humanity.

It all spun around in my mind. I opened the cold water tap and splashed more water on my face. I regarded my own reflection. Another breath, another lungful. I decided then—I'd need to suck things up and take them all in my stride from this moment on.

The recorder. It was in my handbag and still recording audio. I grabbed it out of my bag and looked at it. I hovered my thumb lightly over the stop button. How could I use what was recorded? Who would ever believe my story? How would it go down with Chief? There was no evidence, just words. Just innuendos. Nothing concrete. If I was going to use it, I needed hard evidence to back it up. Could I get that evidence? And what would be the consequences if I *did* break the story? Almost certainly, it would ruin my relationship with Nathan. Almost certainly, it would go viral around the world. With absolute inevitability, it would cause an upheaval. Perhaps even world-wide panic. I'd already caused an untold amount of damage with the *Steinbeck* debacle. Could I risk anymore? Did I have what it took? My hand trembled lightly as my thumb hovered over the stop button. I didn't stop the recording. I placed my phone neatly into the side pocket of my handbag and left.

* * *

I returned to the table just in time to see the manager of Busby's talking to Nathan. He was a man as tall as a professional basketball player, jet-black skin that was black as onyx. The man had his notepad out, jotting something down. He nodded to Nathan and left as soon as I approached. I sat slowly and stared at Nathan sitting there. "Did you manage to get him with your luminol trick, Nathan?"

"Funny."

"Well, how would you know?"

"That guy's been here forever. He's not one of them."

"Are you sure? I mean, every black person in the world is now potentially and alien."

Nathan said nothing, choosing only to stare out of the window.

"Anyway, you were going to tell me how this is all connected."

I asked the question with the sole purpose of getting it on the record one way or another.

Nathan came back from the window, eyeing me intensely as he picked up the plastic floppy disk from the table. At first I thought he was going to break it and toss it away. But instead, Nathan took a deep breath while shoving it back in his pocket. "It's all on the disk but there are some pieces missing. It forces me to draw my own conclusions about what's to come."

"So, what're your conclusions? And don't bother telling me the Chinooks have nothing to do with it, because I know they are. You can't hide from that."

"Nobody can hide from them, Angel."

It was the first time Nathan admitted the Chinooks were all part of what was about to happen. To get the complete picture on the record, I only needed one more thing. What is it exactly that threatens to topple the human race? I looked at Nathan with my best stern expression and asked.

"Something *is* about to happen. Something major," Nathan trailed off and paused. I saw it in his eyes which became red with concern. That told me one thing. Whatever it was, he could do nothing about it.

"Milestone is here," Nathan continued. "It's no longer a theory." Nathan looked away then back. Moving in closer and leaning forward, he whispered. "I've been tracking increasing activity at Pine Gap. I seriously believe The Guardianship have activated Milestone."

Nathan retrieved a hundred dollar note from his wallet, folded it in half and thrust it beneath the menu holder. "Now that you know everything I know, believe me—this is just the very start. There's more I'm certain we all don't know about, and won't find out until we see for ourselves. We need to take extra precautions. The Guardianship are everywhere. Furthermore, I think a Guardianship soldier sent that message to your phone. The question is why? It's obvious they're making a play. We must now make this stop before it's too late."

"We?"

Nathan seemed not to hear me. He ignored me while he got up from his chair and threw his coat over his shoulders.

"Wait a minute. We?"

But this time Nathan wouldn't have answered. He was already making for the door. I noticed he'd left the napkin with the sketch on the table. I was about to pick it up, but something inside me told me it was of no importance compared to where we were about to head.

CHAPTER SIX

Spies Like Us

I WOKE UP. THE AIRCRAFT shook wildly, dropping suddenly, then came the inevitable seat-planting upward thrust. A tone came through the overhead speakers, and the fasten seat-belts warning light flashed on. I shot a sideways glance at Nathan. He appeared oblivious to the rattling and jostling, sitting there comfortably with a novel in his lap. The aircraft bounced hard again. I flung back in my seat. I dug my fingernails deep into the armrests.

Oh, god . . . It's the Oodnadatta Track all over again.

My mind went back to Nathan's ex-army Land Rover. Why did he love that beast so much? I remembered back to the time I was violently bounced and shoved around as Nathan drove the Land Rover down the Oodnadatta Track, with the little diesel engine running at its maximum revs. The flight to Alice Springs felt the same. I braced for more.

Nathan looked up from the pages he was reading. "Relax, Angel . . . Just a little turbulence." Nathan lingered for a second and smiled empathically before dropping his eyes back to the pages he was reading.

I stared out of the aircraft window. The aircraft cruised high above the outback desert. There were no clouds. The Sun was low on the horizon. I reflected briefly on the flight we'd missed in Melbourne. We'd spent nearly an entire day at the airport, and I was tired. I was tired and miserable. I just wanted to get this finished and back on the ground.

Sprawling out to the horizon below was a vast, open desert, abstractly patterned by red dust, trees, and rocks. I looked out on squarish spaces of different earthy hues as far as my eyes could reach. The view briefly made me feel better.

The Lake Eyre Basin came into view with its massive plane of white salt which could only be appreciated from a high vantage. I felt Nathan gently place a hand on my elbow. “Lake Eyre is the lowest point in Australia. It’s thirteen metres below sea level, did you know that?”

I viewed Lake Eyre with a sense of nostalgia. “I remember. It seems so long ago.”

“It *was* long ago. Twenty years since we stopped down there. You were only ten.”

“I never asked you why we took the Oodnadatta Track instead of the Stuart. I’ve wondered about that over the years.”

“Do you regret it?”

“I remember how rough the road was. That old Land Rover of yours wasn’t all that good in the suspension department. And I remember we stopped at William Creek.”

Nathan laughed. “It was a rough ride, but there’s nothing like the simplicity of basic engineering in the desert. That’s why I loved that Land Rover. Hardly anything to go wrong.”

“Oh? How many times did we stop because the engine overheated?”

That was enough to cease Nathans nostalgia. It made me smile for the first time in hours. “So, why did we go down the track? Surely the highway would’ve been better?”

“It seemed like a good idea at the time. The Stuart is boring. Flat, straight nothing. There were lots of things to see on the track, didn’t you think?”

"Yeah. Roos and snakes. Ruts and potholes. A sore arse and a mouth full of red dust. It was a blast."

I surprised myself by saying those words. Nathan seemed to start as he and sat upright. "Hey . . . Are you okay?"

"A headache," I said, reaching for my handbag. I took out my absolute favourite thing that was ever invented. A peppermint Migrastick. I dabbed the essential oils about my temples and at the nape of my neck. The scent of peppermint hung in the air and it was powerful enough to turn the heads of a few fellow travellers.

The flight smoothed out a little. I reclined my chair and settled back. I wondered what might be waiting at Alice Springs after we arrived. I thought about the event of Milestone Nathan had told me and I wondered what it might entail. But even everything, I still wasn't totally convinced it was as bad as Nathan described.

Glancing sideways at Nathan, I was surprised to see he still seemed engrossed in what he was reading. He looked up as though felt my eyes on him.

"How's it going? Is that peppermint stuff working yet?"

"I like the smell. I forgot to bring some meds, so I'm in for it, unfortunately."

"I'll get you something to drink," Nathan said while reaching up and pressing the call button.

"What're you reading?" I asked.

"You wouldn't like this one. But I find it interesting the way it was written. *Gerald's Game* by Stephen King."

"And what makes you so sure I wouldn't like it?"

"It's seriously dark, Angel. I've never known you to read this kind of stuff."

"I've read a couple of Stephen King's novels."

I placed a hand up to my forehead and massaged my temples. Sometimes massaging worked. Sometimes it didn't. I did it anyway, hoping glean some relief.

"Really? Which ones?" Nathan asked.

"*The Stand*. Another one called *Needful Things*."

"You're kidding."

"Why so surprised?"

"I dunno. *Needful Things* is a great book. But I can't picture you reading *The Stand*."

"I read it when I started Uni. Come to think of it—*The Stand* is kind of like what you've told me about Milestone. And I reckon your Milestone thing is the reason for this damn headache."

Nathan dog-eared a page as a bookmark and neatly tucked the book away in the seat pocket in front of him. "It's gonna be fine. We'll be on the ground in a couple of hours."

"You know, I really don't know why you decided to put me in the loop."

"It's as I've already explained, Angel."

"But what am I supposed to do with it? As if I can make a difference. As if I could change anything. I thought I was on this journey to find out who sent me the message, and to find out about the Chinooks. But no. You go and put all this shit in my head. Look at me. I'm a mess. I think my head's about to explode."

In my mind, I was only a second away from a confession about the audio recording that was on my phone. I opened my mouth. To stop words flying out, I tried to think of something else. But no matter what I thought about, I knew I had one thing to do. I had to get rid of that bloody recording. Then, nausea. It came in a wave, and I lunged forward, and grabbed an airsick bag.

Nathan reached up to the overhead and tapped the call button again. "I'm sorry, Angel. The hostess is taking her time." He promptly got out of his chair and made for the rear of the aircraft.

* * *

Nathan was gone for more than several minutes. I wondered what was taking so much time. Water. I needed water. I was tired and miserable with a migraine that had made me sick to the stomach. How I wanted just to fall asleep.

Finally, Nathan returned to his seat and sat down quietly. I locked eyes with him as he refastened his seat-belt. "The message sent to my phone was from Maggie, wasn't it?" I don't know why I had that in my head. But Nathan's reaction surprised me a little which also told me there was an element to all of this that involved Maggie in some way. Somehow, I now felt more confused than ever. I should've kept my thoughts to myself.

Nathan kept reacting by saying nothing at all. The warning sounded in my inner voice as I noticed Nathan biting lightly on his bottom lip.

"Well, was it from Maggie?"

Nathan shook his head. "Why would you think that?"

I leaned over and pushed up the sleeve of Nathan's leather jacket. "This is why." I ran my hand over the tattoo on Nathan's forearm that bore the winged and bannered dagger. *Who dares wins.* The mark of the Special Air Service. The tattoo was old and slightly blurred, but I could still make out the words in the banner. "One night when I was at Maggie's, I saw someone talking with her from my bunk-room window. He had the same tattoo as this. It was you, wasn't it? You were talking with Maggie outside. I saw her give you that floppy disk. I remember it now. So, what other bullshit are you feeding me?"

Nathan was about to answer . . .

"Hello, sir. Glass of water?" the air hostess said.

"Thank you so much," Nathan said as he unclipped and took his tray down. I heard him sigh and I knew it was out of relief. The air hostess passed him a bottle of Evian and a long plastic cup filled halfway with ice.

"Miss?" I'd noticed the air hostess's accent, and it was as though she was from two continents at least. "Yes, please." I politely took the bottle of Evian. The air hostess beamed while passing me some Panadol in a small plastic cup. My eyes met her then. Her eyes of sparkling green. Maybe they're coloured contacts. It seems everyone has them these days. But I couldn't get my eyes away from her hair. The silkiest bright auburn I'd ever seen accentuated her pale complexion with a light sporadic dusting of freckles. And the thing was, her face was familiar.

"How did you know I wasn't well?" I asked the hostess while studying the shape of her face. How did I know her and from where? I could've been a memory from somewhere in recesses of my mind.

"Your partner asked for some headache medicine. I'm afraid Panadol is all we have. I hope it does the trick and you're feeling better soon."

The hostess turned to walk away. I guessed Nathan had already been acquainted and called her by name. "Natalie-Jade, before you go . . ."

Natalie-Jade stopped and faced Nathan, beaming at him with a set of expensive white pins.

"Thank you so much," Nathan said. "But do I detect an accent?"

"Born in the US, Lincoln, Nebraska," she replied.

"And what brings you out here?"

"Family. I live in Alice Springs. We all packed up and moved down here after I finished up with college. My Dad works at the copper mines not far from Alice Springs."

"Copper mines? My Fa . . ." Then it hit me. The copper mine where my father worked was a complete lie. Perhaps there was no copper mine at all. Perhaps the cover story my father was issued with was as generic to him as it was to others. That being the case, the word 'danger' appeared in the mind like a beacon.

Just then, the fasten seat-belts warning light illuminated in the overhead, which was accompanied by the all familiar tone.

Natalie-Jade's smiling face drained slightly. "There's more turbulence I'm afraid. I'm so sorry. Please be sure to stay seated and your seat-belts securely fastened," she said, with a small amount of concern in her voice, as she turned and stepped away.

"I don't know what to make of it, Angel. She resembles someone I knew long ago. Her face is almost the same."

"I was thinking the same thing."

"And she wasn't part of the crew before our flight left Melbourne. Something isn't right," Nathan said, taking me away from my thoughts. He pushed his bottle of water away. Suddenly, the aircraft shuddered, and the bottle of water I was holding fell away from my grip and tipped over. "Shit."

Nathan looked at me sideways with the same sort of expression he had after Natalie-Jade had left us. "When you opened your bottle, did you feel it click?"

"Ahh . . . As a matter of fact, . . ."

"Lucky it tipped over. Mine didn't click either."

"What're you saying?"

Nathan cared not to answer.

The aircraft hit the turbulence like a hammer. We suddenly yawed left and then violently pitched up. The captain announced a diversion over the speaker which to me just spelled more delay into Alice Springs. I gripped my armrests and held on tighter.

CHAPTER SEVEN

Cold Steel and the Odd Explosion

AT ALICE SPRINGS AIRPORT, Nathan Placed a hand under my elbow and moved me with urgency toward the airport locker array. We arrived at a locker marked 2157. He scanned the area before opening the locker and retrieving a small amount of cash and a handgun. After pushing the handgun under his jacket and behind his belt, he scanned the area one last time.

I stopped in front of him and folded my arms. "Are you going to tell me why you're carrying?"

"Not now. No time. Let's go."

Nathan put his hand under my elbow and moved me away.

Trolley bags in our grip, we pushed our way through the crowd of tired and dazed travellers who'd arrived on the bumpy flight up from Melbourne. As I looked outside the airport front window, I couldn't help but notice how dark it was out there. We'd have made it to Alice Springs several hours before; if we didn't miss the flight, and perhaps we'd have some time to take in some of the scenery.

We stepped through the main terminal exit to the footpath outside, and I attempted to hail a taxi. Nathan stepped in front of me and pushed my arm back down to my side. "Not that one, Angel. The one over there."

Nathan pointed in the direction of a parked black car, and its engines turned over and the headlights illuminated. After the black car rushed over and stopped abruptly, Nathan opened the rear door and pushed me unceremoniously through.

"Jesus, Nathan!"

Nathan stepped quickly to the rear of the vehicle and stowed our baggage, then rushed to the opposite side of the SUV and flung himself inside, thudding the door closed.

Nathan quickly introduced me to the driver. "Angel, this is Bosco . . . Bosco, this is Angel."

"Hey, Canter. Glad you could make it," Bosco said in what I thought was an American drawl. His driving position on the left-hand side of the vehicle confirmed it. Bosco's eyes studied me from the rear-view mirror. "Nice to meet you, Angel."

What else could I say? "Nice to meet you too." I politely shook his hand and winced as he almost broke it with his grip. It took an amount of effort not to show him how much it hurt.

Bosco studied me again in the mirror. Then he shot his eyes to Nathan. "You didn't tell her, did ya, Canter?"

Tell me about what?

"My bad. I was in the shit deep enough. Get going, Bosco, will you please?"

"Roger that."

The SUV responded after Bosco put his foot on the throttle, pushing me back into my seat. Moments later, we were accelerating away from the airport and motored north along the Stuart Highway, headed for Alice Springs town centre. I stared out of the dark tinted windows to an empty highway that was devoid of any traffic and couldn't help but wonder why that was the case. So, I spoke up. "There's no traffic."

Bosco and Nathan exchanged glances in the mirror. Nathan checked his wristwatch. I was able to make out that Bosco checked his. They exchanged glances again. "A little weird for 16:42, wouldn't you say, Canter?"

"Probably nothing. Maybe it's punter's night at the local."

"Yeah, you Aussies are big on that shit. I keep forgetting."

I smiled to myself as the possible explanation was at least plausible enough. It suddenly occurred to me that at least soon, I'd have a good opportunity to erase the recording that was on my phone. But then there was another thought. Welcome to the world of spycraft. Is that what I am now? A spy? Like my father? Do I need to swear in somewhere? Do I need to take an oath to Queen, god, and country? The thought of it played on my mind. I rewound moments in time. I played back everything Nathan had told me back at Busby's. I was starting to believe every word. Now, where was I headed? What was this journey about? I thought about everything from the time of my interview. But something was missing to all this. The Chinooks. The reasons why they're here still eluded me, and nobody was saying anything. Why?

I turned to Nathan, who seemed preoccupied as we drove. "I want a gun, Nathan. If I'm now in this with you, I want a gun."

"That's not how this is gonna play out. You're out of the equation."

"No, she's not out of the equation," Bosco interrupted. "The lady needs a firearm. We *all* need them where we're going." Bosco laughed to himself. I saw that Nathan wasn't amused. But what was even scarier was the fact that Nathan didn't say anything else. He sighed and pinch rubbed his eyes as though he needed sleep.

On the other side of a small rise, red and blue lights flashed through the outback darkness. Bosco announced it just as I thought it. "Oh, nice timing. Random breath testing ahead."

The police random breath testing station was set up on the side of the road just before town.

Bosco slowed and followed the orange and white reflective cones into the RBT waiting area. Several cars had stopped in front. Bosco pulled up and reefed the gearshift into park, cranking the handbrake up with force. He then reached into his glove box and retrieved a handgun. "You better pass yours over, Canter."

Nathan said nothing at all while he passed his weapon the Bosco as though he'd done it several times before. I noticed there was a section cut away on the floor of the SUV. Bosco pushed the weapons down into the compartment without any trouble. He closed the lid and covered the flap of carpet back over it. After catching my gaze in the rear-view as Bosco sat up straight and cleared his voice. "Yeah, I know. We might be on government business, but we still need to hide this shit from the cops. It saves the paperwork if they start kicking up a stink."

"And Maggie hates the paperwork," Nathan added.

The night was lit up with the dancing of red and blue flashing lights. Bosco's headlights outlined the silhouettes of a few cops, and out of the darkness, a cop appeared at Bosco's window. The cop tapped lightly on the glass with his knuckle. Bosco tapped a button in the center console, and his window whirred down. The cop bent down slightly. "Good evening, driver. Random breath testing. Can I have your license, please?"

After the cop walked away with Bosco's license, somehow, I started to feel uneasy. Something wasn't right. I felt it. And Bosco appeared to have doubts. I saw his expression of concern in the rear-view mirror as he and Nathan shared something that was like a code. Bosco suddenly stopped chewing on his gum and eyed

Nathan again. I shot a sideways glance to Nathan. His expression told me his apprehension. But then Nathan came out and said what he was thinking. “That guy’s not the real deal, Bosco.”

“Jesus! That’s what I was thinking.”

“Wait until those cars are gone then get us out of here.”

“Copy that.”

I wound my window slightly down, and a soft breeze pushed past my face, making my headache feel a little better. After Bosco had his license back and they’d finished with his breath test, I watched as more cops waved away the cars in front, and I thought at the same time, we were also good to go.

Suddenly, from behind me, someone reefed open my door and grabbed my hair. Another cop had Nathan’s door open and had pulled him out and to the ground. Bosco jumped out of his seat but was taken to the ground by cop number three. I instinctively pulled back and away, but it was no good. I was dragged by my hair away from the car at a furious pace.

“Angel!” I heard Nathan yell from behind me. Then, after loud punching noise, I heard his voice get sharply cut off. Through the pain of being dragged by my hair, I managed to spin my body, and I was able to make out the cops who were laying blows into Nathan and Bosco.

I screamed, kicking out as he dragged me. “Fuck you! You arsehole! What the fuck are you doing?” I fought the cop as much as I could, only to be answered with the words, shut the fuck up, bitch.

He threw me into a chair within the RBT bus, and I realised for the first time how deep I was in it. Before he punched in the face, I managed to notice the RBT bus was not what it was supposed to be. It was as though we were all caught by an elaborately planned ambush.

After I came back from a semi-unconsciousness, I found myself zip tied and bound. My head hurt. I felt congealed blood stiffen the skin below my lips. And, two cops were standing before me who were smiling as though they'd achieved the impossible.

One of the cops stepped closer to me and announced that he'd beat the shit out of me if I screamed. He took off my gag. But all I was interested in was what happened to Nathan and Bosco. "Where are they and what have you done with them?"

"That's none of your concern, girly-girl."

"Why are you doing this? What do you want?"

As soon as I asked the question, I heard the popping noises of gunfire from somewhere outside. Both cops exchanged glances, and in my mind, I knew they'd killed Nathan and Bosco. I screamed out. "NOOO!"

One of the cops lurched forward and bare-fisted my face. I felt the earth beneath me, shatter, and spin. Blackness was coming to take me away, and I welcomed it.

"I said don't fucking scream, didn't I? Why didn't you follow my instructions?" He punched me again. My head spun to the side, and I was sure an amount of blood spurted from my mouth. I heard the cop walk a few paces away and pick something up. Then I felt cold water over me, and I again was brought back from blacking out.

"What do you want?" I repeated with words that wrapped around my burning pain.

"We want you, little Angel. All we have to do now is wait for the bird to come and pick us up, and we're outta here."

"Bird?"

"Oh, fuck. You're a journalist. You're supposed to be smart. Can't you figure it out?" After he said it, he and the guy with him started to laugh in a most sadistic way. Then I concluded. Bird equals flight. They planned to capture me and fly me away to somewhere, but how? Then it struck me hard. *Chinook.* It seemed as every moment passed, I was getting myself deeper into this mess.

They were both standing in front of me, eyeing me intensely, scrutinizing me as though they'd won a most precious prize in some sick and twisted competition. I reached down into the pit of my soul and pulled out the courage to ask the question I needed answering. I needed to know one way or another. "You're going to take me somewhere. But I need to know about the Chin . . ."

Instantly, one of the cop's head exploded, and then the other. Blood and gore showered me. Through the cloud of red, I saw Nathan and Bosco standing there checking their weapons. They both rushed forward and scooped me up by my elbows.

* * *

We'd left that grizzly scene behind us, and through the eyes of my injured face, I gazed out of the window and stared up at the night sky. The lights of Alice Springs town centre cut through the darkness as we entered through The Gap.

"Can someone tell me what the fuck just happened?" Bosco yelled, cutting the silence.

"We've been made, Bosco. Everything is dead in the water."

I wanted to add something meaningful, but all I could think about were those cops. "Slow down, Bosco. The last thing we need right now is a frigging speeding ticket."

I was surprised that Bosco eased off the throttle, bringing his vehicle back down to a much more legal speed. Nathan eyed Bosco in his rear-view mirror and shook his head. "Hollow points. Seriously, Bosco, you loaded our weapons with hollow points?"

"It did the trick, and we're Oscar Mike."

"You okay?" Nathan asked me in a soothing tone.

I tried to speak, but I couldn't manage anything. Nathan put his hand on mine. It made me feel better for a few moments until my enquiring mind, ignorant to the pain I was feeling, started to work again. "They said they were going to take me away."

"Angel. Those guys weren't real cops."

"Yes, and I knew that pretty much straight away. But why me? What did they want with me?"

"Remember what I said back at Busby's? You're our last hope. You're humanities last hope. Do you believe me now?"

"Shit!"

Nathan's words burned deep into my mind. Why now did I feel so small? I felt as though the entire world now rested with me. It was an awful responsibility, and I didn't want it. I preferred not to have it at all. I was nervous as to where everything I'd learned was about to lead me. Lead us. "You need to head straight through town and keep going," I said.

Bosco replied, "Why's that?"

"We need to get rid of the evidence."

I don't know why I thought of it. But Nathan agreed. "Do it, Bosco. We'll need to trash everything. Find a place where we can put a match to your lovely Chevvy."

"Aww heck. That makes two, Canter."

"A worthy cause, Bosco. A worthy cause.'

"Yeah, I get it."

Everything familiar to my early years in Alice Springs went whizzing past the window as Bosco drove. The township was familiar, but oddly smaller compared to how it lived in my memory. Shops and structures started sparsely, then concentrated, then got sparse again as Bosco followed the Stuart Highway north.

Again, there was no traffic on the roads. As we passed through the town, rural machinery yards replaced the car yards. Bosco pulled over roughly thirty kilometres north of Alice Springs. He parked his vehicle almost with seasoned ability down in a ditch, somewhere in the middle of the open desert. Nathan got out of the vehicle and limped around while tapping a message out on his phone. Within a moment, he had his reply. "Shilo will be here shortly," Nathan said as he placed his phone back into his back pocket.

I walked over to Nathan, and my inner voice told me to see if I could help him in any way. From his beatings, he looked incredibly injured. He looked at me with a bloodied smile as he took my hand. "What is it?" I asked. "You've got a strange look on your face."

"Do you remember when you were ten years old, and those men took you away?"

"Yeah, I do. Those guys. Do you think it's them again?"

"There's no doubt in my mind. We're in their killing zone this time. We need to take the fight back to them. But Angel, you also did something for me when you were so young. Can you remember?"

I tried to cast my mind back to the time, but most of those early memories refused to resurface. "I'm sorry, Nathan. All the memories I have are so distant. I don't seem to be able to recollect them."

"I'm about to show you for the first time what you did for me back then."

Nathan grabbed both my hands and took them into his. "You're a healer, Angel. You have this gift. The only way to prove it to you is for *you* to try it out on your own. Look at me. I'm injured as you can see. They broke my face. You've done this before."

"You're scaring me."

"No, Angel. I want you to see for yourself. Don't be scared. I know you can do this."

I closed my eyes and concentrated. Immediately, I saw Charlotte again. I had her picture in my mind as she flew high above the MacDonnell Ranges. I drew the memory back to the surface. I saw Charlotte had joined other eagles; there were seven of them, high up on an updraft circling, then all of a sudden, they all seemed to hover line abreast. They all seemed to be looking down on me. I wondered what they wanted. Then, I felt an immense amount of energy wash over my body. Pure energy. It flowed over me and through me. Through me and out of me. I opened my eyes to see that Nathan was fixed into position and not moving as though he was simply switched off. But as I looked closer, I saw with my own eyes that his wounds slowly began to heal. The dry patches of blood on his face disappeared. His complexion began to glow. But as I looked down at his hands, the finger that had been missing for so many years had remarkably returned.

Almost in shock at what I'd done, I let Nathan's hands go and he came back to life, stepping back a pace. I sucked back a huge gulp of air and immediately felt giddy to my stomach. The world around me spun and forced me to sit on the ground if only to catch my breath once again.

It felt as though an hour had passed. Nathan placed his hand under my elbow and helped me up to my feet. I noticed Bosco was standing right next to him. I wouldn't have believed it if someone had told me what just transpired. But what made everything even more surreal was the fact that I also had, somehow, healed Bosco.

"No. I don't believe this. I . . . I can't . . ."

"It's always been your gift," Nathan told me. "You just didn't realise you had it."

"They're after me because of my gift?"

Nathan nodded slowly. "That. And many other things.

"You're our top priority number one," Bosco added in a military kind of drawl. "Now we need to think about *how* to bring all this up when Shilo gets here."

"Shilo? Who is this Shilo?" I asked.

"It's Maggie," Nathan answered.

"Nathan is Canter. Maggie is Shilo," Bosco put in.

"But why is Maggie, this Shilo? She owns a shop in Alice Springs. She's a retail shop owner. She's not one of you. Is she?"

Nathan coughed lightly in his hand and turned away. I saw Bosco smile a little as he pitched stones into the distance. Both of them didn't answer my question and chose to avoid.

"What do you think, Canter? It's time to go off the grid for a spell, huh?"

Nathan nodded, then answered. "Going dark isn't as it used to be. We'll need to dump everything. Phones, devices, hard drives—we need to trash everything."

Trying desperately to get my head back, as soon as Nathan had said it, I realised my phone still had the recording. If I had to dump my phone, the recording would go with it. It was like someone had lifted a heavy weight off me. The realisation made me relax a little, but I also felt some regret that I'd failed in breaking the story. Nonetheless, it was a relief, and I no longer had that burden. It was at that moment I realised how the importance of breaking this story now paled into insignificance. I needed to get rid of the evidence. That's all that mattered.

Bosco walked up close to Nathan and eyed him. "You know, Canter, I can't for the life of me figure out how those Guardianship assholes got the jump on us."

"The must've intercepted Angel's phone. The CIA pinged it and locked it down."

"Serious? And you didn't think to bring this up with Shilo?"

"I was about to. Things happened so quickly."

"That's mighty unprofessional of you, big hoss."

"Maybe. Let's see if you could do better."

"Well, we're all screwed now," Bosco said, pitching another stone harder than before. "And not only that. Firebird Station is screwed."

Nathan added something else into the mix. "Something else happened on our way up. I'm sure an air hostess on our flight into Alice Springs was a Guardianship soldier. Don't ask how I know. I just know."

"Awww no! Are you shitting me? I mean look where we are now, big hoss. It's not good. We're compromised. There're five dead G-men on the ground with gunshot wounds in the heads, and we're no closer to our target. The mission has officially gone to shit. It's over."

"It could've been much worse, Bosco. They could've captured Bunjil."

"Bunjil?"

"Oh, that's your codename, Angel."

"Wait a minute. I have a fucking codename now? And when were you going to tell me that part of the story."

I felt as though Nathan was about to confess everything this time. But as usual, he was interrupted by something else. In the distance, a set of headlights pierced the darkness. A Landcruiser with a broken muffler and rusty old bull bar parked close to where we were standing. The motor was killed with a loud pop from the exhaust. Out of all the emotions and everything I'd gone through; I somehow became thrilled and overjoyed to see a familiar face when Maggie wound her window down.

* * *

Before leaving the area, Maggie had handed Nathan a large canister of petrol. He and Bosco dowsed the Chevvy and all the evidence we had, including my phone, was left on the back seat. From the window of the Landcruiser, Nathan aimed his suppressed handgun and fired a volley of shots in quick succession. The Chevvy burst into flames, and after a few moments, exploded, casting debris far into the desert wilderness.

CHAPTER EIGHT

Welcome to Firebird Station

IT WAS THE SAME SMALL, fibro clad cottage as I always remembered. After twenty years, nothing had changed. The typical Alice Springs landscape still surrounded the house. There was no lawn and only a few native trees that were still the same as I remembered. Even though it was dark, I knew I'd returned to the place where Maggie had taken me in all those years ago.

Bosco left the driver's seat of the Landcruiser and ran around to open the door for Maggie. She got out of the car, aided by her walking cane. Nathan and I followed Maggie up the driveway to the front door, where Bosco was already at the doorstep. Bosco waited momentarily before turning and knocking on the door in a sort of code. The door opened, and a face greeted him. "Guten abend," the young woman said, then she quickly corrected with, "Oh, Hallo Bosco." The door widened, and Bosco nodded to the young woman, stepping through while at the same time helping Maggie over the doorstep. Nathan and I followed and stepped into the small but well-decorated hallway which was adorned with all the trimmings of a house that sat frozen in time during the late 1980s.

The scent was exactly as I remembered. I recalled the musty old house smell that seemed to arise from the foundations and work into the walls where it would stay until the house gets knocked down in some distant future. The furniture was the same as I remembered. Maggie never updated or replaced anything, and I was somehow thankful for that. Maggie only got new things when old things broke down or completely busted. I remembered Maggie once saying, "If it ain't broke, why get rid of it?" That was Maggie. That's just how she was.

The first port of call was to the bathroom if only to wash off thousands of kilometres of travel and stress. While there, Maggie came in, reached into the shower, and turned on the taps. "You'll feel better soon, love. I'll get Nathan to get your bag, and I'll bring you some fresh clothes." Maggie left and returned a little while later with fresh, lavender infused towels and a brand new fluffy white bathrobe. I lingered long enough in the shower for the water to run cold. It seemed like only minutes.

I heard a polite knock on the door, and Maggie peered into the bathroom just as I was finishing up.

"Are you okay, love?"

"I feel like I've been knocked over," I said, holding a towel up to the side of my face and staring at my bruises in the mirror. I wondered briefly why I was able to heal Nathan and Bosco but not myself. My left eye was almost completely closed over. My lips were thick and engorged with blood. But the smell of lavender in the towels was gorgeous. The softness of the towels was something Maggie was expert at. "I've missed your towels," I said, smiling.

"I only ever did the lavender thing for you. I never liked it much myself."

"So, you must've known I was coming to the Alice?"

"Nathan said so, yes."

"Oh." I was surprised. "Nathan keeps in touch with you?"

"He has to. It's his job."

I wondered why it was Nathan's job. But before I could ask, Maggie had already left.

With my fluffy bathrobe on, and my wet hair wrapped up and twirled high, I walked slowly into the living room expecting to see only Maggie. But they were all there standing in a circle discussing things in low voices. Everyone stopped speaking abruptly, making me feel as though I was an outsider. I did a sharp about-turn and was about to step away, but Maggie's words invited me in.

"Oh, don't be silly, love. We're all in this together. You're among friends now. Come."

I stepped past the smiling face of a woman in her mid-twenties. She was frightfully thin, as though verging on anorexia, yet at the same time, she was stunningly beautiful. I stopped momentarily and put my hand out. "I don't know you—I'm Angel."

Maggie then apologised profusely. "Oh, where's my head these days? Angel . . . This is Christina Schumacher. Christina is our IT specialist. We managed to steal her away from German Counterintelligence. The Bundesnachrichtendienst. I challenge anyone to say it correctly the first time. It took me literally months of practice."

Christina nodded and smiled brightly. However, I was a little confused. Maggie must've noticed. "Oh, we call it BND for short. It's much-much easier."

"Yeah, I understand." I smiled and received Christina's handshake. Her greeting was as strong as a set of vice grips and went longer than was comfortable. It must be a German custom of some kind. "I've heard of BND," I said. "I've also heard that German Counterintelligence is supposed to be the duck's nuts."

Christina looked a little confused. Maggie giggled lightly. "Duck's nuts is slang and means that something is outstanding, Christina." Maggie smiled warmly, then instructed Christina. "We'll need eyes on the area south of The Gap, Christina. See if you can requisition the Keyhole Satellite from our friends in Chantilly." Christina nodded and left to go downstairs.

"I guess sleep is out of the question?" Bosco asked while hovering in the background.

"Go and get yourself a couple of hours of rest. But be sure to be up and running no later than 07:00, Bosco. That goes for you as well, Nathan."

Bosco and Nathan left the living room without so much as a good night. I half expected Nathan to give me a peck on the cheek as he'd done for almost twenty years. But this time it was as though his personality had changed. Nathan seemed harder. He seemed almost like a soldier around Maggie. I wondered why that was the case.

Maggie turned and faced me. "We've got ourselves a huge day after the sun comes up. Get some rest, love. The bunk-room has been kept the same as it ever was. You may need some earplugs, however. Bosco. He's louder asleep than he is standing up."

"I'm on all pistons now. Any coffee?"

"Oh, that sounds like the Angel I know. There'll be some brewing if I know Christina. She's like you. She loves her caffeine." Maggie paused, and her expression hardened a little. With one brow raised, she asked the one question I was most dreading. "You're off the fags, then?"

How could I answer? I didn't. I looked away to the Norman Lindsay etchings, which still hung above the mantelpiece after all these years.

"Smoking is bad, Angel. It'll be the death of you. Asthmatics who smoke won't do." Maggie winced and turned slightly. "But

I'm not going to harp on it. I've said my piece. Now, let's relax a little before we work out what to do about this trouble Nathan and Bosco have managed to get us into. We'll also discuss your future with Firebird Station," Maggie smiled. "Now that you're here with us, you can consider yourself as an inductee to intelligence."

The word spiralled around in my mind. Intelligence. I was still thinking about it as Maggie sat me on the sofa.

"I have to tell you a few things. You may not fully understand, considering what's happened. But I'm afraid there's not much time. So, what I have to tell you may come as a shock."

"Maggie?"

"There *is* no good time for this," Maggie said, looking slightly away. "And it starts with Eagle Shield."

Talk about a sudden slap in the face. Eagle Shield? I had no idea what Maggie was talking about. But I didn't have to ask. It came out in Maggie's next breath.

"Nathan's mission," Maggie said. "Eagle Shield was funded by ASIO. The mission was all about your safety and upbringing from when you left here as a child. Up until *this* day, as it turns out. Now that you're with us, Nathan can rest easy, and Eagle Shield is concluded."

"That's why the change of my name?"

Maggie nodded. "We changed everything so they couldn't get their hands on you."

"They almost did."

"So, Bosco tells me. That's twice, Angel."

"Twice?"

"You still can't remember, can you?"

"Nathan has always told me about those men when I was ten, but no, I can't remember anything. So, you're telling me that those guys are the same guys as back then. Nathan thinks exactly the same. I wish I could remember those events instead of having people telling me everything all the time. It's so frustrating."

Maggie grabbed my hand and held it. "There's a reason why you can't remember. And I think it's to do with you being so young at the time. What you went through was traumatic, and young minds have a safety net which tends to shut out traumatic experiences."

"I'm not a child now. Why hasn't Nathan said anything?"

"He sees you as his daughter. He's still very protective of you. Perhaps in Nathan's mind, you're still the ten-year-old he'd risked his life to protect. And that's why he's never said anything in great detail."

"I'm not an idiot. I can put things together."

"I'm sure you can. But there has always been one thing that in my mind at least, has scared Nathan half to death, although he's not willing to admit it. He's had counselling for several years over this one issue, and he's never been able to shake it, Angel. Imagine his pain."

"What issue."

"The day you fell from the helicopter."

I didn't know exactly how to take it. It was the first time I heard anybody tell me of such an incident. As I thought about it, if it was true, I was thankful that I couldn't remember.

Maggie went on. "Nathan rescued you from the hands of the Guardianship, but in the process of getting you away to safety, the helicopter you were in came under attack. You were thrown out. But later, Nathan found you on the ground, unharmed. How you were unharmed remains a mystery and can't be reasonably explained in any way. And this is something that Nathan still struggles with. He loves you like a father with all of his heart, and he has *never* forgiven himself."

"But I survived."

"Yes. But you have to imagine what Nathan went through before he actually found you. He had to struggle with the fact you couldn't have survived from a fall at such a height. He prepared himself to find you dead. He's a soldier. He's seen and done many things. But nothing could've prepared him for that."

As Maggie explained it, I teared up, and all I wanted to do was run to Nathan and throw my arms around him. I wanted to tell him that everything was alright and he could finally let it go. Maybe this was something I could heal so he could finally have peace in his life. I decided there, and then; I would use all my power to heal Nathan if it was the last meaningful thing that I did in my life.

Maggie held my hand for a few moments of peace as I thought everything over. But my train of thought stopped abruptly at something I just couldn't get passed.

"Do you mind if I ask a question?"

"Go ahead, Angel. What is it?"

"Just who are you, Maggie? I thought you owned a retail shop. But you're among these . . . spies and it's as though you're boss to these people."

Maggie let go of my hand and stood up. She folded her arms, and she instantly became somebody else. "Okay, love, I'll be brief. ASIS runs Firebird Station. Everyone here is an ASIS operative. Do you remember Andrew?"

"Yes. I remember. He's your stepson."

"That's right. Andrew is with ASIO. He's been with ASIO even from when you were so young. Andrew is currently away on a mission but will join us again soon."

Maggie relaxed a little and sat down next to me again, not saying anything, but at the same time, she appeared to brace for more of my questions. She seemed still and rock-steady, but at the same time, she appeared less hard like a soldier.

"And your photography shop?"

"The shop is a legitimate business owned and run by ASIO. Profits from the shop are back-channelled into both ASIO and ASIS assignments. Eagle Shield was one of those assignments."

"So, what's the deal with this Firebird Station?"

Maggie laughed at my abruptness. I wanted to get to the answers quickly. "Of course," said Maggie, clearing her voice. "We're in the business of counterintelligence. But we're a little different to most of ASIO operations and task forces. You see, we sit much deeper as an undercover taskforce with one sole objective to carry out. You'll no doubt learn more about what we do, but for now, you must rest. Now you're part of the team; you'll get to learn more after a bit of rest." Maggie patted my hand as she stood slowly up.

"Maggie. What makes you think I'm part of this?"

"It was always planned that way."

"Planned? How? This so-called Eagle Shield thing?"

"Well, yes. As I've already explained."

"You're not hearing me. I have a life. I can't run away from everything. My job. My home. Jenny . . ."

Maggie walked away. She left me there to wonder. Then Maggie turned and eyed me. She had an expression that suddenly seemed hard again. She appeared much harder than I've ever known her. "There's more Angel. I was going to save this for another time. Perhaps now is the time for you to hear it."

I held my breath, wondering at the same time what was about to be said. But it was without any delay and with next to no emotion at all. "This will be hard on you. You need to hear it, and before saying anything, you need to think about it. Do I have your understanding?"

I nodded. "This is serious, right?"

"More serious than you could ever guess, unfortunately. But here it is. You're now aware you have a natural gift. But this natural gift has been given to you not *solely* by birthright. The gift was bestowed upon you by external events. And it's because of this gift, you are a target, my dear. This is the reason they made an attempt on your life. Not once but three times now. What I'm trying to say is this . . . Your father . . ."

I put up my hand and stopped Maggie. "Nathan has told me everything."

"He did? Well, I'll be bloody-well damned. That one was meant for me. I'm most annoyed, Angel. I'm most annoyed, indeed."

"Don't be. Nathan was looking out for me. As he always does."

"What else did he divvy up?" Maggie snapped.

"Everything on that was on the disk, I assume."

"Milestone?"

"That too."

"Hmm . . ." Maggie pushed a finger to her lips. "So much for the Official Secrets Act. There'll be backlash over this I'm afraid."

"He had no choice. I probed him, and I wouldn't stop."

"You'd think a man of his calibre would know how to deflect. I'm a little disappointed, Angel. I'll have words when he's up. But anyway," Maggie changed her tone. "You must know your mother was an innocent party in this. She was always your mother. In every way."

"Any ideas about my . . . *real* father?"

"We don't know." Maggie hung her head and went silent for a while. She began to walk around in tiny circles while studying the pattern in her worn carpet. "But, Angel, perhaps we'll find out in due course. Perhaps we'll all find out. Consider your past concluded. You're one of us now."

"And Jenny?"

Maggie said nothing. She appeared as though my relationship with Jenny wasn't important. The Maggie I once knew wasn't hardened in this way. It was as though I was in the company of a complete stranger. The Maggie I once knew was gone!

"No," I said. "Maggie. I can't be part of this."

"Your old life is OVER, Angel. The quicker you come to terms with it, the better. We must now think about what's coming and get our heads back in the game! Is that understood!"

"Ah . . ."

"That's yes, colonel."

"Maggie?"

"Look, I've got Christina working on getting us over the area where they ambushed you. From what I've learned so far, it sounds like the Guardianship was prepared for you long in advance."

I immediately thought about the air hostess. "Nathan felt odd about an air hostess while we were on our flight up from Melbourne. I thought Nathan was just paranoid."

"Nathan never gets paranoid. He sees and hears everything. If he's flagged something, it'd be for a damn good reason. Do you know if this air hostess was still on the plane when you left?"

"Of course, she was. She couldn't have jumped."

Maggie laughed to herself. It was at that moment she became human again. "I'm sorry, love. I'm a little tired. What I meant to imply is the possibility of her being a Guardianship soldier. She might have dumped her disguise and melted away into the masses. Guardianship soldiers happen to be good at that."

"Come to think of it, I can't remember seeing her again," I said while thinking it over. "You'd think if she *was* kosher, she'd be one of the crew at the end of the flight, but I can't recall."

"It sounds like she's a soldier. She'd most likely sent the tipoff even before you left Melbourne." Maggie held her breath for a beat. "Come. We'll see if Christina has managed to get eyes over The Gap."

"What? In my bathrobe?"

Maggie blinked, shaking her head almost apologetically. "Of course. If you're up for it, go and get changed. Feel free to come down to the ops room. Come down when you're ready. Okay?"

* * *

As I followed the stairs down into the ops room, I was illuminated only by cool, bluish lighting. The smells of hot electronic devices and computer equipment hung in the air. Several large LCDs were hung on walls which displayed scenery high over Australia. Christina was seated and looking at her computer screen while Maggie stood behind her. I noticed the surprise in Christina and Maggie as I came down. Maggie smiled warmly and gestured for me to come closer. Christina looked up from the computer screen as though she'd accomplished the impossible. "Sehr gut . . . ist sehr gut!"

As I walked across the floor past several computer terminals—one of which appeared to be an ancient, ragged old box that they should've scrapped—I saw first-hand what the fuss was about.

On the screen was a bird's-eye view of the area just south of The Gap. Christina had managed to hijack one of the most hacker proof satellites in space. *The Keyhole Three Satellite*. "A genius, isn't she?" Maggie beamed. "All we have to do now is wait and see what happens next."

After approximately thirty minutes of eyeing a monitor with nothing of interest, several vehicles suddenly appeared out of the early morning darkness with red and blue lights flashing. Figures in police uniforms sprang from the vehicles. They scurried around the scene at a frantic pace before they then appeared to become more organised.

"They're not real cops. They're more of the guys who ambushed us."

Maggie nodded. "I think you're right."

From the back of one the vehicles, two figures retrieved stretchers. They ran and knelt beside the bodies Nathan and Bosco had put to death. While unravelling what appeared to white body bags, the figures went to work packing up the bodies and getting them ready. But the question was, getting them ready for what?

"I'd have thought the real Alice Springs police would be on the scene by now."

"It's weird, isn't it?" Maggie replied. "Yet there's been no police chatter at all. Another thing—there's been absolutely no traffic past the location. None."

I remembered as we drove up from the airport that there was no traffic. Maybe I was about to find out why this was so. "Can we look further down the road to the south?"

Christina nodded and tapped on the keyboard, commanding the satellite to a new location. After a few moments, the camera slowly moved away and followed the Stuart Highway to the south.

"There. Look." Maggie pointed. "They've set up a roadblock with a diversion across the river. That's why there's no traffic." I saw Maggie's eyes sparkling with excitement. "They're bloody good at what they do. See what we're up against? Okay, Christina, move us back to ground zero again, will you please?"

Christina nodded again. She tapped on the keyboard. The camera changed position back to The Gap. After the camera arrived, I felt both my legs almost give away under my weight. A Chinook helicopter had already landed just metres away from the RBT bus.

"Maggie?"

"I hear you, love." Maggie seemed as equally stunned.

"What're they doing?"

"It looks like they're clearing the scene of evidence. Hence the traffic diversion. Oh, they're cunning pieces of shit, aren't they? They'll have the entire scene cleared before sunrise."

"So, it seems."

Christina noticed something. She pointed to the screen, where from under several floodlights, sparks were flying from some kind of cutting device.

Maggie peered a bit closer at the screen. "What the hell are they doing now? Is that what I think it is?"

"I know what they're up to. They're grinding the identification numbers from the chassis. I think they're going to leave the bus where it is."

"That makes sense. It's not the genuine article. Chances are the bus is stolen anyway. It'll be interesting to see what happens next. This is all so elaborate, isn't it?"

"But how is it that there's no police at the scene?" I asked.

"They look like the police. No one will ever bother reporting if they think the police are already there. The Guardianship is literally calling the bluff of everyone. That said, it can only last for so long. Hence their need to hurry things up."

The Guardianship soldiers picked up the pace. The Chinook helicopter now contained the five dead bodies, along with crucial parts of the bus that could most likely lead back to them. Then their activity slowed, and the figures hurled themselves into the fake police vehicles. The rotors of the Chinook started to spin. After a couple of moments, it lifted into the air, swung around and took off in a westerly direction. There was one lone figure left standing at the side of the bus.

"Christina, can you zoom in a little closer on that man please?"

Christina punched a few keys, and the camera moved in.

"What do you suppose he's doing?" I asked.

"I'm not sure," Maggie said. "It looks like he might be planting explosives. You know what? I reckon he's got Semtex all over that thing."

Maggie's words were confirmed the moment the lone figure raced back to a waiting vehicle which took off with its wheels spinning. A blinding flash erupted, and the bus disappeared into a cloud, exploding into fragments. The very thing that would get the real police urgently on the scene.

"We'll need to find that Chinook," Maggie said. "That's now our utmost priority."

In the back of my mind, I wondered if the Chinook was one of the six that left *Steinbeck.* The notion of my concern caused me to shiver on the spot. Were they Guardianship who left *Steinbeck?* If they were, this now brought *new* questions into the mix. I decided to keep that question to myself and leave it unanswered for now.

CHAPTER NINE

Going Dark

Nathan stepped through the door as I was at the coffee machine. Wiping the sleep from his eyes, Nathan busted a yawn, and gave me the same good morning as he'd always done; a peck on the check and warm glowing smile. He stepped up to the glass jug on the counter containing hot black get up and go. Glancing sideways at his wristwatch, he grabbed a mug down from the cupboard. "0700," Nathan said. "Any sign of Bosco?"

"Hear that sound? That drilling sound?"

"Yeah. What the hell is that?"

"Bosco. Snoring." I rolled my eyes.

"Figures. Is there a bucket around here anywhere?"

"Well, I think there's one in the laundry. Why?"

Nathan didn't answer me. He stepped past me and into the laundry. I heard unmistakable sound of running water filling a bucket. I smiled to myself as Nathan again stepped past me, armed with a bucket of cold Alice Springs bore water. I knew what he was about to do as I sat down at the dining table. I waited for the inevitability with both hands wrapped around my hot mug of coffee. After a few moments, I heard Bosco's yelling emanate from down somewhere down the end of the hall. Bosco was up and alive. No more drilling snoring.

Christina bounced through the door wearing her flannel PJs. I felt my heartbeat pick up as I saw the outline of her figure at the coffee machine. At first, I thought she wasn't going to say anything. But as she turned and face the dining table, she greeted me in German. "Guten morgen."

"Hello, Christina. The coffee is fresh. I hope you enjoy."

"Danke." Christina smiled warmly as she pulled out a chair and sat down. "Wurden sie ein fruhstuck mochten?"

I didn't know how to speak German and I let Christina know with a few universal hand signals.

Christina tried again. "Es tut mir leid . . . umm . . . sorry." She tried again. "Vood du like some breakfast?"

"Oh, breakfast? No thanks, Christina. I have my coffee, and I'm about to step out back for a cigarette. It's a Journo's breakfast, don't you know. But that doesn't appear the be the case any longer, does it?"

Christina shook her head again. I looked down at my mug and smiled to myself. I then gestured the sign language of having a smoke. Christina responded. "Ja . . . bitte. Smoke . . . yes?"

I waved my hand toward the back door. "Okay. Come with me."

The early morning sun floated; peaking just above the fence line, which drew long shadows on the dusty red ground. It was cold for an Alice Springs morning. Dry and cold. No vapour from my breath, only the bluish cigarette smoke as I exhaled letting the nicotine do its duty.

As I found a place and slouched up against fibro cladding, I realised nothing outside had changed. It was the same backyard I remembered but seemed smaller. As I scanned the area, it was as though time had frozen, and I was again a ten-year-old. Over toward the shed was the swinging bench seat that I'd sat on as a child every morning before heading off to school. The dry earth was absent of grass. Beyond the bench seat, was the Hills Hoist, which was still kinked and stood slightly askew. The aluminium fence needed some paint but it was still the same as ever. And there . . . I pointed. "See that?"

Christina looked over to where I'd pointed. She shrugged her confusion, then looked at me curiously with her big beautiful blue eyes.

"Come with me. I'll show you."

I walked toward the back fence; Christina padded lightly behind. A small spear of light poked through a hole in the fence. I bent down slightly and placed my finger over it, remembering how close I came. Christina looked at it momentarily. It appeared now; she was more confused than ever.

I lifted my hair around my ear and showed Christina what was missing. Christina looked up again and reacted with a hand toward me. "Sie habe geschossen?" She was surprised, but at the same time struggled with her English. "Err . . . shoot. There?"

I nodded. How could I answer in words?

"Mein Gott!" Christina placed a hand over her mouth and ogled me. She raised her hand and placed it gently on my face next to my ear. In that moment I felt a warmness. I felt a genuine caring from someone I didn't know. It surprised me and cause me to sharply look away. But also in the moment, I didn't notice Bosco who was standing at the back door. "Hey, you two. 0730." Bosco tapped the face of his wristwatch. "Time to get to work."

After returning inside, I found Nathan already seated at the table, cradling a mug of coffee as though he was cold. To Nathan's left sat a man with a face that was familiar; and I knew who this man was. "Andrew? Is it you?"

"Angel, it's good to see you again." Andrew smiled and I knew it was out of genuine affection. I stepped around the table and I took Andrew's hand. His grip was strong but welcoming. Not forceful like Christina's. Andrew's hand was warm, and he withdrew it with satisfactory timing. He kept smiled brightly, just the same as he did way back then . . .

"T," Andrew said, breaking my train of thought. "You're one of us now, so it's T."

I'd forgotten where I was. I'd forgotten that all these people are players and they have their own callsigns.

"Short for Teflon," Nathan looked up from his coffee and offered.

"Huh?"

"T is for Teflon." This time Nathan took a swig of his coffee in a nonchalant way and I suddenly realise he was different. How different? I couldn't say.

"I hate that name, Canter," said Andrew. "And we don't *all* get to choose our own call signs, do we? You'd know!"

Nathan smiled a big cheesy grin. "Well T, it was you who implied that nothing sticks. The fact you became Teflon was inevitable."

I finally pushed past the banter and offered my own to Andrew. "It's been such a long time," I said. "And I never realised you were ASIO."

Andrew laughed. Nathan almost choked on his coffee.

"I don't normally admit it to anyone if they ask me," Andrew replied. "And your question has never been asked so casually, by the way."

I couldn't help but feel rookie small at their laughter. Where was the nearest corner small enough for me to hide in?

Andrew grinned in a way that told me I shouldn't worry. I remembered he'd done that a few times when I was a child.

"It's okay, you'll get the hang of it. Just . . . try not to say anything in public and we'll do just fine."

Shrugging it off, head down, I immediately bee-lined for the caffeine. While pouring coffee into my favourite mug as a child, I said to Andrew, "Maggie tells me you were on assignment." Andrew said nothing. It then occurred to me that perhaps he couldn't answer. Not even if he was amongst other players. I realised then that even under the one roof, there're many layers. This was something that I now had to somehow come to grips with.

I snuck back to my chair and silently joined them all at the table. To my left, Nathan was grinning and sharing jokes. Opposite him, Christina was smiling brightly, but hid her lack of understanding well enough. Bosco sat beside her, also joking, wearing his baseball cap tilted back while chewing on gum. And there was Andrew, seated exactly on my right.

I didn't know what it was about Andrew. He had a certain magnetism, almost pulling me in with his charm and charisma, and somehow, I found that I adored it. Andrew even took the trouble to stop mid-sentence and give me an expression that I knew in my heart was just for me. I melted. I felt things I shouldn't have felt. I wanted to stay in that moment forever. But then Maggie's voice drilled through the delicious moment and shattered it into fragments. "You people get your backsides down here. It's time to get to work."

* * *

Down into the bluish, electrically charged ops room, Bosco and Christina stood behind the main computer with their arms folded. Maggie tapped madly at the keyboard, then replayed a video recording that was captured by the *Keyhole Satellite Three* over

The Gap, south of Alice Springs. When it was over, no one said anything, and the silence was deafening.

Finally, Bosco was the first to break the silence. “That’s it; it’s all over. Our best choice is to go dark.”

“For once I think Bosco’s right,” Nathan added. “We need to break away from whatever it is that they know about us.”

Maggie acknowledged Nathan and then turned to Andrew. “Your thoughts?”

Andrew shrugged then replied, “It is what it is. I agree. There’s no option for us but to go off the grid.”

Maggie turned and asked for Christina’s opinion. She was about to speak when Bosco cut her off. “This isn’t for BND to decide,” Bosco said sharply then stomped away.

Maggie stepped forward and grabbed Bosco by the upper arm. “What in god’s name is wrong with you? Get a grip. We all have a job to do. Christina is part of the team. Do I make myself clear?”

Bosco said nothing.

“Is that clear! And don’t make me pull rank Bosco. We’ve survived without the formalities for so long!”

“Yes . . . Colonel,” Bosco huffed as he sat heavily in his chair.

Christina then began to speak. “If ve must go dark, ve must destroy our netverk, vich includes hard drives and surveillance. Ve cannot hold any recovered data. Everything must be destroyed.”

Maggie nodded in agreement. “It’ll be expensive. No doubt about it. Angel? Your thoughts?”

Still feeling the perfect rookie in their company, I never expected to contribute. I took a breath before I said, “The photography lab for starters. Won’t that need to be shut down also?”

"Good point, Angel. The shop will have to go. No more funding for us. The problem is how? We can't even sell it as a legitimate business. It'll draw too much attention."

"Is there a way for the shop to stay operational?" Nathan asked.

"Too risky, big hoss," Bosco put in. "I say we put a match to it. The place is full of chemicals. It won't seem suspicious."

Maggie put her finger up to her lips. She was actually considering Bosco's proposal. But then, Maggie again turned to Christina. "Anything further to add before I decide?"

"I think Bosco's idea ist sehr gut. But ve don't vant to cause damash to ze shops next doors."

"That's true," I added. "We can't cause undue stress to innocent parties. We don't even know if they *have* the appropriate insurance."

"I disagree," Bosco put in. "If we go down this road, it'll have to look realistic. If it's done surgically, it *will* be suspicious. I say burn, baby, burn. If the other shops get lit up in the process, then that's how it is."

I'd had enough of Bosco's attitude. "I've not known you for long, Bosco. But already I can see how much you're a complete arsehole."

Nathan laughed. Christina laughed. Maggie was most annoyed. "Enough! You're like little school kids! Bloody-well get your heads back in the game!"

There was a certain awkwardness after Maggie silenced everyone. She turned slowly, walked to her chair and sat down. "Okay. I take it we're all in agreement then?" One by one, Maggie made eye contact with everyone in the ops room. We all nodded including myself. I wasn't happy knowing innocents would be part of the collateral damage. But what Maggie said next was completely unexpected.

"Andrew and I have discussed your next assignment, Nathan. Now that Eagle Shield is concluded, we'll be needing you abroad."

It was to be the first time in twenty years that Nathan and I would be separated. I wondered how drastically things change in so little time. Nathan was going to leave me and I had no control over it. My eyes filled with tears.

"Okay then people. The ayes have it." Maggie looked away, seeming to be a little upset. "Sad, isn't it? All the work we've done. Everything we've achieved. It just gets destroyed. We were so close."

"I'll get a report back to Canberra, and I'll request our redeployments," Andrew said almost under his breath as he stepped past me.

Maggie agreed with her stepson. "We'll start with the hard drives after our meeting concludes. I'll get a clean-up detail from HQ to deal with the photo lab. Angel, I'll need you here with me this morning. We'll have a chat about getting you some training at Swan Island."

As soon as I heard the words from Maggie, it was like everything became set in stone. Nobody goes to Swan Island without the one sole purpose of becoming a spy. Secretly, I'd always wondered about that place. I was almost excited to go there just to see what existed behind all those doors. The excitement, however, melted away as I realised after graduation, I was almost certainly destined to do time behind a desk. It wasn't how I saw myself.

"How do you feel about going straight into ASIS?" Maggie asked me. After she asked it, I realised that maybe the desk job I thought about was never on the agenda. Maybe this was all intricately planned from the time I was so young.

* * *

It was easy to say goodbye to Bosco. It was a little harder with Christina. It was especially difficult to say goodbye to Maggie and Nathan. But after Andrew dropped me off at Alice Springs Airport, he unexpectedly kissed me soflty on my cheek. It was no ordinary peck, however. It wasn't one of those things that was done with the speed of light, as though it never really happened in the first place. Andrew had left me with a kiss that had a special something that can't be pulled from the air. I felt myself fall to a place I'd never visited. There was something about Andrew, I kept thinking. It was so strange; I'd never felt an attraction to men. Andrew was different. But he had the same effect on all women, apparently. Even with young thin women who struggled to speak English. I saw it as though he had his own force of gravity. But I was in love with Jenny. I like girls. I might like boys too . . .

Andrew left me on the footpath with my luggage outside the Airport main entrance. I waved to him as the white government limousine pulled away. I never waved to anyone in that romantic way. But this time, It was something that I couldn't have helped if I tried.

CHAPTER TEN

Graduate

THE OLD BITUMEN TRACK THAT SPIRALLED it's way around the Swan Island facility never seemed empty of young candidate joggers. They ran dressed in their official grey Swan Island tracksuits, most of them were firmly plugged into their music devices. I ran hard. I made a habit of putting everything I had into it. I ran on. I ran to forget.

After doing laps around the facility, I slowed, and walked it out as I sucked huge gulps of air down into my lungs. I sat down on the edge of a jetty that overlooked Port Phillip bay to the north. I could just make out the tall Melbourne skyscrapers that pierced the horizon. I thought about Jenny. She was there, somewhere. I couldn't help but wonder what Jenny would be doing right now.

I drew my knees up and I wrapped my arms tightly around my legs. I sat there enjoying the cooling breeze as it pushed past the sweat on my back. As I looked out across the water, a lone figure stood on a nearby boat who was tossing out burley, while flocks of noisy seagulls fought over the spoils. In that moment while looking out across the water, I felt peace. I felt peace even though I missed Jenny and my heart broke every time I thought of her.

As I sat there, my thoughts were rudely interrupted by someone's sudden appearance. I glanced sideways to the person who sat heavily down beside me. "Nice job," I said.

"Even if you *do* say so yourself."

"Sorry."

"No. Don't be. Now I know we've trained you well."

"It looks that way, doesn't it?" I said smiling a little.

My instructor briefly echoed my expression, then he lifted his hand to his broken face. "Normally I'd say you deserve a few shots tonight, but somehow . . . I don't think I'm able to partake."

"I don't like tequila that much. It gives me reflux. Besides, I'd much rather be elsewhere right now. My old life. My old home. My old job . . ."

"You know that's not an option."

"So you keep saying. What? Am I in some kind of a jail?"

"Candidate. This is a seriously important institution. Of the hundreds that apply for intelligence each year, only six get to graduate. You're one of the six. And not only that, you've leapfrogged them all. They'd all kill you for the chance you've got."

"And that's supposed to make me feel special."

"Check your attitude, candidate. You've got small arms assessment to get through, at 1400. After that, you're officially on stand-down, awaiting deployment."

"Then what? No one's said anything. Just gossip. I don't do gossip."

"You'll know soon enough. HQ will let you know. Just do me one favour. When you're out in the field, do as you're instructed. Don't go on gut. That way you won't get your own arse handed to you. ASIS *will* kick your arse severely if you stuff up. Make sure it doesn't happen. Number one above everything; back up your players. Got it?"

I shook my head and looked away. “You’re all the same. You’re all on the need to know. I seriously doubt if I’ll spend the rest of my days as a player.”

“You will. That’s the way it is. Now you’re with us—you’re with us for life. We’re your family now. You’d better get used to it.” I heard my instructor breathe deeply before looking away. “Okay, Angel. Here it is and you didn’t hear it from me. What I’m about to tell you is rumour. It’s innuendo. It’s speculation. Get what I’m saying? There’s no graduation for you. There’s no ceremony, or anything like it. Not like the others. Those guys are bound for that desk job at Ben Chifley you’ve been worried about. But you know what? This one comes from the top. From the boss, himself. Make no mistake about it; you’ve already been assigned and deployed. And I’ll repeat it, in case you didn’t hear me. It’s rumour and speculation.”

I took noticed of my instructor’s serious tone and when I did, all the memories of the time at Busby’s with Nathan bounced back. Just *what* was I getting into?

“You’ll deploy from 0700.”

“Deploy to where?”

“Forward ops. But it’s rumour and speculation, remember. You’d better get your head in the game, Angel. I shit you not.”

I thought about it momentarily. It just didn’t sit well in my mind. “I don’t believe you. It’d be suicide for everyone if Firebird Station came out of the shadows.”

“It’s no longer Firebird. That’s finished with. Firebird station is dead in the water. Colonel Mack requested your reassignment. You belong to her as of 0700 tomorrow. I will not disclose the location of your ops post. It’s for everyone’s security including mine. Report to the range before 14:00. That’s all I have to say.”

My instructor slowly heaved himself up, wincing in the pain from the injuries that I bestowed upon him. Without anything further to add, he walked with a slight limp toward HQ.

"Wait!" I shouted after him. "I need something!"

"What is it?"

As I walked toward my instructor I wondered that it may not even be possible. But I asked it anyway. "I need something before I deploy. I need a new look. Some new clothes. A new hairdo. Can you get me out of here for a while?"

My instructor scrutinised me up and down as though he was looking at some object that was far from human. "Don't change your look too much. Canberra has sent new travel documents including your new passport. Rumour has it, you're going to Langley after you deploy to forward ops."

"Langley? Why?"

"You're going to help the CIA locate the whereabouts of a stolen Chinook. Apparently. Rumour and inuendo, kiddo. Remember? I'll get Andrea to take you into Geelong. I need to go there myself. Nose straightening sucks big time. And not only, you've made my testicles feel like they're the size of St Clement's bells. I hate this job sometimes, just saying."

"Sorry."

"Don't be. But your ops post needs a name. Colonel Mack tells me you have an idea."

"Charlotte," I shouted as my instructor turned and walked away. "We'll call it Charlotte Station."

CHAPTER ELEVEN

Jenny

I'd SPENT THE MORING SHOPPING for clothes. It wasn't an easy choice—there're so many options. With only two hours at my disposal, I scampered around the main areas of the Westfield's Shopping Centre in Geelong. I hurried along at a frantic pace, almost running, while at the same time checking for time on my brand-new smartphone number three.

In and out of the dozens of boutiques I blurred, stopping occasionally for a few moments before moving on to the next. Andrea followed closely behind me. "Hey. Slow down. We've still got time."

It was the smell of leather that caught my attention. The smell of a saddlery. It reminded me of home. The scent brought back images of a much younger me, who grew up in Alice Springs. I pushed on toward the scent and stepped through open glass doors into a large area of an RM Williams retail outlet. At last I could choose. At last, poor Andrea was likely to rest and catch her breath. I took several garments from hangers and stepped into the change rooms to try them out for size, then rushed to the checkout, knowing my hairdressing appointment was just moments away. Out of the shop, I lugged several large orange plastic bags with big RM Williams longhorns printed on the sides. Andrea still followed closely, and it was in that moment I wondered why she was along in the first place. I didn't need a minder, and I knew Geelong quite well. It didn't matter. I strode on, loaded up to the chin with bags upon bags.

After I'd finished with the hairdresser, I asked if I could use the back room of the salon to change into my new outfit. I needed the final picture immediately. The salon manager agreed, and I stepped through into the back.

I stared into the mirror, and I was happy with my new me. But I wondered about my passport photo—I'd changed so much. My long, flowing raven hair was now dead straight, cut, shaped and styled into a short bob and glistened blue-black under the salon lights. I smiled as I ran my eyes up and down my reflection. I loved the way my new white blouse – which was open-necked and buttoned low – accentuated my complexion. I loved the hint of my pink lingerie under my blouse. Everything was masterly measured and properly fitted. My nails were freshly polished with a neutral tone and manicured to just beyond the tips of my fingers. A chocolate leather waist jacket which was tailored in the classic Australian rural style, and a pair of figure-hugging beige jodhpurs that clung to my curves. My new look was finished off with a pair of leather, knee-high RM Williams boots. I was no longer the city slicker of my former self. I was no longer the journalist everybody knew on evening television. I was no longer the conservative chick that lived high up over Melbourne's skyline. My look returned me to my rural origins, and I was happy.

* * *

Returning to the range at exactly 1400, I wondered what would be waiting for me tomorrow at 0700. As I placed my ear protection over my ears, and a set of amber safety shields over my eyes, I stood there and waited for the command to check weapons, aim and fire. I knew what I had to do to pass. The question was, was I capable of doing it? With all that training behind me, it now came down to this moment. But in my mind, I still had a choice over my destiny. I could fail. And if I did, I'd return to my old life. I'd return to Jenny. It'd be like old times. I could get back to were I was before all this bullshit started.

"Candidates! Welcome to your final objective! Fail this test and it's a handshake before you return to civvie street. Take your time and make every round count. Remember. This is for MPI, and not the perfect bullseye. Ready . . . At your own time, begin!"

I was still thinking about Jenny as I squeezed off my first round. Miss this shot, my inner voice kept telling me. Miss it and you can go home. I didn't know the reason why I opted in. Perhaps I felt as though I was now duty bound to my country. Nathan was right. Something dreadful was about to happen to everyone on this Planet Earth. It would happen over my dead body.

After I fired five rounds, the paper targets came whizzing back via overhead snatch rails. I smiled to myself at the outcome. My mean point of impact was small enough to pass my exam. I was on my way.

* * *

0700 the next morning was heavily overcast and with rain. The rain came in horizontal sheets that was carried in on gale-force winds. As I stood alone at the facility guard house, my umbrella offered only momentary cover before the howling southerly wind turned it inside out. Dressed in my new full-length black trench coat, I bobbed up and down on one spot with my arms tightly wrapped around my body. I tried desperately to keep out the cold. But suddenly, a set of headlights speared through the gloom.

A white government Holden Statesman with black licence plates embellished with the State Crown of Victoria slowly motored over and stopped by my side. The dark tinted windows prevented me from seeing inside. I waited momentarily for someone to step out and give me a hand with my luggage. It never happened, but just as I thought about it, I heard a click and the boot lid rose slightly up. After putting my luggage in the back I jumped inside and shut the door. The government vehicle then moved off slowly and did a wide U-turn, and I left that lonely place forever.

There wasn't much in the way of conversation on the way to Tullamarine. The traffic was heavy on the Princes Freeway, up from Geelong. It was even heavier approaching the West Gate Bridge. And by the time the government car made a left turn and headed for the Bolte Bridge, the traffic was almost at a standstill.

I finally got up some gumption and seized the moment. "How about a small diversion to Port Melbourne," I asked my driver.

My driver flatly refused my request in a cold, formal tone. I said nothing else for the rest of the journey to Melbourne Airport.

On arrival at the domestic terminal, I grabbed my baggage from the boot of the government car – all by my bloody self. Head down and bent forward, I fought my way through the rain and the wind.

New electronic technology made check in a breeze. With my luggage checked, I decided to take a seat and rest before doing battle with airport security. VIP or not, all passengers were given the same treatment. Pain in the arse.

The scent of freshly brewed, real coffee hung in the air. How could I *not* have a Starbuck's. I took a large paper mug of unsweetened black coffee back to my very uncomfortable chair. Glancing down at the screen of my phone, I realised it was an hour before my flight was due to board.

We could've easily accommodated a diversion to my apartment. But now there was no hope of seeing Jenny for one last time. There was no hope of collecting some of my belongings. And there was no hope for closing the book on a chapter of my life, once and forever.

Countless times I'd tried to contact Jenny. After dialling home, there was no answer. The phone rang a couple of times and then went directly to voicemail. I'd left dozens of messages, but it was impossible to leave a phone number for Jenny to return my call. I made inquiries using the techniques that were not readily available to the masses. Everything I tried came up empty. The line was disconnected the last time I called home. Later, I'd discovered Jenny had deleted her social media. It was as though she'd already moved on.

But then, there was the title of our Port Melbourne apartment. That was something that could never be taken away. It was a purchase we'd both made. I instantly checked my bag for my apartment keys and they were there. If only my driver diverted after I asked him. Now, it was too late now.

Coffee finished, I decided to get one more before boarding. On the way to the Starbuck's kiosk, I passed by the noticed board and checked for boarding in the hope of an early departure to Darwin. To my horror, the flight was delayed due to weather. Three hours. But maybe it wasn't a bad thing after all.

I quickly did the sums in my head. Leaving the airport to go to Port Melbourne then getting back before boarding was going to be a tight squeeze but not impossible. I'd need to get going right now. I picked up my belongings and sprinted for the exit.

Outside, thunder and lightning cracked through the greyness as I hailed for a taxi. It took more than a few goes, before eventually, a yellow Melbourne taxi stopped and I flung myself into the back.

* * *

The first thing I noticed after I placed my key into the lock was how easily it slid in. It never did that before. But also, the door wasn't locked at all. It was slightly ajar. My brain thumped hard. Something was wrong.

"Jenny?"

I pushed the door open and stepped inside. Somebody had ransacked our apartment. Stuff was strewn all over. Things that stood up right now lay on its side. Bookcases, shelving, chests of drawers, kitchen bureau, everything. The floor was littered with broken and smashed debris.

"Jenny!"

I murmured Jenny's name at first then shouted it. The horror of it all. There was no reply.

"Oh god. Jenny!"

I stepped through the mess on the floor and headed into the kitchen. Cupboards were open. Plates were smashed. Things were strewn and thrown from one corner of the kitchen to the next. Even our outdoor furniture on the balcony was upturned and tossed about.

I tiptoed over debris from the kitchen and stepped into the bedroom. Everything was a mess. Everything was everywhere. Even our mattress stripped and ripped up and upturned.

On the floor, in the rubble, there was something that caught the corner of my eye. It glimmered for a second. I tiptoed over to it and picked it up. My rock crystal figurine—the one Jenny had given to me as a birthday present. I retrieved it, wrapping it up in tissue before putting it deep in my trench coat pocket.

Getting my head back took a few moments. I fought through the urge to start cleaning the place up. But now, time was getting away. Reluctantly, I stepped back through the front door, closing it behind me. Out on the street, the taxi waited just as instructed. Dodging the downpour, I flew in the back, and departed for Tullamarine with a great amount of speed.

TWO

Stand-To

CHAPTER TWELVE

Red Bandana

AFTER LANDING IN DARWIN, I was still feeling the stress with what I'd discovered back in Melbourne. I remained seated while passengers got up and prepared to leave the aircraft. I was still sitting, daydreaming out of the window after all passengers completely vacated the aircraft. I held the figurine Jenny had given me in my hand. I twirled it around, eyeing it, running my fingers over it. My mind ran like a silent movie over the memories I'd shared with Jenny. Happy memories. It was Jenny who'd kept me grounded. It was Jenny who'd listen—often late at night—to the stories of my stressful days. At times, I caught Jenny at the edge of falling asleep, but she never did. She was all ears. Jenny my rock. Jenny my sounding board. Jenny my soul mate. Jenny my lover . . .

At that moment, I was brought back from my thoughts by a polite touch on my shoulder. "I'm sorry, Angel. It's time to leave the aircraft now," the flight attendant said. I looked up and nodded. "Thank you. And thank you again for listening to my worries. I was a bit of a mess, wasn't I?"

"It was no trouble. But I'll let you in on a secret. It's all part of our job." The flight attendant smiled warmly before disappearing down the aisle toward the business class bulkhead.

I pulled myself up from my seat. It felt as though my heart was heavier than the rest of my body. I got up slowly. I collected my things from the overhead locker and stepped forward toward the exit.

In contrast to the weather in Melbourne, Darwin was stiflingly hot and sticky. I was overwhelmed by the humidity as I stepped out of the aircraft door. With my trench coat dangling around my forearm, the first thing I thought of was, what to do with it? Darwin was no place for a trench coat. No one in Darwin would ever need one—much less own one.

Arriving at the baggage carousel, I waited patiently for it to start moving around, indicating bags were on their way. I held back from the crowd that gathered there. I was in no hurry and I couldn't have cared less if I was the last to leave. I was sluggish to react and I felt as though some kind of invisible force was weighing me down. Head down and sad—I waited by the carousel.

My bags passed by. I knew they'd already passed by several times. I'd collect them the next time around. Then they passed again. And again. After a while, the carousel was empty with my two bags floating on the conveyor, passing me by—lonely, as I was alone. They passed by another time. I made no attempt to retrieve them. I stood motionless, still, like some porcelain statue. And then suddenly, my breath left my lungs.

Dizziness attacked me. I spun from the carousel and headed to an empty seat at the edge of the large open space. My mind wound and twirled. I felt inner heat rise. My skin prickled and I gasped for air. I felt tiny beads of sweat break out over my arms. With the back of a hand, I wiped perspiration from my face. Then the tears came. I tried to control it. I tried hard. I failed. I bent forward with my head almost touching my knees.

I tried to breathe. I wanted to scream. Wave after wave, it came. I buried my face in my hands. I screamed out. As hard as I could. Uncontrollable. Overpowering. Overwhelming. I was so sad. So angry. So heartbroken. Alone at an airport, devoid of souls. Souls that had long since left and returned to their lives.

Bent forward in my chair, I did my best to hide. But then, I felt a comforting hand on my back. I imagined a stranger had come to comfort me. Someone who took the trouble to console me. I was such a blubbering mess. Wiping my eyes, I grabbed some composure before looked up and I recognised him straight away.

"Bosco?"

Bosco said nothing but only nodded slowly. Perhaps even empathetically. Something I couldn't imagine coming from Bosco.

"I was expecting Maggie," I said.

"Maggie's got things on. I'm here to pick you up," Bosco said, gazing down at me. He patted his pockets then took something out. "It's not a tissue, but it's clean, and you can have it," he said as he sat down next to me. Bosco passed me what I thought was a red bandana. I took it with thanks and used it to dab at my tears.

"I don't leave home without it," Bosco said. "And Maggie keeps making sure it's clean."

"And why do you have a red bandana in your pocket?"

"A long story. But it's a lucky charm, I guess. I think knowing what's coming, maybe I don't need that lucky charm no more."

"Oh? I never saw you as the superstitious type."

"We all have something. Canter has his dummy round. Maggie has her Norman Lindsay etchings. Andrew has his father's police badge. And I had my bandana. A story for another time. You good?"

"Getting there. I just had a moment . . ."

It was roughly thirty minutes before I had the strength to stand up. During that time, Bosco sat next to me, silent, not a word said as I explained what had happened to Jenny. It was as though he wasn't there at all, but somehow, I knew he was listening. He put a hand on my shoulder occasionally. It was somehow odd to find comfort Bosco's company. But certainly, it was better than nothing at all.

"Your bag," Bosco said, pointing, breaking the silence. "A guy just got it off the carousel. You'd better go get it before these guys start jumping around."

"Shit. I forgot."

"Yeah. You can thank 9/11 for that. But don't worry, I'll get it."

Bosco sprinted away, and after collecting my baggage he strolled back with a big smile on his face. He looked kind of goofy. A big muscular military type trailing a very feminine looking bag behind him. It made me return his smile and for the first time I found myself warming to Bosco. I stood from the chair, still feeling heavy as he approached me. After passing over my bag, he stepped back. Bosco's eyes scanned me up and down and he smiled again. A very different kind of smile.

"It's just a haircut," I said, handing him back his bandana. But he took my hand and closed it. "I said you can keep it. It's yours. I know you're not into guys. But you're a fine-looking woman, Angel."

* * *

There wasn't much in the way of conversation out from Darwin domestic. Much the same as the ride up to Melbourne from Swan Island. I tried to hide my sadness as it attacked me in waves. There were a few moments where I thought I'd succumb to tears all over again. And then there was Bosco's lucky charm which he gave to me. The scent of wonderful lavender in the bandana helped me immensely. I had to wonder. Maggie did the lavender thing for me, she'd told me. Now Bosco? Maybe it was Maggie's way with everyone.

Bosco glanced at me sideways occasionally as he drove. I knew he avoided the chit-chat, and I was quietly thankful. On the other hand, Bosco seemed almost glad about something. I caught him smiling—then he'd snap his head forward, eyes back on the road.

"Not long now," Bosco said. "It's just up ahead."

"Are all original Firebird players deployed?"

Bosco nodded. "We've got a newbie with us this time."

"Really? Who?"

Bosco glanced sideways again. "I think I'll let Maggie do the intros."

"And Nathan?"

I caught Bosco's expression drain a fraction. Something was wrong.

"Canter is about to jump on a flight from Seoul International. He's due into Darwin International at 2300."

* * *

The white Holden Commodore drew to a halt out the front of an inconspicuous, timber clad cottage that was raised off the ground on stilts. I noticed a shipping container that was out the back. I wondered what it was used for. The place was new. Perhaps the container was for supplies or for storage. But I also noticed a light that was set up on a pole in front of the container door. Even more strange was some kind of antenna on top of the container.

Bosco reefed the handbrake lever and killed the engine. "Welcome to Charlotte Station," he said. "I heard it was you who'd given the station the callsign."

I nodded as I looked from the window. The obviously newly built cottage had no lawns or gardens and sat raised on a patch of bare earth. I left the vehicle, still feeling heavy as I followed Bosco up wooden stairs that smelt of new cut pine and fresh paint.

Bosco stepped forward and knocked on the bare wooden door. After a moment Maggie's smiling face appeared as the door opened.

"Shilo," Bosco said. "Mission accomplished."

Maggie beamed and stood to one side. The smell of home-style cooking wafted through and was instantly spoiled by the awful smell of freshly painted walls. I couldn't help myself. I flew into Maggie's open arms. "Goodness, love," Maggie said as she wrapped her arms around me. "Whatever is the matter?"

I could say no words as my tears erupted and I'd succumbed to my sadness all over again.

"You didn't tell her, did you?" Maggie said to Bosco. Bosco shook his head and quickly disappeared down the hall.

"Told me what?" I asked.

"Come inside, love. We can't stay out here any longer."

Again, Maggie asked as I stood in the warm light of the foyer. "What is it, Angel. Whatever is the matter?"

As the words came out of my mouth, it seemed as though it was no longer a thought in my head. It was real, and there was nothing I could do about it. "It's Jenny. She's missing."

"Missing? But Angel . . ."

"I thought it might be an idea to catch up with her before leaving Melbourne. My apartment is a mess. Everything is ruined, and Jenny's gone!"

"And when, may I ask did you go there? Did your driver take you there? Damn it. I specifically requested for that *not* to happen."

I was amazed at Maggie's choice of words. My sadness left me and shock took over. "You knew she was missing?"

"We knew about what happened at your apartment. That's why you were not to go there. Under *any* circumstances."

"My flight was delayed due to bad weather. I had the time to go there, so I did."

"God no! I'm so sorry Angel. That was something I was not expecting."

"Maggie . . . How could you *not* tell me what happened? And now Jenny . . ."

"We couldn't tell you, love. You were training. If we'd contacted you even on a secure line, we might've been compromised yet again. It was much too risky, you must understand. We're all far too deep in the game, and there's no room for risks. Not now."

"But Jenny . . . she's missing."

Maggie took a step back and folded her arms. "That Bosco. I'll kill him. He was supposed to tell you about Jenny the moment he saw you. Jenny is here, Angel. She's safe."

CHAPTER THIRTEEN

Canter

MY SPRITS LIFTED IMMENSELY at the sight of Jenny. Jenny padded quickly to the front door. She reached for me the exact moment I pushed past Maggie. The embrace was a long one. Tears again. Happy tears. I witnessed for the first time I'd ever seen Maggie with red-rimmed eyes. Her hardness disappeared and she was the Maggie I'd known as a child.

An old-fashioned lamb roast, cooked old-school, was my favourite. Around the table, hoeing into plates piled high, were all the familiar faces. Christina, the lovely polite German girl who'd been smuggled from the BND for her obvious talents. Maggie's stepson, Andrew. 'The ASIO guy,' I'd once called him. I winced slightly at my own recollection. Even among operatives, the mere mention of the word was deemed taboo. Bosco sat beside Andrew with his baseball hat that he never, ever took off. Maggie was sitting opposite, beaming with her chin resting on the back of her hands, watching on proudly. And Jenny right beside me. Thank god Jenny was safe.

Nathan, of course, was more than a few hours away, on a flight out from Seoul International. When he finally arrived back, all originals would be reunited. But there was one other seated at the table. The newbie Bosco had mentioned. A man with skin the colour of ebony. A man who was as tall as an NBA major league player and a grin that lit up the room. The introduction to this man was one of my biggest surprises. I recognised him before any words were exchanged. "I know you. I know you from Busby's. You're the manager. You were there when Nathan and I were there." It all started to sink in. He nodded and began to belly laugh. A very weird sense of humour, I thought.

This man's real name was non-existent, as was his history. He was known only under the codename of Xenon, and all referred to him simply as Xe. It wasn't clear what Xe's mission entailed. However, Maggie explained everything I needed to know. Somehow, I knew there was much more to what she let on. Xe was ops forward. Black ops, mostly. But the biggest shock of all came after Maggie went on with the details. There were many layers to the operations of ASIS. Xe was deep below the layers of secrecy. He'd been assigned a security level equal to that of the Director-General himself. He moved among the world silently unknown to all but a few and answered only to the Prime Minister. His cover was cleverly cloaked, and his whereabouts at any point in time was classified. Xe had the luxury of autonomy. He could plug in and unplug as he saw fit. And Maggie explained it in words that now seem like slow motion. He's Oudarretian. The realisation was an explosive moment in my mind.

Around the dinner table, with Jenny's help, Bosco began clearing up plates and taking them back to the kitchen. Wine, beer, spirits, everything, cluttered the table with half-full, half-empty glasses. The was the chatter about this and that. Small talk and shared jokes, to which bouts of laughter rang out. But among all the chatter, I decided to change the subject. My words stopped everyone and a silk sheet of silence fell down around us.

"So, what's in the shipping container out the back?" I asked. Everyone held their voices, and quickly glanced at one another. I thought their reaction was guilt. But why?

"Don't tell me," I said trying to make light of the situation. "You've got someone stashed in there, right?"

It was taken as a joke; it was a bad one. No one laughed.

Maggie looked across and eyed me directly. "Well, love, that's for you. Consider it your dessert. Now's the time you get to use some of your training," Maggie said, smiling.

"High priority, huh? Who do we have in there? A G-man?" I laughed a little under my breath. Surely not.

Maggie smiled wryly before winking at Xe. "That's right, Angel. We have ourselves a Guardianship soldier. How about that?"

"You're kidding."

"It's true. However, we've already extracted all the intel we're ever going to get out of the man. Xe was tacking him. He got hold of him as he was making a play on Jenny."

Jenny placed her hand on my knee and she gave me that expression that told me not to worry. But now, I was angry. I thought about what the G-man did to my home. I thought about how Jenny must've felt when it was going down. I was angry. I tried to keep it in check. "Did you manage to extract any intel on the CIA's stolen Chinook?"

"Xe had a go at it. So did Andrew. There's nothing else forthcoming from the man, unfortunately."

"I bet I can drag it out of him."

"If Xe can't, then I'm afraid we're at our wits' end. However, you may interrogate him as part of your growing experience. Show us what Swan Island has taught you. But I want you to do it constructively and by the book. Am I clear?"

I was about to answer Maggie. Suddenly Christina bounced through the dining room door. “An email received from Canter. Schnell! Schnell!”

* * *

The email from Nathan was only one line. It was something I never wanted to read. Nathan words were by using the code known only to those in our tight intelligence community.

canter@bya.net; Airline has lost baggage.

Maggie stepped back from the laptop and half turned away. Others scrutinised the screen in horror as Christina began the various stages of verification. After it was complete, she turned away from the screen with her wide eyes.

“Jesus,” Maggie said. “We don’t need this right now.”

As I realised what was happening, I felt my heart plummet. “Nathan has a watcher? Who?”

“We need more code,” Bosco said. “Maybe it’s Gs. But maybe it’s Norks. If it’s Norks, god help him.”

“Norks?”

“North Korean spooks,” Maggie answered me almost under her breath. “We can only speculate as to how this has happened. Can’t we Andrew!”

Andrew said nothing but his expression of embarrassment said everything. Nathan was in danger. Surely there were friendlies who could help.

Everyone crowded around the laptop, except Andrew who began to pace around with his hands stuck in his pockets.

Maggie asked, "Christina, can you verify a secured SMTP server back to Nathan's emails?"

Christina tapped out a string of commands, then nodded. "IP encryption enabled."

"Reply to Canter's email to disengage, will you please."

Christina opened a new email with the new encryption settings locked in.

charlotte@bya.net; Check airport lost and found.

"No, wait," I said just before Christina had the opportunity to press send. "If I know Nathan, he would've already long ditched his countermeasures procedure."

"That's true, Angel." Maggie said after thinking it over. "It would've been his number one. We have to think more like Canter. What would he do instead of the standard ops?"

I leaned over the laptop and typed.

charlotte@bya.net; Check your travel insurance.

I hit send.

"Good work. If he says, 'no insurance,' at least we'll know where we stand, and we can use Alfa Two Bravo for his extraction."

It only took only a minute for the reply.

canter@bya.net; Airline will on-send baggage.

"Log Canter's IP will you please, Christina?" Maggie asked sternly after stepping back from the screen.

Christina responded and typed out a string of commands. "Hess connected to Vi-Fi via Seoul International."

"That means no Nork watchers," Bosco said.

"Not necessarily, Bosco. Norks are all over the south peninsular. I wouldn't rule it out just yet." Maggie went back to the laptop. "Cristina, see if you can access the passenger manifest of his flight out from Soul."

Everyone went silent as Christina worked her magic. Nathan was in serious trouble. If he failed to board his flight from Seoul International, it could only be for one reason. He was trying to tag his watchers. To my horror, I realised Nathan was not about to disengage.

After Christina accessed the passenger manifest, she looked up from the screen and shook her head. "He's not on ze list."

"He's not disengaging, damn it! Christina, we need to get him to safety. Initiate Alfa Two Bravo. Extraction priority."

Maggie started pacing the floor then she turned and scorned into her stepson. "Andrew, what the fuck have you done! Didn't I tell you *not* to break his cover! Didn't I tell you to bring him home under code black!"

"Another email received," Christina said loudly over Maggie's shouting.

canter@bya.net; Baggage recovered at Lost and Found.

I looked at the email. "What does that mean? It's not part of our cypher."

"Canter is trying to tell us the Norks have disengaged," Bosco put in. "But I don't like it. They never disengage from an active target. And Canter knows that."

“Cristina! Initiate Alfa Two Bravo! Immediately!”

“It’s too late for Seoul friendlies,” Bosco said. “They won’t get there in time.”

We stood around the computer. My eyes never left the screen. We waited for updates. I held my breath. My heart thumped in my mouth. Moments ticked by. A blinking lone cursor against a white computer screen. I hoped for the confirmation of Nathan’s departure out from Seoul International. The clock showed thirty minutes had passed since the flight had left the ground. Nothing. No confirmation of anything. It was as though Nathan had stepped off the edge of the world.

CHAPTER FOURTEEN

Mea Culpa

AT 0344 HOURS, I lingered alone by the tactical laptop. I sat and stared at the blank screen, at the same time clinging to any hope I had left. A lonely cursor blinked in steady rhythm on a white background. I stared at it, willing it to make letters but nothing changed.

Padded footfalls were loud enough to take my mind away from the computer. Jenny appeared at the open door and peered at me through eyes that were hardly awake. She stood there in her new nightclothes and her new fluffy slippers. Her skin glistened from the humidity. "Coming to bed?" she asked as her eyes struggled to adjust in the darkness.

"A few more moments, please Jen. Don't be angry. I need to know if Nathan's . . ." Then the tears.

Jenny came to my side and placed an arm around my shoulder. "C'mon hon. You need to sleep," she said. "How would it be if Nathan resurfaced and you were too tired to do anything? Put the laptop in sleep mode. The chime will wake you if he sends another email."

I nodded. "Okay. You're right. I'll be there in a bit."

"Besides," Jenny added. "We have some catching up to do if you think sleep won't come." Jenny's face lit up with a wicked smile. She kissed me softly and left, almost skipping with cheeky intention. It made me smile. But how could I get in the mood knowing what's happened?

* * *

I was still at the laptop as the first signs of a new day began to lighten the night sky. I hadn't moved from the chair. Every muscle in my body hurt but I didn't care. I was determined to be the first set of eyes on Nathan's next email and I'd stay seated there for however long was required.

0722. The first up for the morning was Andrew.

"Morning," Andrew said as he strutted past me, wiping the sleep from his eyes. "I'm about to make a brew. Can I get you one?"

"I need a cigarette. Got any of those?"

"I can do coffee. Smokes, I don't have. And Maggie . . ."

"Don't give a shit about Maggie! I want a fucking cigarette!"

"Hey . . . You okay?"

I didn't answer Andrew. He had the ability to read my body language. If he couldn't do that, too bad. My thoughts of Nathan began to fade. My hopes diminished, and by that time, I didn't quite know what it was that held me there. I slowly put my hand out for the shutdown key and hovered.

Andrew stepped up beside me, and took my hand, helping me to shut down the computer.

"We'll get those fuckers," Andrew said. But there was no comfort in his words. None. Somewhere deep inside, I could no longer keep my anger from growing into something of a monster. It rose silently like the black, evil thing that it was. I needed retribution. I needed it, and I was going to get it. The shipping container. That's where I'd go and get my revenge. I desired it like something delicious; something delectable. Payback. Something I could taste, swallow, and enjoy. That evil thing inside me. It lay down swishing its tail, looking up at with dog eyes, baring its teeth. I gave the thing a pat; said sit, good dog. Now, its calling me. I'd take the leash out and go for a walk. Meet my evil twin sibling; that horrible dark me that stayed mute at the back of my mind. Not anymore! They say hell hath no fury. I scoff. I say, my fury hath no hell!

I got up from the chair and faced Andrew. He stood there smiling as though Nathan's demise no longer mattered. I placed a hand softly and calmly on Andrew's cheek. I echoed his smile. I felt his smooth skin beneath the tips of my fingers.

"What?" Andrew asked me while smiling his sexy smile.

"Your skin is so smooth. You've shaved." I looked at him closer and continued to run my fingers softly over his face, tracing my fingers along his cheekbones and neck. He smiled again. "You're flirting with me?"

"I don't know, am I? But I do want something of yours."

I noticed Andrew's Adams apple bob up and down and I knew I had him where I wanted him.

"What is it, Angel. What?"

"I want your straight razor. I know you have one; I've seen it. Go and get it for me."

Andrew turned and disappeared upstairs without adding another word. Spinning around, I grabbed the pump-action sawn-off shotgun from the rack inside the steel locker. I cracked it open and checked for rounds in the chamber. Two brass eyes stared back at me; a welcoming sight. I was loaded and ready to spit death. I slammed the twin barrels shut at the same time as I saw it. Just what the doctor ordered, I told myself. A nine-millimetre

Beretta in a holster was slung over the door of the locker. I grabbed that too.

Andrew bounced down the stairs as I shoved more shotgun cartridges into my pockets. He eyed me curiously, pausing momentarily, looking more confused as ever. “Angel?”

I stepped forward and took the straight razor from Andrew’s grip. I turned without any hesitation and made directly for the back door.

I bounced down a set of wooden steps to where the large paint-peeled and dented shipping container stood. Andrew called out after me. I heard him. I didn’t respond. My head was elsewhere. I turned sharply just to give Andrew a wink. Why? I had no idea.

“Don’t do it, Angel.” Andrew called out from behind me. I ignored it.

I ducked around the edge of the container, oblivious to Andrew’s words. I felt my heart pumping madly at my breastbone. I grasped the handle of the shipping container and wrenched it up. The large container door creaked open and I stepped inside.

The inside of the shipping container was *not* as I’d expected. There was a concrete floor and a stairwell going down into the earth. A pole stood next to the stairwell. An electrical box and a set of light switches were positioned on the pole. I threw all the switches one by one and lights lit my way down.

Below the cold, cold, earth I heard muffled cries coming from behind a main door at the end of a small corridor. I paced myself forward, opened the door and entered.

He was in there; the son-of-a-bitch. He was seated and tied with nylon zip ties into place. I stepped up closer and leaned forward, peering into his blackened eyes. As he made eye contact with mine through his contusions, I noticed he shuddered in his chair.

"Hello there, little man. Know who I am?"

His eyes immediately widened and bulged but he shook his head.

"Oh? Well let's make it a little easier for you to remember, shall we?"

I leaned forward a little closer and flicked my hair around my left ear. "Surely you'd remember that?"

He *did* remember. The guy shouted something from behind the gaffer tape that trapped his voice. I laughed most heartily. I enjoyed my retribution. I ran my eyes over him, smiling at him up and down. I reached out. The tips of my fingers just hovered above the backs of his hands.

I studied his injuries. The bruises on his face. The nose that sat crooked. The cuts beneath his eyes. I could do better. So much better. "No real damage done that I can tell. Let's see if I can change all that, huh?"

Getting out Andrew's straight razor from my pocket, I unfolded the blade in front of his eyes. He immediately flinched back in his chair.

"Let's call it an ear for an ear then, shall we?"

I reached forward and grabbed his ear, pulling it forward. With the razor in my grip, I cut through the gristle and sawed the thing clean off. The son-of-a-bitch screamed so hard, the gaffer tape flew off his face. I laughed at the same time placing his severed ear in his shirt pocket, giving it a pat just for good measure. I stood back and eyed him. Tears streamed from his contused and closed over eyes.

"Uh oh. That looks a little odd to me. I'll probably need to even it up a bit, don't you think?"

The yelling and screaming stopped me from taking his other ear. A moment of weakness.

"What the fuck, lady! You fucking crazy bitch!"

I wiped the razor blade clean on his shirt, choosing to ignore his cries. I brought the razor to the side of his face. I could've finished him right there. But I relented. He flinched back. I decided it was moment of pity. I was human, after all.

"Let's have the location of the Chinook," I asked him. "We both know you're privy to its location. So, be a good little man and tell me where it is. Then all this will go away."

"BITCH! You fucking crazy bitch."

I got my mouth up close to the hole in the side of his head that was once an ear. "THE CHINOOK! WHERE IS IT!"

"Bitch! You'll never end what's gonna happen. Kill me now; just do it!"

"Oh, I will. You can count on it," I replied calmly. "It's up to you, though. Slow or fast? Which way will you have it? Killing you will be easy. Quick, and painless, or . . . you can die with a great amount of pain. Isn't it lovely how you get to choose?"

I stepped away to the corner of the concrete room and dragged a chair over. I sat down in the chair and eyed him; patiently eyed him until his breathing started to slow.

"Tick-tock," I said. "Fast or slow? Which way will it go?"

He looked up almost empty of soul.

"Oh well, this was fun." I shrugged as I got up from the chair, making sure he would see me. I reached into my pocket and got out a set of iPod earbuds and plugged the cord into my device. "Oh. It's for my benefit. Shotguns are unbelievably loud. In a room like this? I could go deaf. That isn't happening."

I pressed play. *'Sad But True.'* by Metallica played loud. The bastard sat there wincing up at me. I brought the shotgun over and aimed at his left kneecap point blank. I pulled the trigger. His patella exploded into a thousand bloody shards that scattered, clinking around the room.

I laughed. “Fuck . . . that was loud, huh? And Guess what? There’s another one of those.”

His screams began to chill me. But I pushed on.

It seemed he was about to black out. “This won’t do. I’m not done with you yet!” I gripped the warm barrel of the shotgun with both my hands. I held it up like a baseball bat. With a decent wind-up, I stepped up and belted him across the face. His teeth flew from his mouth. “THE CHINOOK! WHERE IS IT!”

He hesitated answering me. Big mistake. An instant later, another kneecap exploded. A bone fragment landed on my lips and I spat it away.

“TELL ME WHERE IT IS!” I screamed and cracked open the weapon, ejecting the spent cartridges. I reloaded the shotgun and pointed the muzzle at his left hand. “TELL ME!” He hesitated and winced again. I pulled the trigger. His hand blew away in an ugly red cloud. I held the shotgun to his other hand, knowing he was moments from death. Time was running out.

“ALL RIGHT!” he finally choked. “Okay, I’ll fucking tell you what you want to know!” The muthafucker had the audacity to eyeball me. “Nurrungar. You’ll find it there . . . Nurrungar.”

I looked down at him. A wave of pity pushed through my mind. I pushed it back and away. I stepped forward and clutched his hair, tilting his head back. He opened his eyes for a second or two and closed them again.

From my holster, I retrieved the nine-millimetre handgun. I placed the muzzle to his temple. I held it there. But I did not pull the trigger. “No,” I said. “No neat hole for you.”

One last shot in the shotgun chamber. I held the shotgun barrel up to the side of his head, but far enough away for maximum damage. Bosco and Andrew burst through the door. Too late.

“This is for Nathan,” I said and squeezed the trigger. His head exploded and disappeared in a cloud of blood and bone.

CHAPTER FIFTEEN

Unity

I HAD NO IDEA HOW, OR WHY, I resorted to such measures. What was it that overcame me? It was as though a dark force had taken over and invaded my body, pushing me forward, taking control, getting me to do things I never imagined it was ever possible for me to do. I was never the monster who made violent choices. But now, I cannot undo what's become apparent. I must somehow accept the fact that I'm capable of doing evil just as easily as I can do good. Just *what* . . . have I become?

The disappointment in Maggie's eyes was something I couldn't ignore. It was the mere act of her turning her back on me that made me feel ashamed. Maggie said nothing. After she was informed about my bloodshed, she simply retreated to her quarters and closed the door quietly behind her. But my shaming didn't stop there.

Xe shunned me big time. His shunning disappointed me, no end. He avoided eye contact and chose silence, much the same as Maggie. Bosco openly belittled me, choosing the words, 'rookie cluster fuck' to describe his disapproval of my actions. Under the circumstances, however, Andrew and Christina seemed to evince some empathy. They to looked beyond my act of carnage, to see the person behind the things I'd done.

The truth of the matter was clear. I'd succeeded in extracting the valuable intel from that Guardianship arsehole. Pending confirmation, and eyes on target, I realised the mission to assist the CIA in the US for their stolen Chinook was likely to be scrapped.

Maggie announced that all operations were on hold pending updates from Charlotte Station's parent ASIS Task Force known as Crossfire. As time slipped by, she continued to spend her days locked away in the solitude of her quarters. She came out briefly for the necessities of life, only to wordlessly retreat again. And also during the days that dragged on, Andrew and Bosco spent a large chunk of their time either on their iPads, or on the Xbox. But their laughter and chatter fell silent whenever I approached. Xe, however, came and went as he saw fit, with no questions asked.

During the backlash that never seemed to end, I kept my promise to Christina. I did my best helping her come to grips with perfecting her English skills. Then after a while, I began to long for my former life.

I was tempted to just walk out and leave them all to it. If it wasn't for Jenny, I most likely would've walked out; no matter the politics; no matter the logistics. But in the end, it was Jenny who reminded me of my position and the oath I'd taken to protect and serve my country. I was at odds. Just as I was to decide to stay with it or run, Maggie again changed all my plans.

"News in from Task Force Crossfire. My ops room at 1200."

CHAPTER SIXTEEN

Gloves Off and into the Muck

CHARLOTTE STATION'S OPS ROOM WAS MUCH LARGER than the ops room I remembered at old Firebird. I entered through a big double door that looked as though it was made from Tasmanian Oak. The command post was filled with cutting edge, state-of-the-art electronic equipment, computers, LCDs, and communication equipment. There were several high-back leather chairs positioned around a large dark timber boardroom table in the centre. A large LCD was positioned on the wall at one end of the table which showed a green background displaying the Kangaroo and Emu of the Australian Coat of Arms. It was obvious Canberra had splashed a truckload of money, with no expense spared.

Maggie was present, shuffling through papers as I looked on. Other members of Charlotte Station filed through the double door and casually made their way to their chairs. No one spoke, not even Maggie. Her expression was serious, I noticed. It was time to get into the game. No more fucking around—In my heart, I knew it was gloves off and into the muck.

Bosco nudged me gently with his elbow as he sat down next to me. He pointed to the LCD and whispered, "That's direct optical link back to Ben Chifley. It's the only way to guarantee a secured connection. You can imagine the labour and cost to install."

By the time we were all seated and waiting, Maggie held up the blue plastic computer disk which I instantly recognised. It was the same disk from Scotty-Blue, who'd expressed such urgency for it to arrive in Maggie's safe hands all those years ago. It was the same disk my mother had slid into my rucksack. It was the same disk which had blood all over it. My mother's. My father's. Even Charlotte's. And also, the blood of all the dead Guardianship soldiers who'd tried to take it back. I wondered briefly how Maggie obtained the disk back from Nathan. Back at Busby's, Nathan was always adamant that it was his property, and served only as a reminder of his early years protecting it. I wondered what I was missing.

Maggie then stepped to the whiteboard and wiped it down, then turned and faced everyone. "Some of you know, and some of you don't. So we'll start from the beginning to bring everyone up to speed." Maggie then gestured for Christina to take a seat at an antique Pentium 386 computer. Christina took the disk from Maggie and plugged it into the drive. Maggie passed Christina a yellow folder. Christina opened it, then began tapping commands on the old and aged looking keyboard.

After several moments, the contents of the disk appeared on the overhead LCD. The first page showed an emblem that appeared to be the same as the seal of the US Central Intelligence Agency—a blue circle bearing a star-encrusted shield with an American bald eagle above it and looking left. Underneath was the yellow banner with the text 'United States of America.' In block print above the shield was, 'THE GUARDIANSHIP OF MILESTONE.'

"Hey, that seal belongs to us," Bosco blurted out. "The Guardianship just can't grab it and make use of it!"

"That depends on which you look at it, Bosco." Maggie went on to explain how among Guardianship ranks, there existed retired top American officials and more alarmingly, a former US President sat at the top of the Guardianship tree. "Clearly, these former American officials see it as their right to use the seal of the CIA. The only thing that's changed is the text as we see here."

Maggie reached to her console and made a few clicks with the mouse. A portrait appeared on the monitor. I was stunned, straight away recognising who the former US President was. I was almost about to shout out his name. Maggie raised her hand and instantly silenced me. "Don't even think about it, Angel. This man no longer has the right to his former title. To us, he's just one more of those pricks who mean to do us harm. Sad, isn't it? And, he now controls all of Milestone operations. I know what you're all thinking. I'll make it absolutely clear right here and now; decapitating this man from his position in the Guardianship is *not* on our agenda. We'll leave that to our overseas counterpart. Our mission takes us elsewhere." Maggie faced Xe and nodded before returning to her chair.

Xe stepped over to the main LCD and plugged a USB stick drive into the side. On the screen, several yellow folders appeared. With the tip of his finger he double tapped and opened a folder which contained several digital images. "These photos of *Peacemaker* were taken by Canter during his close target reconnaissance mission, while he was embedded with the South Korean 707th."

Immediately, my head screamed the word back to me. *Peacemaker*. Where had I heard it before? Where? Then it erupted in my mind, spewing my memory back at me. The dream I had as a child. Nathan was with me in William Creek when I was sick. I had that dream then. The black man with the white teeth grinning back at me. He'd screamed the word *Peacemaker* and scared the bejesus out of me.

"*Peacemaker* is well secured within the city of Pyongyang," Xe continued on. "Intercepted intelligence suggests *Peacemaker* is essentially an Atlas Five vertical launch vehicle with a modified guidance system."

"That means any continent on Earth is within range," Bosco said.

Xe nodded to Bosco. "Correct."

From the images on the screen, I could tell the Atlas Five rocket towered upward roughly twenty stories high. There were zoomed shots and wide-angled shots. My mind reeled with shock as Xe flicked through the images on the screen. Then it dawned on me. The words Nathan told me back at Busby's were true. Realising it almost took my breath away.

Xe continued, "*Peacemaker* is a thermonuclear hybrid super-bomb. The explosive yield of *Peacemaker* is speculated to be within the vicinity of 1.1 gigatons of destructive force."

I was about to react. Bosco butted in "Hybrid? Hybrid to what?"

"Thank you, Bosco. That was my next point. On *Peacemaker*, the deuterium shell has an outer layer to magnify the explosive yield by three-hundred-fold. Helium-3. How the Guardianship have managed to procure the large requirement of helium-3 isn't clear. However, our intelligence suggests helium-3 in a crystallised state encasing the entire deuterium outer shell. This is something horrifying to say the least. To get our heads around this, let me give you some comparisons.

"Imagine one ton of high explosive. It would be enough to fill a small truck, measuring five metres in length and three metres wide. Imagine the damage one ton of high explosive is capable of doing. To give you an idea, it was estimated as one tone of high explosive that was used by the Oklahoma City bomber. Now multiply that picture in your head by a thousand. Imagine a fleet of trucks that now stretches five kilometres long. We've just arrived at one-kiloton of destructive force. Now imagine a multiple of that by twenty, and we get one hundred kilometres of high explosive. We've arrived at the twenty kilotons, which was the destructive force that destroyed Hiroshima. We move up through the range of kilotons and then through megatons to reach one-gigaton. We now have the equivalent of one *billion* trucks, loaded with TNT. Your fleet of trucks now stretches five-*million* kilometres; the same distance from the Earth to the moon and back by seven times. It's hard to imagine, but here's another perspective. There is now a truck full of high explosive for every one square kilometre of land on Earth. A 1.1 gigaton detonation has enough destructive power to dwarf the asteroid strike of the K-T extinction, sixty-five million years ago. That said, if *Peacemaker* is ever deployed and used, it alone will be the end of all life on Earth. The debris in the Earth's atmosphere will cause a darkness lasting long enough to push into another ice age, and perhaps, even into the theoretical Snowball Earth."

Xe clicked the folder closed, then stood back. "Questions?"

"Yeah," Bosco said. "Seems odd if *Peacemaker* was ever used, the senders of the package would be toast along with everybody else."

Xe immediately responded to Bosco. "It makes you wonder about their motivation, doesn't it? I'll address this in a short while."

Christina raised her hand and added, "This ist madness, how can the destruction of life ever be considered as some means to what end?"

"It *is* madness," Xe agreed. "And we'll stop it from happening. That's our objective."

"So, what's the Guardianship's motivation?" I asked. "There must be something behind all this insanity."

"Good question, Angel. Here's what we know. The early intelligence we managed to procure suggests this. It's about oil. Or, on the other hand, it's about not having enough to meet world supply and demand. It's also about world financial collapse. Overpopulation. Also, the never-ending war on terror. Added to this, the runaway cycle of global warming. The Guardianship see all these issues as a situation that requires a means to an end, as Christina suggested. In other words, they think humanity cannot return from the damage humans have done to the Earth; directly, indirectly, or otherwise."

Xe paused, taking the opportunity to sip at a glass water before continuing. "Let's start with the world oil reserves. It's finite, and as world supply recedes, the addiction to oil will intensify. China currently possesses more than ninety percent of world manufacturing infrastructure. Without oil, China's manufacturing capability will fail, and their economy will collapse. The knock-on effect will resonate around the globe, directly causing other economies to fall. If China collapses imagine the logistics that's required to bring manufactured goods back to the consumer. It wouldn't be possible. Why? Because there are simply not enough alternative manufacturing infrastructures set up to meet world demand. With an end to China's manufacturing capability, world stock markets will crash. So, then what? It's frightening to contemplate. How can a world population survive without ability to manufacture the missing ninety percent of consumer products?

What will happen if no-one has access to the items we all take for granted? Shops and supermarkets will literally empty in days. Businesses will close. Transport industries will grind to a halt. People will begin to starve. The list goes on. The result is mayhem and anarchy on the streets. Rioting and looting. The entire world is thrown into a chaos never previously imagined. And all this is just the very start of a very dark picture.

"Now consider the direct effects on the oil-producing nations just by themselves. If they had no more oil to sell it would mean there'd be no income for them to purchase food, supplies, and commodities for their people. Terrorism will strike back. Islamic fundamentalists and radicalised jihadists will put the blame squarely on the capitalism of the western world. We all see the effects of terrorism every single day. Terrorism by itself is a war without an end. As jihadists die for their cause, babies are born into Islamic State and are radicalised from early childhood. It's a never-ending cycle with fresh soldiers to replace those who've died and entered their so-called paradise."

Bosco raised his hand. "That's not a dark picture. That's a goddamn black picture you're painting, Xe."

"You'll certainly think it's a black picture when I'm done, Bosco. What about global warming? This is now accelerating at a pace where there is little chance humanity can change anything. We—humans—have released a billion years of carbon into the atmosphere through burning fossil fuels. A billion years of carbon released in just shy of a hundred and fifty years. Fifty to a hundred years from now, the Earth will have a climate that is out of control. Crops will die. Food will run out. People will fight and die over something as simple as a can of fresh water. The fine balance of Earth's ecosystems as we know it will be annihilated. Added to that, as the world's oceans warm and expand, the waters will swallow most of humanities coastal cities. All these issues are now considered unstoppable. A snowball effect, running away after each and every day. It needn't have come to this. Clean and renewable energy has been available, and viable, for many decades. It was never exploited nor embraced. With the many trillions of dollars tied up in oil, clean energy was left behind and never truly included. Now, before I go on, let me add that everything I've covered so far was our first school of thought. Our early intercepted intelligence lead us to believe all these issues stopped there. But there's more to this. And it goes much deeper than all of the items I've touched on so far."

Xe stepped to the LCD and double tapped a folder. A folder named, '*The Blue Enquiry.*' He went on.

"The Blue Enquiry began with leaked intelligence in 1996 suggesting a need for helium-3. It sparked interest concerning a genetically modified plant that released helium-3 into the atmosphere. The plant seeds also contained the helium-3 element. Our investigations led us to the location of where the seeds were stored. McMurdo Station in Antarctica. Operation Cobalt Blue, launched in 1996, destroying the seed vault known as Vitae-G. Along with the seeds—the sole parent genome codenamed Hadgitol was destroyed, so no further genetic modification of the Coffea Arabica plant was possible."

"And your point?" I asked.

Xe took a breath. "Thank you, Angel. I was getting there. You all must know how hard this is for me. You all know my origin, and due to that, some of these things are quite uncomfortable to share. As an Oudarretian, and as all Oudarretians are, we require a certain amount of helium-3 to survive. We metabolise helium-3 in the same way Earth humans metabolise complex carbohydrates. Although the required amount of helium-3 is vastly less in comparison, it is, still, a necessity for our existence."

"And what'll happen if you guys don't get the helium-3?" Bosco asked.

"We die slowly. There's no other way to say it. First, our protection to Ultraviolet and Gamma radiation will diminish. Cancer will be the end of us all."

"How much time?" Christina asked.

"Years. Sometimes it may stretch to a decade or two."

"And that tells me you guys already had access to helium-3," I said. "Or you wouldn't have been here as a race for so long."

Xe nodded. "That's true, Angel."

"So, where'd ya get it?" Bosco asked. "Helium-3 is rare on Earth. It's much too rare for you guys to procure in the quantities you'd need."

Before he continued, Xe began to appear a little ashamed. He struggled bringing his words to the surface. "We've had access to the modified version of Coffea Arabica for many decades. Simply put, coffee with helium-3. The Hadgitol, or parent genome I described previously. That by itself has kept us alive. Now, and from the time Cobalt Blue destroyed the seed stores in McMurdo; all Oudarretians are on time they no longer own."

Then it erupted in my mind like a strobe light. "This has got something to do with the *Peacemaker*," I said. "The Oudarretians are going to destroy Earth for the helium-3? The helium-3 harvested from the radioactive decay?"

Xe winked. "We're not going to let it happen. Now, that may seem odd coming from me."

"You're right, Xe," Bosco said. "Coming from you, it's just weird."

"But there's more." Xe put his head down and sucked back a heavy breath. "This is most uncomfortable as you can appreciate. Helium-3 exists in vast quantities elsewhere. I'm talking about Earth's Moon. Everything is geared toward that end. Mining the

Moon of its helium-3 remains the prime Oudarretian objective. The destruction of life on Earth is their number one mission only because they could never accomplish mining tasks with . . ."

"With a living human race," I said out loud.

Xe made eye contact with me and for the first time, I saw tears welling in his eyes. I couldn't believe what I was hearing. The things Nathan had told me back at Busby's were all true. But now, this was worse than ever. I sat there nursing the tiny shockwaves that rippled through my mind. But I also had a question that needed an immediate answer. I stood from my chair. "You people travelled ten thousand light years to mine Earth's moon of its resources? That's hard to believe, Xe. You could've found Helium-3 closer to your home world. So now, that tells me something else. That tells me our tiny Moon must be one of many. So, assuming that's the case, Xe . . ."

Xe immediately deflected. "You need not worry, Angel. We won't let any of this happen. You're exactly right with what you're thinking. The subject of the Helium-3 wasn't on today's agenda. But it seems now, I owe you all an explanation, so here it is.

"In 1961, Frank Drake, an American astrophysicist theorised the possibility of intelligent life within our galaxy. His famous equation leads to the speculation that at least fifty thousand *intelligent* lifeforms exist somewhere in the Milky Way. But the Oudarretians were already aware of this fact before Drake even penned out his formula. Like you, we have become explorers. As we traverse the vastness of space, we rely on the resources we find to get us from one place to another."

"Helium-3?"

"Got it in one, Angel. But, through our journey, all of the lifeforms we'd encountered on other Earth like planets inhabiting a Goldie-lox zone around a star, were nothing more than what you'd refer to as 'extremophiles.' That's to say, life has evolved in its early stages, *before* becoming the free-thinking intelligent individuals as we, ourselves are. We look for the Earth like planets that have a moon, or moons, such as Earth. We harvest the resources, and then on to the next. That's how it's been for countless millennia. Until we have the required resources to move on, we cannot continue to explore. Earth's Moon is the Oudarretian target and also their objective."

By the time I had the right words in my head, Bosco cut in. "But what about the Guardianship?" he asked. "They're not the same as you guys. They'll die from the *Peacemaker* like anybody else. Why would they even *want* to be party to this?"

"My next point," Xe put in. "Milestone will begin with the deployment of *Peacemaker.* Then the exit strategy. The Guardianship plans to escape Earth and come back at a time in Earth's future. It will then be the time for the Oudarretians to carry on with their moon mining objective."

"But escape to where?" I asked. I shot a look to Maggie, who appeared equally surprised. My eyes darted back to Xe. I realised for the first time the predicament he was in. Who'd know what the case would've been if we didn't have him on our side.

Xe gave a sharp nod and went back to the LCD. He double tapped a folder on the LCD labelled '*Exit Strategy.*' He began by describing the dark earth after *Peacemaker.* He also explained how post *Peacemaker;* mother nature would begin her fight back. It would take many millennia, Xe went on and explained. And, he described the passing of thousands of real time Earth years using the Oudarretian exit strategy; a neutrino particle cannon that was set up to strip organic matter down into subatomic particles and blast them into deep space. On their return, Earth would be theoretically habitable again. "To a degree," Xe then added. "After Milestone, Earth will certainly need more than twenty thousand years to heal. However, after some time has passed, there will be locations that will allow for repopulation more readily."

"Vhere?" Christina asked.

"Antarctica for one. Parts of Alaska and Northern Canada. Also some parts of Southern Australia."

"How many years," I asked.

"Re-inhabitation in the areas I've described may begin after a hundred and fifty years, give or take."

"How in the hell can the Guardianship expect to repopulate with only a handful of individuals?" I had to ask. "I'm sorry. It doesn't sound possible. And didn't you just explain the need to move on? Why even *consider* re-inhabitation?"

Xe smiled avoiding my question. Perhaps he'd had enough of the embarrassment. "I'll hand over to Maggie for this one."

Xe gazed down as he went back to his chair. I wasn't happy about his body language. But I understood, knowing he couldn't be pleased about his origin. Then it settled heavily in my mind. All of the issues Xe touched on a moment ago—the addiction to oil, the threatened collapse of world economies, the runaway global warming, the never ending war against terror. And now, the threat of a nuclear war that loomed and was a real possibility. All of it, cleverly put into place over the last two centuries. I collapsed in my chair, numb to the realisation it would take nothing short of a miracle to turn anything around.

"You have a right to your scepticism, Angel," Maggie said while stepping up and taking over from Xe. "And you're right. The whole idea of Milestone is extraordinary, and yes, I'm aware of my understatement. When I first came to this operation, it took me a long time to come to grips with the data we'd found. I didn't want to believe it at first. That was until we retrieved the disk your mother gave to you as a child. Without that disk, we wouldn't be sitting here now. We'd all be unaware, and there'd be nothing in place to counter the entire situation. We have a chance, and we're going after the Guardianship's Achilles heel," Maggie said while stepping up to the LCD and double tapping a folder labelled *Project Amber.* Maggie eyed us individually, with intense resolve. Her eyes locked on with a sternness that hardened her facial lines. "This, my people, is the Guardianship's highest playing card. It's also their weakest link. Our mission? Find and destroy Project Amber. What is it you might ask? We know of it so far as an immense gene ark. Amber carries all the required DNA for human repopulation. We know the DNA profiles contained in Project Amber are engineered specifically for the purposes. So, Project Amber encapsulates the hopes and dreams for starting a new a new world order. With Amber destroyed, Milestone is effectively, and immediately nullified."

Maggie briefly smiled and nodded to Andrew. She stepped to one side, allowing Andrew room on the floor.

"Project Amber is our target," Andrew began. "Find it. Destroy it. It's as simple as that. But it'll be anything else other than simple. Our intelligence so far suggests Project Amber is located somewhere within the Pine Gap facility. The precise location, however, is unknown."

"What are we physically looking for?" I asked.

Andrew replied while staring back at the LCD. "It's an unknown quantity, unfortunately. As you can see for yourselves, our intelligence has been heavily redacted. So now we can only speculate about Project Amber's size, shape, colour, smell, taste, whatever. We won't know what Project Amber *is* until we actually get our eyes on it. We'll begin by leading close target reconnaissance on Pine Gap. After that, we can begin to formulate our objectives."

Bosco raised his hand. "Yeah, but without further intel, it's gonna be like trying to find a blowfly in a dust storm."

"And that's why we need the Chinook, Bosco. There're at least five Guardianship bodies that we know of, possibly more. We speculate the Guardianship are using digital security to access Pine Gap. Therefore, recovering the digital security devices will increase the chances of finding our target."

"What if the bodies have been cleaned?" I said. "And that's assuming the bodies are still there."

Andrew nodded and coughed lightly in his hand. He took a sip of water then answered. "We just don't know, Angel. We have to play this one up against the odds. We also know there're other security devices the Guardianship are using. Fingerprint scanners. Retina scanners. This is our plan B. Xe has this one covered and it's Xe's responsibility should the plan B become a necessary diversion. At this moment, we have a US Delta team on the ground at Nurrungar. We'll patch in with them shortly. We must not forget; the Chinook is US property. They have the right to recover it."

"And the bodies?" I asked.

"That's why we're patching in. The bodies are ours if they're there." Andrew then nodded to Maggie and stepped aside.

Maggie stepped back in and gazed directly into my eyes. "I'm not going to stand here and lecture you, Angel. You know exactly how this intelligence was recovered. But you also got us closer to Project, so thank you."

Bosco then stuck up his hand. "When do we start kicking Guardianship asses?"

"Immediately," Maggie said. "We're patching into Canberra as we speak."

"Almost there," Christina said, while working at the main computer. After a couple of moments, the LCD went blank and then sprung back into life showing a background with an empty executive chair and bookshelves stacked with books. A steady tone sounded. Then, the smiling face of the Director-General appeared on the screen. He took his seat then said, "Colonel Mack. Everyone is up to speed, I take it?"

"Everyone has been briefed. We're ready to proceed."

"Excellent. We're still waiting to go live with Langley. There appears to be a minor technical problem with the satellite uplink. Our techs are working on it. I'm sure we'll have the situation in hand soon. A moment ago, we had received confirmation of boots on the ground at Nurrungar. At this time, operation Clean Skin is on standby awaiting a go."

"Very well, Sir," Maggie responded.

A female voice erupted from the Director-General's phone, announcing the successful satellite uplink. Christina worked feverishly at the computer. "Ve've established za link to Nurrungar. Ve're live with Ghost Recon. Patching us through."

The LCD flashed. An image appeared showing the dusty surrounds of Nurrungar with the various outbuildings in the background. The video moved around with the motion of the Delta operator's helmet. A few more clicks and the LCD came back in split-screen mode. A second later, the large main screen divided into three, with the arrival of the CIA uplink. Dressed in casuals, CIA Director Petersen stared almost devoid of expression from his office location in Langley, Virginia.

"G'day George," the Australian Director-General said with a very aussie grin.

"It's fucking 0300 here, Phillip. Let's get this over with, shall we?"

"Do you want the honours? Or shall I do it?"

Director Petersen laughed. "You Aussies are all the same. Just patch the audio through. I'll get this shit started, if you don't mind."

Maggie nodded to Christina. Christina patched Ghost Recon's audio through to Langley. From across the Pacific, the audio arrived without any delay.

"Hardball. Ghost Recon . . . Radio check. How copy?"

"Ghost Recon. Hardball. Five by five. You are go for Operation Clean Skin. Repeat. Go."

"Copy that, Hardball. We are go."

A set of gloved hands signalled the advance of troops. The helmet camera video feed moved forward. The team of Deltas cleared their way across and around abandoned outbuildings, bunkers, and concrete structures. Then the feed stopped suddenly in forward momentum as the Deltas' advance halted. The helmet camera showed several figures lurking. Then the feed slowly backed up as the Deltas retraced their steps, finding cover behind a pile of rusty steel diesel fuel drums.

"Hardball, Ghost Recon. Tangos twelve o'clock, ROE, how copy?"

Director Petersen replied, "Stand by for ROE, Ghost Recon." He suddenly broke off.

I stood tall from my chair. I placed my finger lightly on my lower lip as I stared at the LCD. The Australian Director-General placed his head in his hands, then looked up red-faced.

The video feed lowered as the Deltas went prone behind cover.

"Hardball, Ghost recon? ROE?" The Delta operator spoke with experienced resolve.

"Ghost Recon, Hardball. We need numbers to decide your ROE."

The video moved slowly forward and showed three figures standing almost motionless at the doorway of a large aircraft hangar. Three more figures walked slowly back and forth from a position roughly twenty metres south of the hangar door. The video moved back again behind cover.

"Hardball, Ghost Recon. Tangos six. Maybe seven."

"Roger that, Ghost Recon. Please stand by."

Director Petersen stepped away from his desk, leaving his Delta team in limbo. He came back and sat down again with a glass of water. I noticed our ASIO boss biting down on his bottom lip. "George? What's your game plan, mate? Your guys need your ROE."

"We weren't counting on any enemy contacts; Phil. Rules of engagement weren't specified."

"Are you telling me you sent in special forces with no actions-on? George, you can't be serious."

Director Petersen didn't reply, only, his expression told me he'd really fucked up.

Again the Delta operator demanded. "Hardball! Ghost Recon! ROE. How copy?"

"Stand by . . ."

"George! Get in the game or get out, will ya mate!"

I stepped closer to the LCD with an incredible sinking feeling. I glared at Maggie. Maggie echoed it back.

"George. In or out? Don't leave your guys hanging."

A most urgent voice from the Delta operator broke through. "Hardball. Ghost Recon. ROE."

"Ghost Recon, Hardball. Engage the target, Critical stealth, I say again, critical stealth."

After a long pause, the Delta operator responded. "Copy that, Hardball. Critical stealth."

I held my breath but I had enough air in my lungs to whisper, "Maggie, I don't like it."

Maggie ignored me and said nothing.

"Maggie . . . this isn't how it's supposed to go," I pleaded.

The video streamed the Delta's gloved hands signalling to move forward. A lone operator went prone behind a concrete pylon and peered downrange through the scope of a suppressed M107.

"They need to fall back," I whispered. Maggie again didn't respond.

"Maggie. Please."

After a moment, a voice crackled over the speaker. "Hardball. Ghost Recon. Eyes on target, ready to engage."

"Roger Ghost Recon. You're go to engage."

I stepped back from the LCD and looked away, expecting to hear an exchange in gunfire. But there was a nothing. I held my breath. I briefly closed my eyes but something else inside me kicked in. I looked back to the screen. I couldn't believe what I saw. The same Delta operator's voice I'd heard a moment ago crackled over the speaker and confirmed what I'd seen. "Hardball. Ghost Recon. Tangos bugging out."

CIA Director Petersen drew a long breath with a hand to his face as he watched the live feed. "Roger that, Ghost Recon. We see it."

I watched on as the figures in the foreground scurried away then jumped into several Humvees and sped off in a cloud of red dust and black smoke.

"Hardball, Ghost Recon. No fubar. I say again. No fubar."

Director Petersen sighed and appeared to relax a little. But our ASIO boss seemed exactly the opposite. I noticed how he bit down harder on his lip. That was a bad sign and I reacted while I remained glued to the LCD. The bastards had left in a hurry. The question was why?

"It's not over, Maggie. Something just doesn't add up."

Maggie eyed me curiously and finally, she reacted. "Get your men to fall back, Hardball. The mission is compromised."

"Negative, Colonel Mack. We're moving ahead as planned." In the same breath, Director Petersen ordered his team of Deltas to advance toward the hangar.

"Copy that, Hardball. Advance on the hangar."

The video showed the Delta operator wave his team past. Moving out from behind cover they advanced with speed. They cut across the dry dusty plane, weapons hot, clearing the area as they went. Moments later, they arrived at the aircraft hangar's towering sliding doors.

"They need to fall back. Get them to fall back," I said urgently.

Maggie nodded and repeated her words more sternly than before. "Tell your men to fall back, Hardball! Abort the mission!"

"Negative, Colonel. We'll have our Chinook momentarily."

I stood rock still with both hands up to my face. My heart thumped from beneath my chest cavity. "Maggie!"

Maggie gave another sideways glance, then looked back at the LCD. "Director Petersen! Stand your men down! Immediately!"

"I outrank you, Colonel. The mission goes forward as planned."

I thought our ASIO boss might use his powers to force Petersen to back down. He said nothing, only watching with stun in his eyes.

The Deltas continued plastering Semtex around strategic positions on the hangar doors. When they were done, they sprinted back behind cover. "Stand by for breach . . . BREACH!"

THUD

The main hangar door came clean off and landed several metres away with a loud metallic clang. The Deltas moved forward through the dust and the smoke. They sprinted into the hangar. As the dust and smoke settled, the video streamed the

Deltas silhouetted against the sunlight in a large open area inside the hangar. It became apparent the moment the Delta announced it. “Hardball, Ghost Recon. No package. I say again. No package.”

The mission was over. The mission had failed. I knew it in my heart the worst was yet to come. “Maggie you have to do something!”

“It’s over! Damn it, Director Petersen . . .”

But if not listening to anything at all, Director Petersen instantly yelled to his men. “Fall back! Fall back! Abort, goddamn it. Abort!”

“Copy that, Hardball. Getting the fuck ou . . .”

A blinding flash bright enough to dazzle my eyes lit up the LCD screen, then, the video feed cut to grain.

CHAPTER SEVENTEEN

Eyes of The Reaper

THE VIDEO LINK BACK TO LANGLEY ended. Maggie stood fixed as though hypnotised by the grey static on the LCD. Andrew stepped up behind her. He placed a hand on her shoulder. Maggie shrugged him away and turned slowly to face us all. “Well. Isn’t this a fine piece of shit we’re in now?” Without another word, Maggie turned and disappeared from the ops room.

I got up from my chair. Andrew raised a hand, gesturing for me to remain seated. “Give her a moment, Angel. It’s been a bugger of a day.”

In the same breath, Andrew asked Christina if she could get the *Keyhole Satellite Three* up and running. Christina nodded vigorously and made for the keyboard.

Bosco got up from his chair and made for the door. “You can have this shit. I’m done with it!”

The next to leave was Xe, following Bosco without saying a word.

“Sohn einer hundin!” Christina yelled as she thumped the tabletop with the heel of a closed fist. But after a pause, she went back to typing out strings of commands. Her fingers moved so fast, they became a blur of movement until finally, she sat back clearly delighted with her accomplishment. "It vill be up soon. I promise it."

We waited, not moving, eyes fixed on the screen. The screen flickered into an image above the area of Nurrungar.

"Danke Gott!" Christina clapped her hands and blew a kiss to her computer.

Andrew leaned in and inspected the scenery. He pointed to a section of land that had his interest. "Move the camera there, Christina."

Christina went to work on the keyboard. The camera zoomed down. After a few minutes we realised we were looking in the wrong location.

"Take us back up," Andrew said. "We might get a better view."

Christina tapped keys, and the camera responded, lifting up higher.

I fought the urge for a cigarette, as I viewed what was going on at the computer. But something caught my attention. As I moved in closer to the computer screen, I noticed an area that didn't seem quite right. I leaned forward and trained my eyes while looking over Christina's shoulder.

Andrew came in closer and I felt his presence up behind me. I could feel his breath on my neck as he spoke softly about the situation. Oddly enough, knowing full well the state of affairs we had on our hands, all I wanted to do was push back toward him. My head ran away for a second. There was work to be done, but something else had surprised me. It was all about Andrew's magnetism. How I wanted him, and I was sure, Andrew knew it.

Dragging my head back, I forced myself to re-focus. My eyes went back to the one thing that looked out of place. Another outbuilding, but the colour was all wrong. What I'd seen was much darker to the others areas. “There. Move the camera down on that spot,” I asked Christina.

A few taps on the keyboard and Christina had the camera zoomed down. It was horrible to see what had happened to the hangar. “That’s what’s left of it? Ghost Recon had no chance. What could have caused all that damage?”

Andrew peered in closer, pausing, I could almost hear his magnificent mind ticking over. “I know what happened. The bastards used AGM 114s. Probably more than one.”

“What are they?”

“Hellfires, Angel. Air-to-ground missiles.”

Andrew stepped back from the computer, thrust his hands in his pockets and walked away. “If that’s the case, this thing has just become a whole lot worse than we can ever imagine. If I’m right in what I’m thinking, the 114s came from a Predator. That means only one thing. The Guardianship have access to top military spec weapons. If the Guardianship has access to a Predator, our momentum to Project Amber had just hit a huge roadblock.”

“We need the Chinook. If it’s not in the hangar, it has to be somewhere.”

“Yes, Angel, I know. It’s all about that, isn’t it? But where is it? We now know it was never at Nurrungar. We’re back to square one.”

I thought about what Andrew said but somehow, I couldn’t have believed it. I saw it in the eyes of the Guardianship soldier before executed him. He wasn’t lying. The Chinook was there. But perhaps not as we’d expect. “You know, Andrew, what if it *was* there but not as we’d imagine.”

“What do you mean?”

“Well think about it. If you were trying to hide something the size of a Chinook, how would you do it?”

Andrew shook his head. "It's a bloody big piece of kit, Angel. I can't see it being anywhere else other than in a hangar or out in the open. Both options are no longer."

"Chinook equals hangar, we both know that. Don't you think that's a bit obvious? I reckon it's not even close to any *sort* of hangar."

I had Andrew's attention. He stood there staring at me with a hand to his chin. "So, what're you thinking?"

"I think the Chinook is no longer a Chinook. I think it's in pieces somewhere. I think we may be looking for something in all the wrong places purely because of its size. Maybe it's not about size anymore."

Andrew began to smile. "Okay. Let's assume they've dismantled it. That's not implausible."

"Implausibility isn't what we go on. We work with probabilities that lead to facts. It's possible they've cut it up into pieces, so I reckon we go looking with that in mind. Let's look for something smaller and out of place."

Christina heard and pre-empted what to do next. She moved the camera to different locations above the Nurrungar site. She zoomed the camera in and then out.

"There. Look," I smiled and pointed to what appeared to be a series of shipping containers which were lined up side by side. At first glance, the containers didn't appear to be out of place. There were various objects and debris scattered around Nurrungar that sat out in the open. But now, with a different perspective, the containers were exactly what we were looking for.

"Zoom down, Christina," Andrew asked.

A closer inspection of the containers revealed the absence of desert dust, indicating they'd recently been positioned into place. I also noticed fresh tyre tracks running up to the sides of the containers.

“A little closer please, Christina.” Andrew asked and the camera zoomed in.

“There. Look.” I pointed. “There’s footprints around the area. And that means . . .”

“That means recent activity,” Andrew smiled. “And the idiots left an oxy kit behind. Can you believe it?”

“Yeah. That’s what they’ve used it to cut the bloody thing up.”

“Holy crap, Angel. Holy crap. We need to get this up to Langley, Angel. Most pronto.”

“No. We do this ourselves this time.”

* * *

It was as tough Maggie had a new life to her step as she appeared in the ops room.

We were all seated and expecting good news after what we’d discovered at Nurrungar. I looked around and felt an enormous boost in moral, noticing at the same times, Bosco slouching in his chair while chewing on gum. Bosco’s demeanour had changed. This time Bosco wore his baseball cap backward. I wasn’t used to it, and it looked odd for Bosco.

“Bosco only wears hit cap backward when he knows something’s about to happen,” Andrew whispered as he sat himself down next to me.

At the time, Andrew’s words registered but they weren’t important enough to take my mind away from other thoughts. My mind was elsewhere. I felt as though I wanted to ask Andrew how he slept, and did he have a nice breakfast. It was surprising how all of a sudden, I wanted to know more about him. How I wanted to be closer to him. But Jenny! Why was I doing this to myself?

I’d spent part of the night with Jenny. Our lovemaking became rushed and somehow inconsiderate. It wasn’t slow and delicate as it used to be. It wasn't romantic and not even erotic. It was over shortly after it started. And then sleep came for Jenny. I lay wide awake, staring up, fighting the urge. It was almost a primal need that was just as much confusing as it was exciting. So I left Jenny's side.

Dressed in nothing more than my white undergarments and a smile, I stepped with speed toward Andrew's door. There, I'd discovered Andrew awake as I quietly entered his bunk room, silently closing the door behind me. Soundless by word, I went to Andrew, and he immediately drew me in, taking my body close to his, feeling his steamy skin next to mine. My body spoke to Andrew, and he spoke back. We entered a new chapter with all the words, sentences and paragraphs until, by the end, a new book had been written in my life. As we climaxed together, I noticed tears in Andrew's eyes. Then his smile. How could I help not loving him? I knew in my heart something had changed, and as I left him and closed the door, my thoughts returned to Jenny. My god, what have I done? What have I just done to my Jenny?

Now, here was Andrew, sitting, sending out is magnetic charisma all over again. An internal battle over Andrew and Jenny began to overwhelm me. But . . . His eyes. His smile. That smile. That chin. The irresistible profile of his face. His hands and fingers, strong and slender, soft—not calloused. I had no idea how I was ever going to recover and come back to being normal again.

Then, Xe bounced into the ops room. His sudden appearance brought me back from wherever I'd gone. Getting my head back, I noticed Xe had brought a large green canvas bag draped over his shoulder. He dropped the bag in the centre of the room, then settled in his chair at the meeting table. Something was in the air. Bosco's demeanour was exactly spot on.

I scanned their faces, sitting there, staring up like a bunch of eager school kids who were bright eyed and bushy tailed. I stopped at Xe, and I remembered the *Star Trek* series that I watched all those years ago. Xe reminded me of Mr Spock. Xe was devoid of any emotion. He said little. His eyes said more than words. And when he did speak, it was worthwhile and to the point. I even wondered if he had *the grip*. I smiled a little to myself at the thought.

There was Christina. She danced around the place as though in preparation for something. She moved quickly between terminals and keyboards, shuffling things, picking things up and placing them back down. She was also smiling and had a new something to her step. Christina, the lovely German girl. Too skinny. Much too skinny. She never ate much; just like a sparrow. She was the only member of Charlotte Station that smoked all day and probably well into the night. Her English was improving, and her intellect was breathtaking.

Sitting there, I wondered about Nathan. Where are you, Nathan Masters? What's happened to you?

After I thought about Nathan, I noticed a bottle of tequila on the meeting table surrounded by shot glasses. On a tray to one side were slices of lime and salt. It was customary to toast to absent friends before deployment. I felt saddened, and my eyes became unfocused as my tears once again rose to the surface. I missed Nathan so terribly.

Maggie came to the centre of the floor and took away my sadness over Nathan "Welcome to day one of Operation Mogul, my people," Maggie said as she smiled brightly. It was such a long time since I'd seen her looking so eager. "Our first mission won't be easy. But it appears we have a leg up, and every bit counts." She then turned and nodded to Christina.

Christina bounced an image onto the main LCD. Everyone sat silent and stared.

"This is an image of an MQ-9 Reaper," Maggie went on. "It's the deadliest UAV of them all. It's equipped with the AGM-114 Hellfire air-to-ground missile and has enough capacity to carry the same firepower as an F-16 fighting falcon."

There was an almost overbearing silence in the room as the news settled on everyone.

"So, our mission is to shut down the Reaper?" Bosco then asked.

"No. Unfortunately we don't have the intelligence to suggest where it may be piloted from. It could be anywhere, even a location outside of our shores. So, shutting it down is not an option. We'll have to accept the Reaper is always looking down. The Reaper is equipped with one forward-looking and two ground-trained IRCs. What makes matters worse, of course, is the heat-seeking hardware. It will pick up the heat signatures of anyone on the ground. If the Reaper locks onto body heat, our operation is finished."

"That sounds like a suicide mission to me," Bosco said.

"You're in good hands." Maggie smiled briefly then nodded to Xe.

Xe stood up and stepped to the centre of the room. He upturned thc large green canvas bag that he'd brought earlier. The contents spilled onto the floor. He held up what I thought at first was a full-length wetsuit.

Bosco laughed out loud. "Wetsuits? You gotta be kidding."

"Not wetsuits," Xe explained. "These are thermal evasion suits and will mask any heat signature, making us invisible to the Reaper. But there's a disadvantage. The suits trap body heat. We'll be uncomfortable. We'll sweat inside them. Wear them too long, and it'll be inevitable to succumb to heat stroke. So, therefore, we must be well hydrated before deployment. And we must stay hydrated while using them. Added to that, carrying extra water will slow us down. So, we must develop actions-on strategy to cope."

Andrew was smiling, rubbing his hands together. Maggie was smiling. Bosco appeared determined as ever. Xe was his normal, devoid of any emotion.

"That's a big ask," I said. "Considering the heat down there, we wouldn't last very long—hydrated or not."

"We'll infiltrate at night when it's cooler," Xe said. "But there's a complication. At night, the Reaper will pick up the slightest heat signature. These suits are not one hundred percent protection. They will leak. The Reaper will know soon enough. So, speed and timing is crucial. We'll get to the target, and get out with the package, whatever that package may be."

"We'll need the NVGs," Bosco added.

"Night vision goggles we'll have. Luck is something only the gods can provide. Make no mistake; it's going to be tough. We don't have the intel to suggest if there's Guardianship combatants on the ground. And that's something else to consider."

"So, we can assume the Reaper is in the air at all times?" Bosco asked.

"It may or may not be the case. There'd be downtime. The problem is, we don't know when that downtime is likely to occur. Therefore, we must assume as you suggest."

Bosco adjusted his baseball cap. "Weapons and ROE?"

"We'll have our silenced SA-80s. Rules of engagement have been authorised as echo-charlie engage the enemy at will. We're not about to make the same mistake as Langley. After we find the Chinook, our primary objective is to get us anything we can use to access Pine Gap. Anything we can use to get us closer to Project Amber. The Guardianship bodies. Let's find them. That's the start. We'll infiltrate from the drop-off point, forty-five kilometres south at the position of Pimba and Stuart blacktop.

From there, we'll tab to the Nurrungar facility. We'll be issued GPS coordinates before deployment."

Bosco shook his head and stood up. "Tab a total of ninety clicks dressed up in these thermal evasion suits? Now, you know that's not gonna be easy. The amount of water we'll need to carry goes beyond our human capability."

Andrew then added, "It's probably not an issue getting in. We can tab in with the suits in our bergens. Getting out, though, we'll need to dump the suits before we tab back to exfil. But then the Reaper will target our heat signatures."

Xe nodded in agreement, "Yes, it will. I suggest we wear them for as long as possible. Let's do what's possible to get acquainted with the symptoms of heat exhaustion. That way we'll know how far to push ourselves."

Xe then turned and nodded to Maggie.

"Anything further?" Maggie asked, stepping up again.

"God help us," Bosco said. "God help us all."

CHAPTER EIGHTEEN

Eve of War

BEFORE LEAVING DARWIN FOR Alice Springs, I'd spent time with Maggie and Christina in the ops room, as Bosco, Xe, and Andrew continued formulating actions-on strategy. Christina made use of Chantilly's *Keyhole Satellite Three* system, tracking an increased amount of activity at Pine Gap. Various vehicles came and left the facility. Some of the vehicles appeared civilian, others very obviously military, seeming to be mostly American. We speculated among ourselves why this was so, then learned the American vehicles arrived in Alice Springs aboard the C-5 Galaxy Star-Lifters that were always coming and going. But then, almost as suddenly as the activity increased, it slowed down until there was no movement left at all. Now, the place seemed empty. Christina zoomed the camera down to near ground level. She shifted the lens around. From the outside of the facility at least, Pine Gap seemed to be abandoned.

"The place is deserted," I said to Maggie as she stepped back from the computer and folded her arms. "That's to our advantage. I think we should go there now and look for Project Amber."

"That's called complacency, Angel. Don't be lulled into a false sense of security. They're there alright. The question is, where?"

* * *

The absence of humidity at Alice Springs was a welcome change. At last, I could move around without constantly feeling the need for a shower.

After we arrived on the tarmac, my mind began stepping through the entire exercise, completing all the possible actions-on we'd formulated earlier that day. It was as though I was working out an internal puzzle. What to do if this happens? What to do if that? What to do if things seriously went bad? Every possible scenario was thoroughly thought through, played out, formulated and fixed down. If Nathan was with me, I wondered if our final actions-on scenarios would be similar—or would they be completely different? Either way, it had taken five entire weeks of drilling, thinking, sorting, formulating, and speculating, which had brought me closer to the required confidence I needed to get the job done.

And there was something else. I was late. I was *never* late.

At the time, I didn't know whether to laugh or cry, and letting Andrew know he was going to become a father was a subject I jostled with internally. And then there was Jenny.

I'd hurt Jenny immensely even though she didn't show it. After I confessed to her, she seemed to take things on board. Her only reply was to tell me of my need to be a woman, and of the primal urge to procreate which came at a time of weakness. She forgave me. She never had to, but she did. I fell in love with Jenny all over again, and even though Jenny gave me her understanding, I will spend the rest of my days doing penance for my feebleness.

Outside the airport terminal, our black bergens were heaped in a single pile on the footpath. Bosco, Andrew, and Xe stood together in a semicircle, chatting lightly about anything other than the mission. I wondered about having a cigarette. But now being pregnant, I had even more motivation to never again experience the rush of nicotine.

Almost involuntarily, I found myself pushed up to Andrew's side which confused me even more than Jenny's forgiveness. Could it be that I was in love with two people at the same time? Could it be that I'm now officially bisexual? My head reeled thinking about it, and I made a conscience effort to step away from Andrew's side. Then, more confusion set in and I began to feel a hole in my heart. Suddenly, from out of nowhere, a minibus appeared, rushing to a halt, pulling up just where we all stood on the pavement.

Xe eyeballed, then nodded to the driver. The driver got out, then shimmied around the minibus. Without making eye contact, the driver briefly scanned the area before lifting the rear door. Without any hesitation, he then made his way back to the driver's seat.

We picked up our bergens and threw them into the back of the minivan and I straight away noticed something that was hidden under a dark canvas tarpaulin. My curiosity got the better of me. Under the tarp was a shiny olive-green metal trunk with the stencilled words, *CART H K SA-80 5.56 RNR 6*

As I stood there looking under the tarp and trying to imagine the firepower that was left to our disposal, the others had already climbed inside the minivan. Bosco eyed me with an expression of impatience. "Are you coming?"

I was about to get in, but something grabbed my attention. I looked up and saw a group of eagles circling high above us. There were seven of them that I could make out, one of which was all white, and I momentarily thought back to Charlotte and her demise. Then, the ear-splitting noise of turbofan engines landing on the runway dragged my thoughts away.

"Are you coming?" Bosco asked again.

"Hang on, Bosco. Give me a second." I cranked my head toward Lear jet after it touched down and taxied out from view. I turned to Andrew and asked him, "A Lear jet. Is that strange? For around here, I mean?"

"It's not entirely strange. It could be just some rich guy coming for a round of golf, for all I know. But then it could be just about anyone rich or famous, Angel. Why?"

"I have a feeling. Can we see who gets off and where they go?"

"If we had the time I'd say let's do it. But time is what we don't have. We need to get . . ."

I sprinted back to the terminal entrance, without the chance to hear the end of Andrew's last sentence. By the time I got through security and appeared at the window to look out over the airport, the Lear jet was in the process of taxiing and heading toward the main terminal. It taxied and docked with the nose of the aircraft disappearing just out from view.

The aircraft door swung down and became a set of stairs. Whoever he was—he stepped out dressed in a shiny black suit, the same suit Nathan wore when he was on the Prime Minister's security detail. The stranger walked away from the aircraft and then disappeared under where I stood watching.

I raced over to the other side of the viewing area, hoping to catch a glimpse of the stranger after he reappeared. He stood at a steel door near the entrance to the main hangar. He scanned the area before holding something shiny and metallic up to a device at the side of the door. The door swung open, and he stepped through.

Returning to the minibus, I imagined Bosco's usual sarcasm. But, after I arrived, Bosco was quiet. They were *all* quiet. They all appeared stunned into silence not able to move.

"What wrong? What's happened?" I asked as I jumped into the back of the minibus.

"We've had coms with Darwin," Xe said.

"And?"

"It's started." Bosco blurted out. "This Milestone shit's going down."

"What? How?"

Then Andrew replied slowly. "Detachment 421 reported a subterranean nuclear shot in North Korea. But there's worse news. The US Embassy in Tokyo has been breeched and The US Ambassador, with his family . . . They've been captured."

The words pin-balled around my brain before the reality started to sink in. At first, I thought it was another of Bosco's not very funny pranks. I almost expected him to come clean at any second. Now, I felt slow and in a place of limbo. Was Bosco going to 'fess up or not? After everything we've prepared and trained for. This *can't* be real.

"Shit!" It was all I could manage. "By who?"

"Norks!" Bosco put in. "Bet your ass it's Norks"

"What now?"

"The mission goes ahead as planned, but our drop off point is now by Black Hawk," Xe told me. "We're waiting for confirmation back from Canberra, and the details of when a Black Hawk will become available. Time was against us before, but now? We need to destroy Project Amber before things escalate. And it *will* escalate. The capture of the US Ambassador is an act of war, Angel. The Americans are expected to retaliate. *How* they decide to retaliate is the question."

Xe was about to go on when the tactical laptop sounded. He looked down at it momentarily before lifting the lid. Maggie's sullen face appeared via a secure satellite feed from Darwin.

"It seems things have turned for the worse, unfortunately," Maggie said with sadness. "Canberra has informed us that United States Strategic Air Command has lifted defence condition to DEFCON 2!"

I noticed Christina was in the background, smashing her fingers into a keyboard. Maggie's voice then lowered into a sombreness that I hadn't heard before. "Xe, I'm afraid you simply *must* find a way to Project Amber. There are no second chances. We're sending a Chinook from RAAF base Edinburgh in Adelaide. A Black Hawke won't have the range before it goes bingo, so it's the best we can do on short notice. Stay put until the Chinook arrives."

"How much time do we have?" Xe asked Maggie.

"I think a week. Two at the most. The *USS John Steinbeck*, along with the *USS Minnesota,* and the *USS Dallas* have been deployed to the South China Sea. They're pulling out of Pearl Harbour at this time. If Project Amber is *not* destroyed by the time the fleet arrives, there's no way of coming out of this unscathed." Maggie looked down, then she held up something that looked like an official memo. "One more thing. Something a little positive out of this sad situation. The 707th in South Korea received a tip off from an unknown source. They mounted a rescue mission for an Australian citizen who was being held captive in the city of Kaesong. This all went down during the time the US Ambassador was captured in Tokyo."

Oh my god. I knew in my heart it had to be, "Nathan?"

Maggie nodded. "Yes. Canter is now on home soil. He is at The Royal Darwin Hospital as we speak. He has sustained some minor injuries but nothing he can't bounce back from. He'll be back on deck by the end of the day. Now, use this as positive energy to get the job done. Godspeed to you all."

The news was immensely uplifting. But I also thought about Jenny. Maggie cut off before I had the chance to ask after her. Strangely enough, I wondered briefly if it might've been the last chance to speak with her face to face.

Xe closed the lid and slid the tactical laptop back into the top of his bergen. I noticed his hands were trembling. If Xe's hands shook, something had him rattled and Xe never got rattled. I wondered how bad things had become.

"Are you okay?" I asked Xe.

He didn't answer. Like the logical being he was, he changed the subject altogether. "Did you see anyone get out of the Lear jet?"

I nodded. "Some guy with a very expensive suit."

"People who own Lear jets dress in expensive clothes. Nothing strange about that."

"Yeah, but you'd think even for that guy, he'd have to go through security before leaving the airport. Instead, he took out some kind of device and used it to open a steel door down in the main hangar. Who gets to do that?"

That got Xe's attention. "Show me."

When we got there, the Lear jet had already departed. Xe had his nose up to the glass checking out the steel door with the security locking device at its side.

"Do you know about the message that was sent to my phone?"

Xe nodded. "Yes, I know about the message. What's your assumption?"

"Nathan tracked the origin. The message was sent from Alice Springs Airport. You know what? I think it came from somewhere behind that door."

"We'll flag this one for later. We have a job to get done first. We need to put our efforts behind finding a way to the Project Amber. Let's go, Angel. We have little time . . ."

"But what if Project Amber is down there?"

"Unlikely. Our intelligence suggests Pine Gap. That's ten kilometres due west from here."

"I know. I studied the maps. Pine Gap is exactly west in a straight line. What does *that* tell you?"

"You're suggesting a tunnel?"

"It's possible, don't you think?"

"It's plausible," Xe replied. "We'll still need the digital security to access it. Perhaps you've got us a bit closer, Angel. Perhaps you've saved us some valuable time. I'll inform Shilo while on mission. Let's go."

I went to follow Xe, but my attention was grabbed all over again. I looked up from the window. The same seven eagles I'd seen before circled as though they were trying to tell me something.

* * *

We infiltrated by Chinook roughly ten kilometres south of Nurrungar. Without the moon casting its glow, I struggled to see my own hand. I huddled down with the others in a tight circle, waiting for my eyes to adjust. After approximately twenty minutes, Andrew finally signalled weapons ready. The metallic clacking sounds cut through the silence, as we slapped magazines and cocked breaches. A quick coms check and everyone gave thumbs up.

Dressed in the black thermal evasion suits, weapons hot, we began the long tab under NVG to the target area. Almost immediately my suit began to drip from the inside. I pushed on, Andrew taking point, Bosco scanning from the rear. Soon, it was my turn to take over until someone else slunk up to take point. That's how it went. Every one thousand metres, down and scan.

Drink more water. Change point. Swapping and changing and creeping through the darkness like a centipede on a mission. NVGs showed the path ahead as shades of green. We sneaked on into the night like a machine; silent and deadly.

Eventually, the sparse and irregular Nurrungar outbuildings came into view under a strange green monochrome. We moved silently toward the buildings, stopping only to check our flanks. Through my NVG, several beams from our laser assisted optical sights danced around as they made contact with objects in my path. We snuck up behind the first building, then made tactical approaches to the next, and then to the next, and the next.

Xe was on point at the time he put his hand up, signalling a stop to our advance. Everyone halted behind him in single file, then we all went prone, at the same time trying to avoid the nasty spikes of the desert spinifex.

"Target ahead," Xe whispered over coms while giving the signal to approach under critical stealth. We crept on.

We were approximately thirty metres away from the first shipping container. The NVG gave me a false sense of security. I didn't realise how black it was until I flicked the device up from my face to chase away a huge outback moth.

By this time, my TES was seriously hot and uncomfortable. The amount sweating inside was incredible. Every time I made a move, the suit made squelching sucking noises as I moved forward.

Xe signalled to advance near a concrete pylon, and we all slunk across. "Fall back zone here," he whispered. Everyone nodded, giving thumbs up and dropping bergens. We drank more water, then lined our bergens up in a row to create a last resort barrier in case things went bad. So far, the place was empty. But I also knew that things can go to crap real fast.

We snuck up to the rear of the first container and it was an opportunity for everyone took catch their breath. The door lever on the container was held into place with a large heavy looking padlock. Andrew retrieved a bolt cutter from his chest pack and was about to go at it. Xe stopped him. "Wait, we need to secure the area first."

Xe signalled for silence. We all dropped low. With his gloved hand, Xe signalled for Bosco to scout forward. Bosco crept past Xe with experienced precision. He was gone for a brief time before he returned. "Contacts. Six of the assholes in one Humvee," he whispered over coms. But then without any notice, Bosco disappeared again.

My mind went back to my training at Swan Island.

"Fear," my instructor said to all of us in lecture-one. "Fear, is good. Fear, is healthy. Fear . . . keeps you sharp. Use your fear. Use the energy it provides. If you're down range and fearless, do not stand next to me. I'd rather not have you on my team. Fearless means you're a loose cannon. And we do not do loose cannons on my watch."

Then, the sound of gunfire broke through my thoughts as Bosco engaged our enemy. I was ready to take the fight to them. I was ready to use everything I'd learned. I waited for the command from Xe; he said nothing, only signalled for us to wait it out. Gunfire ceased and everything went silent. We waited in the darkness safe behind cover. My breath shortened as my heart pushed blood around my body. What was Xe waiting for?

"Tangos down," Bosco then whispered over coms.

CHAPTER NINETEEN

Drake Equation

ANDREW AND XE GOT DOWN ON ONE knee at the door of the first container. The head of the bolt cutter was poised, ready to do damage to padlock number one. I crouched down with them—green monochrome images, shining through the NVG. The head of the bolt cutter bit at the hardened steel padlock. Andrew and Xe grunted, putting their weight behind it. After several moments of trying, panting from exertion, they stood up to take a breather.

"Bloody hell," Andrew said. "This isn't gonna work."

"What about a crowbar?" Bosco said.

"We don't have a crowbar, Bosco. If we did have one, it'd need to be longer than the damn container to get enough leverage on it."

As Andrew and Xe got down again and went back to the task with the padlock, my mind returned to the bodies in the Humvee. The dead soldiers would certainly be cause for alarm if the Reaper was in the air. As I thought about it, the scenario went rocketing around my mind. We were all in danger from the Reaper as one by one, the soldiers heat signature slowly went cold.

With the thought racing around in my brain I went down to Andrew. “We have to make this quick!”

Andrew looked up from what he was doing, breathing heavily. “It isn’t gonna be quick or anything close to it, Angel. Why?”

“The Reaper,” I whispered. “The Reaper knows about the dead guys.”

“I doubt it.”

I shook my head thinking Andrew misunderstood what I was getting at. “The dead soldiers. They’re going cold. The Reaper will know something has happened to them.”

Andrew dropped the bolt cutter and stood up. “Fuck!”

Xe looked up from what he was doing, “Bosco, get to the Humvee. When you get there, take your thermal evasion suit off, and start moving around like a guy that’s not dead.”

“Serious?”

“Do it. Don’t run. Just walk over there.”

“Roger. Why do I always get the shit jobs?”

“I think that might buy us some time,” I said.

“It might. Who knows for sure? It’s a start.” Andrew picked up the bolt cutter again and went back to the business with the padlock. He tried harder break it but it seemed it was no good. He and Xe fought on to no avail.

“Andrew . . .”

Andrew looked up to me from what he was doing. “What’s on your mind, Angel?”

“Maybe if Bosco starts the Humvee and lets it idle, the heat from the engine won’t raise any suspicions with the Reaper. They’ll think everything’s good on the ground.”

“Good point.”

Bosco heard the talk over coms. “Doing it,” he responded. The Humvee engine turned over. The sing from the turbo cut through the desert air, and then the engine settled and idled. Andrew went back to the bolt cutter. He and Xe put a massive amount of weight behind it. The padlock was still looking like it was never going to break. "We need more leverage. Look around, Angel. Find something. Anything we can use to get more leverage on these damn handles."

I had an idea. I remembered the oxy kit they'd left behind and I wondered where it might be. But the flame from the oxy would certainly give away our position. I offered my idea anyway.

Andrew stopped trying to force the bolt cutter and stood up almost exhausted. "Okay. See if you can find the oxy. With a bit of luck, we'll be out of here before the Reaper gets eyes on us."

I spun and moved swiftly toward where I'd seen it on the computer screen via the *Keyhole Satellite Three*. It didn't take long before I found what I was looking for. Two gas cylinders sat atop a trolley with the brass burner. I began to drag the oxy toward the container we were working on. Then, I noticed the handles on the trolley were removable. The handles were held into place with simple locking pins. I undid the pins, and the handles slid off. I imagined they would get the extra leverage we needed on the bolt cutter. And it also meant we didn't need to worry about the heat.

Leaving the oxy kit where it was, I brought the handles back to Andrew.

"Good work," Andrew said. He placed the lengths of pipe over the bolt cutter handles. With the help of Xe, they worked the cutter and applied brute force.

With a loud snap, the padlock finally broke free. Xe stood up while Andrew stepped out of the way. The container handle creaked and groaned as Xe tugged at the lever. He pulled. The door squealed open. Andrew peered inside. Nothing. It was empty.

To the next container.

With the bolt cutter at the padlock. Andrew and Xe once again put their weight behind it. Another snap. The padlock shattered. Xe pulled the lever again. The door opened. "This one's empty again! Can someone tell me why they put these here if they're not gonna use the damned things?"

I felt my hopes drain. We had no Chinook and I realised it for the first time—everything might be a waste of our effort. And the Reaper will find us before long.

"Next container. Go," Xe ordered.

By the time we reached the next container, my hopes had all but diminished. Xe had the head of the bolt cutter poised at the padlock.

"Tap it first," I suggested. "If it sounds hollow, forget it and move on. There's still two more after this one."

Bosco came over coms. "Hey guys? It looks like we might have a situation."

"What is it, Bosco?" Andrew said at the same time tapping around the container. As he tapped the metal walls it sounded very hollow to me.

"Radio dude just checked in. Do ya want me to respond?"

"No," Xe said. "Don't do anything. Just make sure you move around. Get out of the Humvee if you have to. Walk around. Just do something so you don't raise their suspicions."

"Copy that."

Xe tapped the sides of the next container. Hollow. He looked up and shook his head, then signalled to move on. I stopped him. "It smells like somethings dead in there. Can't you smell it?"

Xe lifted the NVG away from his face. He put his nose up to the hinges. "You're right. This might be what we're looking for."

Bosco came over coms. "The radio guy keeps checking in. You're gonna have to pick this shit up a pace."

"Bosco. Search the bodies," Xe ordered. "If you can't find anything useful on them, dig out their eyes."

"I already searched them. I found some kind of shiny thing. It's got some seriously strange markings on it. I've never seen anything like it before. But why the eyes? Are you shitting me?"

"Just get it done. Make sure you get a good length of blood vessels. Don't damage them more than you have to. It's my Plan B if we need it."

"Roger that. Beats the shit out of me but I'll do it."

After Xe and Andrew shattered the lock with a bolt cutter that was fast approaching its use-by date, the door creaked open. Xe and Andrew stepped quickly inside. Just as they did so, a pungent stench punched me straight in the face. I covered my nose with my gloved hand as I stepped inside. Several ordinary looking caskets were lined up and stacked along one wall.

Bosco came back over coms. "I got one dead guy's eye out. Now what?"

"I have a cryo cylinder," Xe replied. "Stay where you are. I'm Oscar Mike." Xe sprang away and disappeared into the night.

"Hey! Can I at least ask *why* we need the dead guy's eyeballs?"

"We need the retinas." Xe said over coms. "They'll get us past scanners."

"Nice idea, Boss, but that ain't gonna work. May as well use potato mash. Just sayin'."

"Get the damn eyeballs, Bosco. I'll be there momentarily."

Andrew stepped up to a casket and kicked it over. The lid fell off. A grisly bath of maggots rolled out onto the floor. I turned away, trying to stem the rush of nausea that rose up my throat.

"Angel. Are you okay?" Andrew asked me at a most inappropriate time.

"I need a moment."

I sprinted out of the container and prompt threw up on the ground.

Stepping back in, I looked down at the corpse while holding my hand up to my nose.

"You could've spewed up in here," Andrew said, "This isn't my living room. I hope you kicked some dirt over it. Just so there's no heat signature."

Why didn't I think of that? I rushed back out and fixed up what needed fixing.

After I stepped back inside the container, Andrew leaned down closer to the casket and brushed away the handfuls of maggots. In the casket, under waves of heaving maggots, was the body of someone dressed in a dried-up, blood encrusted, Northern Territory police uniform. Andrew knelt to study the body more closely. At the same time, Xe returned, sprinting back into the container. Xe held up the strange device Bosco had found. "We have our plan A. Also, we have what we need for the plan B if it's required."

Then Bosco came back over coms. "Hey, Boss, I think I need to answer this damn radio. They're starting to freak out."

"Don't fuck it up," Xe responded.

"Roger that."

My attention was split between Xe with his device, Bosco answering his radio, and Andrew searching the dead body. "Found something!" Andrew said while shoving his hand deeper into the dead guy's trouser pocket. Something in my mind told me to stop him. I was about to yell it out, Stop, Stop, Stop! But it was far too late.

CLICK!

CHAPTER TWENTY

Singularity

ANDREW WENT IMMEDIATLEY STILL AND QUIET. "Don't move, Andrew. Please don't move," I said as I pushed my hands out to stop him going any further.

"Do me a favour, guys? Get the fuck out of here," Andrew said in a tone I didn't recognise. "Get out, Angel. Go, go, go."

Bosco then came over coms. "The radio dude's freaking out. Suggest we get our asses into gear."

"Fuck!" Andrew shouted as if not hearing Bosco. "How was I so stupid?"

I couldn't believe what was happening. It was the worst of my nightmares. "Andrew. Just stay calm and don't move."

Xe, crouched down to Andrew's side. "Don't move. Don't even breathe," Xe told him as he began to gently probe around Andrew's hand. He lifted a small piece of blood encrusted fabric away from the dead body. A metallic object with a set of wires was well hidden within the folds of the dead bodies clothing. "Pressure-sensitive trigger. Old school. But where's the charge?" Xe continued the search around the body, then found a long cylindrical object. He stood up slowly as though he already knew how bad the situation was. Xe then looked for other signs around the container.

Ii was in that moment, I saw the same thing Xe was seeing. More improvised explosive devices were strategically placed around the inside of the container. It seemed the entire place was wired for a massive explosion. My mind whirled. This was now no more than yet another deadly ambush. There was no Chinook, nor was there ever going to be one. How did I get this so wrong?

"Get out. All of you get out!" Andrew said again.

Xe again got down beside Andrew and probed a bit more. "Bosco, we need your expertise on this. Get back into your TES and get over here. Move it."

"Oscar Mike . . ." Bosco immediately responded.

Andrew appeared to hold his breath as Xe probed around him. "Don't hold your breath, Andrew. Breathe or you'll faint. We don't need that at the moment."

I relaxed just a little as I saw Andrew begin to breathe again.

Xe put his nose up to one of the devices. He stood up and stepped back more urgently than before. "This isn't your average," Xe said directly to me. "I know what this is. The charges are rigged with helium-3 We've a job on our hands."

Before I had words to reply, Bosco entered the container. "Shit's about to go down if we don't extract digits from assholes. What've we got here?" Bosco stepped with speed toward an a clearly exhausted Andrew. He kneeled down beside him and pulled up sections of cloth, peering under in the same way Xe had already done. Bosco checked it with expert eyes, then stepped slowly away. "Triple loop jury-rigged. We need to find the power source."

As we looked around, I found the main wire we were looking for. A single black wire trailed away from the casket and through a hole in the container to the outside. I followed Bosco, picking up the wire from the exterior that led away from the container to a pile of rusty fuel drums. We all scratched frantically at the ground with our bare hands and after a while, we dug up a plastic box which contained a motor cycle battery as the power source. Bosco studied the battery for a moment then put it back in the plastic container.

"Aren't you going to do something? Please do something!"

"It's no good, Angel. See the circuit board? If any of the circuits become corrupt, the others will activate. It doesn't matter which way we look at it. Disconnecting the power source ain't gonna happen."

"So, what does that mean?"

"Option one—We'll need to maintain the down pressure on the trigger sensor. We'll need to replace the down pressure with something heavy enough to equal the down force. *Before* he can take his hand away. That's the only way we're ever gonna get him out."

Bosco continued to inspect the jury rig in the plastic box. "I've seen these things before. Damn pressure-sensitive triggers tend to activate even if you try to swap them out. I hate to say it. Fatigue is the biggest threat. It's a race against time."

"We can't give up."

"That brings us to option two, Angel. I ain't saying we give up. We can bungee Andrew away from the devices. It was always a last resort actions-on in cases like this. But even so, IEDs either killed, or they were duds. The chances are slim but we'll work with what we have."

"Great. If the blast doesn't kill him, we'll break his ribs, and he'll die from a collapsed lung?"

Bosco shook his head. "If you think he's gonna come out with a few broken ribs, think again. He'll lose something. A leg. Probably both. Who knows? The few broken ribs are a given, but the least of his worries. If he lives, we'll need to make sure he keeps *on* living. What we need to do is get ready for the bleeding. Shell dressings won't be enough. If we can't get it under control, he'll bleed out. Simple as that."

Xe walked away slightly. I knew he was hard at work thinking of a plan. It was as though Andrew heard all the chatter over coms, "It isn't gonna work! You won't do it quick enough. Save yourselves and go!"

"I'll go and get the Humvee to the container," Bosco said, ignoring Andrew's words. "Go grab your toggle ropes."

* * *

"I bloody-well told the lot of you lot to get out of here, didn't I? You've got what you came here for. Go and destroy Project Amber before it's too late."

I kneeled down to Andrew and gently placed my hand on his shoulder. "We're going to get you out, Andrew. Let us take care of things."

Andrew dropped his head and I knew exhausting was catching up with him. Droplets of sweat fell away from his chin and the tip of his nose. "You're just wasting time, Angel. Forget about me."

I didn't respond. I began wrapping the fabric that we recovered from the dead soldiers uniforms around Andrew's waist. Bosco ripped more fabric into shreds and passed it to me. I took it and wrapped more around Andrew.

"It isn't gonna work, Angel."

"It'll work. We'll have you out of here soon; I promise."

Andrew looked at me and appeared to lighten a little. Finally, he had a huge amount of padding around his waist and I was satisfied that maybe we'd only break one or two of his ribs. Xe kneeled and helped tie one end of the toggle rope around his waist. Behind my NVG, my tears were already beginning to blur my vision. I was about to save Andrew's life, but at the same time, I was also going to cause him a massive amount of injury. The extent of his injury, I could only imagine. If Bosco was right in what he'd said earlier, Andrew would at best most likely spend the rest of his years in a wheelchair. I owed it to him to give him the news of his unborn child. Perhaps it would give him the strength to fight for his life.

"Andrew. I have to tell you something."

Andrew looked up at me and I could see it in his eyes how tired he'd become.

"Andrew . . ."

"What is it, Angel?"

"I . . ."

Bosco wrecked the moment as he brought the Humvee to the container, pushing the bumper up to the door, switching the engine off but keeping the lights on. For the first time, the headlights illuminated the grisly scene, and also for the first time Andrew appeared to be losing his will to endure.

"We need to hurry," I said.

Xe and I finished securing the toggle rope around Andrew's waist. I decided could tell Andrew of the news after we finally got him clear.

But the, Xe froze into one place. "Stop!"

Bosco did the same but stepped silently to the door of the container and cocking his head to the side.

Xe got up from Andrew and crept over to Bosco.

In that instant, my heart plummeted. The sound of helicopter blades thumped through the silence in the distance. I stood up from Andrew, not believing how bad the situation was getting.

"Stand-to! Stand-to!" Xe shouted, then spun to Bosco. "Tie the end of the toggle around the bumper, Bosco. Move your arse."

Bosco bounced back in and grabbed the rope out of my hands. The toggle rope unspooled as Bosco stepped back toward the Humvee, clutching his SA-80 with his free hand. He stopped just short of the bumper and dropped his weapon. "It's not fucking long enough!" Bosco yelled.

Bosco gripped the rope with both his hands. He was about to wrench the rope toward the Humvee.

"No! Don't pull on it!" I screamed at him. "If you pull Andrew over, the charges will detonate. Move the Humvee closer."

"STAND-TO!" Andrew yelled from behind me. "Stand-to, Angel. Go . . . Just go."

"I can't get the Humvee closer!" Bosco screamed back at me. "It's already hard up on the container!"

I put my head down and felt so sick, I thought I would vomit again. I turned to Xe. "Do we have more ropes?"

"No. That's all we have."

"Then we'll have to slide the casket closer to the Humvee. Xe, help me, please."

"Get out before it's too late!" Andrew yelled again. "Take the device and fuck off!"

Bosco ran over and with the three of us at the casket, we began the slow process of sliding it forward toward the Humvee.

"Angel, it's no good." Andrew pleaded with me to stop. "The wire. It's not long enough."

I looked down to what Andrew was talking about. The sound of the helicopter was getting closer and closing in. There was no slack in the wire. Andrew was right. There was no room for any movement toward the Humvee. The wire leading away from the casket to the battery outside was already taut.

Bosco raced toward me and grabbed my arm. "We have to go. Now!"

I jerked Bosco's grip away from me. "I'm not leaving without Andrew. You can go if you want!"

"Now, Angel! There's no time," Xe said as he locked and loaded his weapon.

"We'll get to the battery and bring it closer," I said as I got up from Andrew and started for the door. "If we bring it closer to the container, we'll have room to slide the casket!"

Just as I appeared at the door of the container, the chopper came in hot, strafing shots down. The metallic pinging rang out across the top of the container. Shots pierced through just missing the IEDs. Xe stepped out and fired his weapon in a steady burst as the chopper punched overhead.

Andrew pleaded again but I ignored him. I was going to get him out or die trying. I spun and attempted to run back toward him. Xe gripped me by the top of my arm and dragged me back.

"NOOO! ANDREW!"

"No time for this," Xe shouted at me. "We have to move."

Bosco was behind the wheel of the Humvee, engine revving, waiting to go. "C'mon! Hurry the fuck up!" The engine revved. The turbo spooled. The heavy thumping of the chopper returned for a second strafing.

"Incoming!" Bosco screamed. Xe manhandled me into the back, then threw himself inside.

"Go! Go! Go!" Xe thumped the side of the Humvee.

Bosco stepped on the throttle. The Humvee leaped away in reverse. Dust kicked up as he jerked the wheel hard over, sending the Humvee into a controlled one-eighty. With a crunch, he fought for first gear, then stepped on the throttle again. The chopper came bearing down from behind.

THUD!

I was the sound I never wanted to hear. I spun in my seat. Then, the shock wave from the explosion struck the Humvee, jolting it forward.

"ANDREW!"

"He's gone, Angel," Bosco yelled back to me. "He's gone."

"NOOO!"

The chopper came down from the rear, strafing more rounds. Xe immediately screamed out, "I'M HIT! I'M HIT!"

I spun around in time to see Xe buckled over, squirming, blood oozing from between his fingers. I noticed it then. A long green wooden crate on the back seat, jumping around as Bosco drove the Humvee at full speed down the rutted and potholed dirt track. Clouds of dust kicked up from the rear as he forced the Humvee forward. I reached out to grab at the crate. The bumping and jostling bounced my hand away.

"Bosco! There's a launcher!"

"I know. I'm trying to get us to cover. You've got one shot, Angel. It's already loaded and primed. It's not guided so make it count!"

"But you can't slow down if the Reaper . . .!"

"If the Reaper was up there, we'd all be shit-canned by now. I'll get us to cover. Then get the bastards. How copy!"

The chopper came back hot, peppering shots down as the Humvee drove at top speed. The Humvee engine began to gurgle and misfire. Black smoke erupted from both sides of the hood. "Hang on, Angel, I'm gonna go broadside. You'd better get ready with the launcher!"

I gripped tight and braced. Bosco reached to the handbrake lever and reefed it up while at the same time turning spinning the steering wheel hard left. I felt two wheels leave the ground as the Humvee broadsided in the dirt and rushed to a stop. I reached around through the cloud of dust and grabbed at the crate. I lifted the lid away and grabbed the long, cylindrical weapon. Springing out of the Humvee with my heart pounding in my chest and almost out of breath, I sprinted away for several paces. Bending on one knee, I flipped open both ends of the optical sights. I held the weapon up, catching the chopper in my crosshairs and waited for the shot.

I fired. The rocket shot away from the launcher. I dropped the tube and watched on as the missile got closer to the target.

Without any warning, the chopper suddenly banked left. Chaff and flare countermeasures pumped with tiny explosions out from the sides. The rocket flew under the chopper making contact with a flare, exploding but leaving the chopper undamaged.

Out of breath and feeling the failure, I fell on both knees.

"We gotta get to cover!" Bosco screamed at me from behind. "C'mon, Angel. Suck it up and move your ass!"

Xe heaved himself from the rear of the Humvee, holding a blood-soaked hand to his shoulder. "Angel. Run . . . And leave me here. Go!"

I sprinted to Xe and tried to help him to his feet. Xe resisted.

"I said leave me. Get to cover with Bosco. They're heading back this way."

"You're coming with us, Xe."

"No, I'm not. Trust me. Just get to cover with Bosco."

Xe kneeled in the dirt and placed his both palms onto his temples.

"What're you doing?" I shouted at him.

Bosco ran up behind me and grabbed me by the wrist. "You finished? Get a move on!"

I left Xe and ran for cover, dropping down behind a clump of malnourished bloodwood trees. Spinning around, I saw Xe pushing his hands to his temples using force. He screamed out as though he was in extreme pain. The chopper strafed us again.

Rounds hit the dirt and kicking up dust all around us. Xe again screamed out more chillingly than before. Instantly, a bright blue glow appeared in the sky above him. I watched, not believing, as the glow began to move slowly across the sky, then began to chase the chopper down.

After the bright blue glow encapsulated the chopper, it immediately imploded and crunched down into something tiny. It disappeared from the sky. Somewhere out in the desert, the sound of something metallic hit the ground. I stood there both astonished and horrified as I watched Xe's body slump and fall to the ground.

The chopper was gone. The threat was gone. I moved out from behind cover and ran to Xe. Kneeling down in the dirt, Bosco took off his glove, placing his hand up to the side of Xe's neck. Shaking his head sadly, Bosco confirmed the horror of Xe's untimely death.

CHAPTER TWENTY-ONE

Fallen

WE'D BEEN SHELTERING BY THE DEAD HUMVEE for hours. The first light of dawn broke low over the desert horizon to the east. The stars slowly extinguished, and the blackness of space drew lighter into shades of blue. Another hot, cloudless, desert day was on the way. I sat in the bullet-ridden, pock-marked dust, hunched over Xe's body. At first, I wanted to mourn him. But tears evaded me as I sat silently in the arid, red earth. I placed a hand on Xe's chest to check for life one final time.

Bosco sat quietly close to my side, while doodling in the dirt with a stick. "We'll need to bury him," Bosco said sadly. It was the first time I heard Bosco speak with such sadness. I didn't know Bosco had it in him to be sad, but there he was.

Already, flies were doing steady work on Xe's body. I swished them away as best as I could. "It's not over, Bosco. There's a job to do. They might've thumped us this time. They won't get a second round."

"Yeah, I know," Bosco said, as he stared vacantly into the distance.

I eyed him, frowning a little. "You sound like you've given up."

"It's just me and you left in this. Without Canter, Andrew and now Xe, we have ourselves a shit of a job getting to Project Amber in time. I don't know where *Steinbeck* is right now. If she gets to the Sea of Japan, Angel. If she exchanges ordnance with North Korea . . ." Bosco shook his head, pausing a beat. "Anyway. I'm sure you know the consequences if that shit starts to go down."

"That shiny thing will get us there," I said, casting my eyes over the chrome metal object.

"Yeah. I'm not sure why we need those eyeballs, though. Using them for retina scanners seems too ridiculous for words."

"Xe's plan B?"

"Yeah. How in the heck would a plan like that work? You and I both know there needs to be blood supply to the retina before it can possibly be scanned."

Bosco got up and dusted himself down. "I wasn't in the loop with Xe's plan B. Only Andrew. But he's also gone."

I looked away to the horizon, thinking I'd heard something low and thudding. It was faint, and only just audible. Thinking it was just the wind somewhere out there, I put it to the back of my mind.

"We'll need to check in," Bosco said. "For that to happen, we'll need to tab back and get Xe's tactical laptop from his bergen."

The thought of going back was a hard prospect to consider. The first thing I thought about was Andrew. Going back there, I'd need to see him a final time. But I also knew his physical body was gone. What made matters worse was the thought of Andrew not knowing about becoming a father. It almost brought me tears. I caught myself involuntarily placing a hand on my belly thinking of him. Then, for some reason, I smiled at the thought of Andrews

DNA growing inside me. It confused me a little, having that feeling. But it was something I couldn't have helped even if I tried. A smile, when I should've felt nothing but loss and bereavement.

I gazed down at Xe's body while swishing more flies away. "What was that thing he did?"

"Oudarretians do it sometimes. It kills them, though. Xe didn't die from his wound. He didn't die from blood loss. He died giving his life up for us, Angel."

"What? Some kind of telekinesis or something?"

"No . . . Nothing like that. Oudarretians are connected to the universe in ways we only get to imagine."

"So, what did he do, exactly? That blue glow in the sky. And where did that chopper go? It looked like some kind of implosion."

"That's because that's exactly what it was. An implosion. Xe opened a time and space singularity. A point of condensed universe."

"An event horizon?"

"You've been reading science mags."

"I'm a journalist. I read everything."

"You *were* a journalist . . . And yeah, something like that. But it is what it is. The moment the chopper went into the singularity, the forces of the condensed universe destroyed it. I've only ever seen an Oudarretian singularity once before," Bosco said eyeing me with intense resolve. "C'mon. Let's get our asses into gear. It's a long way back, and these suits are gonna kill us if we have to spend daylight hours in them."

Bosco stepped toward the rear of the Humvee and retrieved a small spade. "We don't have the time to bury Xe's body. But we'll bury the shiny thing and the cryo cylinder for safe keeping. We'll grab it back after we make contact with Charlotte Station."

We walked to the edge of a clump of bloodwood trees. Bosco put the spade into the earth and grunted as it made little impact in the dry dirt. As he dug, that faint noise in the distance I'd heard earlier, cut louder through the desert silence. Now, I was sure about what the sound was. It was the steady thumping of rotors.

Bosco stood up, immediately cocking one ear in the direction of the sound. "We gotta move again. This shit ain't over! Quick. Back to the Humvee and get under it for cover."

"No, Bosco. If they decide to blow it up, we're done."

I got Bosco by the arm and pulled him down. We both went prone behind spidery arms of large tree roots that seemed to be screaming for water. I tasted the gritty dust between my teeth as I hit the ground.

Together we watched as the chopper came in closer. The thumping increased as dust blew up in the wind. It came in low, and hovered near the dead, bullet-riddled Humvee.

"Black Hawk," Bosco said loudly over the noise of rushing turbofan engines. "Maybe our exfil. Maybe friendlies. There's no aggression yet. That's something at least."

The wheels slowly padded the ground and the noise of the engines spooled down. The rotor slowed, and the dust began to settle.

"If not friendlies, we're prisoners, Bosco. There's no hiding from this. They'll find us soon enough."

"Yeah," Bosco smiled. "Let's pin our hopes up on exfill then, huh?"

The Black Hawk rotor blades finally stopped. The desert was silent again. The cockpit window slid open, and a voice called out. "Operation Mogul! Are you there?"

I wanted to sit up at the sound of his voice. I couldn't believe my ears and I fought through the urge to get up and run to him. The voice, I recognised. Unmistakable. Distinctive.

"Operation Mogul! Do you copy?" he called out again. "Are you gonna get your arses over here or what? Time's wasting."

Bosco shot me a sideways glance. He was about to get up. I dragged him back down.

"Hold on a second. We don't know exactly who they are just yet. It might be another trap."

Over at the Black Hawk, the door slid open, and someone stepped out onto the dirt. He walked around with a slight limp, the same as Nathan did. He was wearing dark sunglasses and a baseball hat, and he also had a full beard.

Nathan hated beards. He'd never grow one. He always said a beard got in the way of things. I remember I asked him once, what he meant. He just laughed. He said nothing else. So, I never asked him again.

The figure with the sunglasses, baseball hat, and full beard walked over to the Humvee. He poked around, while the pilot dressed in desert fatigues and aviator's helmet stepped out from the helo's cockpit door. The two had words out of earshot.

The figure that walked around and sounded like Nathan did a whirly sign above his head with the point of his finger. The pilot echoed the gesture in response, then went back to the Black Hawk. Moments later, the engines came to life and began to spool up.

"Angel, they're about to leave. Can't you see that's Canter over there?"

"Maybe it is, maybe it isn't. The beard tells me maybe it isn't."

"Are you shitting me? How would he know about Mogul if he ain't Canter?"

I wanted to believe Bosco. I wanted to believe it *was* Nathan. The sunglasses, hat, and beard made it difficult. If it was the enemy, there'd be no escaping. How would I know for sure without giving up our position? But my head wanted to know, one way or another.

I called out and immediately the unnamed man spun around and began to walk over toward us.

"Halt, stand still!" I yelled as he got closer. To my surprise, he stopped as instructed, and for some reason put up his hands.

"We're armed," I said. "Turn around."

He did what I asked without question.

"Get on your knees."

He began go down on his knees. He hesitated.

"On your knees!" I yelled again.

"I'm doing it, Angel. My leg, remember? And I know you don't have your weapons. We already retrieved them from where you left them. And your bergens. And the tactical laptop. Do you want me to go on?"

Bosco and I got up off the dirt in synchronicity to each other.

"Nathan Masters! As I live and breathe," Bosco called out with a big cheesy grin on his face. Nathan got up from his knees to face us. I cut my way past Bosco. I felt as though my face was on fire. I paced toward Nathan, fists clenched, gritting my teeth. Nathan held out his arms toward me with his usual smile on his face. A few seconds later, he was flat on his back, and I was shaking the hurt away from my hand. "Fucking do that to me again, I'll kill you myself," I screamed at him, then promptly burst into tears.

CHAPTER TWENTY-TWO

The Eyes Have it

"I CAN'T GET MY HEAD AROUND HOW you managed to find us out here," I said to Nathan.

Nathan pointed a finger in the air. "Look up and smile to Christina. She had your back. Pity Xe didn't check in. Things might've turned out differently. We also managed to kill the Reaper. We found where it was piloted and shut that shit down. The drone crashed somewhere in the desert. If we could've established communications with you, we would've. Xe stepped outside protocol. The reasons aren't clear—we'll never know now. Maybe he stuffed up. Maybe not. Maybe he decided it was too risky to check in. Now Andrew's gone. Maggie's beside herself," Nathan paused, then added, "Things are about to happen, and I'm talking about worldwide catastrophic events."

"There was so much coming down on us—there was no time to check in. Things got all out of shape. We had no actions-on for what happened back there."

"Nonetheless, you managed to do well under the circumstances. The shiny thing. And the eyeballs in the cryo cylinder. It's a major step in the right direction."

"You know what that thing is?"

"The shiny thing? Yeah. I know exactly what it is."

I waited for an explanation, but it wasn't going to come without applying additional pressure.

I gave Nathan my eyes.

He relented. "It's a microwave emitter," Nathan explained. "It's as simple as that. Nothing more. Nothing less."

"And?"

"They're used to disengage the locking mechanisms that are using the microwave wavelength." Nathan then flipped the shiny thing over and studied it. "The markings are the Drake equation. But they're just for the sake of decoration. It seems a little odd but I get it."

I looked at Nathan using my best blank stare expression. It made him chuckle.

"Xe said there was a plan. For the eyeballs, I mean. They're to be used to get past retina scanners. Bosco seems to think it's a waste of time. He says the eyeballs won't work without blood circulation. I can see what he's on about. They aren't going to work, are they?"

"One—There *is* a plan. Maggie briefed me before getting down here. Two—They *will* work."

"How?" I asked. "They need to be in someone's head to get blood circulation, don't they?"

"Absolutely," Nathan nodded, then grinned. "But . . ."

"You're not gonna tell me something crazy like transplant, are you?"

"A full eyeball transplant has never been done before. Not successfully anyway."

"That's good. I thought the idea was crazy."

Nathan then added something I wasn't expecting. "A full eyeball transplant has been attempted before, and full blood supply was successfully re-established. The problem is the reconnecting and regrowing the optic nerve. Medical science hasn't got that far."

It was enough for me to raise an eyebrow. "You're seriously thinking transplant?"

"Yeah. But not as you might think. The plan is to get them surgically implanted. But . . ."

"But what?"

"Not in your head."

I gave Nathan another of my blank stares. "What do you mean, not in your head? Is it a transplant or is it not?"

"As I said. Implant—not transplant. You get to keep the eyes you have, but we have to supply blood circulation to the implants so they work with retina scanners."

I couldn't help falling back slightly. My legs weakened beneath my weight and were threatening to collapse.

"Relax, Angel. It's temporary. They'll be removed at the first opportunity."

"Okay. So, where are we supposed to have these . . . Implants?" I thought about trying to close my ears, so I didn't have to listen to anymore. My imagination ran away and there was nothing good in the pictures I had in my mind.

"On our wrists; like wearing a wristwatch."

"And who, may I ask, gets to get one of these bloody eyeball wristwatches?"

"Well that depends."

"On what?"

"It depends on how many good ones we have in the cryo cylinder. Knowing Bosco, he'd probably butchered some of them. If they're all good, then we all get to have one."

I looked away stemming the rush of bile in my throat. After a moment, Nathan added more to this grotesque set of circumstances. "It's for the . . ."

"Don't even go there with that 'greater good' crap. I'll do what has to be done. I don't have to like it, though. But if that's the plan, I'm assuming we need a surgeon?"

"Yeah. Soon enough."

"I bet Bosco doesn't get an eyeball wristwatch."

"Yeah, he will. We need to play this one up against the odds."

Nausea attacked me again. I leaned forward slightly with a hand on my abdomen, trying to get fresh air into my lungs.

"You good?" Nathan asked just as I felt I was going to be sick.

"Just the thought of someone's eyeball looking up at me. It seriously grosses me out."

Nathan nodded his reply, then turned away. I couldn't hold on to it any longer. I reached out and gripped Nathan's shoulder before I promptly threw up.

"You're *not* good. I wouldn't have thought this idea would make you sick to your stomach. Like I said, it's temporary." Nathan eyed me up and down. I hadn't seen his expression of compassion in so long. I was beginning to think Nathan wasn't Nathan anymore. "You need to get out of that TES and get some hydration back. There're some fatigues in the back of the helo. They may not fit you as you'd like, though."

* * *

Nathan looked down at the body of Xe before zipping up the body bag. "He was a good man, Angel. He was one of them, but in the end, we all considered him a brother. Such a shame he had to go this way."

I was angry. I tried hard to keep it in check. But there were things that needed to be said. "You know what? I'm sick of you keeping things from me. Why didn't you just tell the whole truth from the start, when we were back at Busby's?"

"I keep telling you, Angel. There're things I can say. And there are things I can't. What would you have done if I told you he was Oudarretian?"

"I wouldn't have believed you. I would've thought you were crazy."

"And you would've walked out on me, right there."

"Yes that's true."

"And you wouldn't have gotten yourself to Tullamarine."

"No."

"And you wouldn't be pregnant."

"How did you know?"

"Maggie told me."

"Maggie? I never said anything."

"Maggie knows everything. And congrats, Angel. I never would've thought . . ."

"Yeah, but Andrew . . . It's not fair."

I adjusted my desert fatigues that were three sizes too long for my limbs. But even so, I was glad to do away with the thermal evasion suit that was wet through with my perspiration.

With the help of Bosco, we heaved Xe's body into the Black Hawk and placed it gently down, next to another body bag that appeared to be much lighter, and much smaller.

"Andrew's remains," Nathan told me out of respect and empathy.

I stood over the body bags feeling extremely saddened. Reaching out with a trembling hand, I hovered lightly over Andrew's body bag and remembered all the good things that Andrew stood for. My mind also replayed all of the happy times I shared with him. I never knew him for very long. Now I wished I had spent my life with him. I did love Andrew. And it was with all my heart. It was exactly the same love as I have for my Jenny. I was sure of it now. It is indeed possible to be in love with two people at the same time. Looking down at Andrew, this was the proof.

Taking a seat, the Black Hawk's engines slowly came to life and began to spool up. Bosco looked at me with a glum expression that I'd never seen on him before. For a second, it wasn't Bosco at all. Just for a second, I thought I was sitting opposite a complete stranger. Then I realised that these hardened men of war have feelings like any human. Yes they're hardened from the things they've seen and done. Bosco was no exception. There was a place and time with combatants to let their true self come to the surface. Perhaps now, it was time for Bosco.

As the Black Hawk lifted away, Nathan grabbed a set of headphones off the rack behind him and gestured for me to do the same. After we plugged in, it became easier to communicate over the noise of the Black Hawke. Bosco produced a packet of gum and offered it around. I waved it away with thanks. Nathan took some with a nod and placed between his teeth before beginning to chew. Bosco bit the packet of gum and forced a few pieces into his mouth. He then reached into his bergen for his blue baseball cap with '*NY*' in white letters embossed across the front. But then, Bosco straight away placed it on his head backward. He eyed Nathan with a sort of expression that told of his frustration. The gum chewing, the hat turned backward, I knew now that Bosco wanted to get back into the fight. He wanted for blood. That was his sign.

"Bosco," I called out over coms, as the Black Hawk lifted higher into the air. "You're a good man, Bosco." Why I said it, I had no idea. But as I looked, Bosco's blush was something that only comes once in a lifetime. I smiled wider. He blushed more. Then we both broke out into fits of laughter. It was something I needed. And I think it was something Bosco needed as well.

After a few moments, the Black Hawk veered left and headed south, high over the position that had seen bloodshed only hours previous. I looked out of the window and saw for the first time how much damage was done to the container. It was no longer the shape of a brick. It was warped up and domed at the top, the sides were twisted out of shape and distorted. Black soot was spattered all over the ground. It sat twisted and askew, like some kid had made it out of plasticine. I realised then that even if we could've pulled Andrew out of the container, he was already dead. The blast radius would most certainly have killed *all* of us. Andrew, at his final moment, had managed to save the lives of his comrades. With the thought, I found myself again involuntarily placing my hand over my abdomen. Then I realised, like Maggie, Andrew probably knew.

The Black Hawk pitched left again and headed exactly south-east. Within a few moments, we passed over the white, salty vastness of Lake Eyre. I looked out and sighed, then met Nathan's stare. He too, now had an empathetic expression, with his head slightly tilted to the side. I wondered what he might be thinking about. Nathan was so complicated. And then, due to his stubborn secrecy issues, maybe I'd never know.

"Mind telling me where we're going?" I finally shouted, probably a bit too loud in the microphone. Both Bosco and Nathan simultaneously winced.

"We're first going to stop off at 4 Military Hospital," Nathan said. "Andrew and Xe will start their journey north from there. After that, we'll make our way to Adelaide repat, where we have an appointment with an ophthalmologist."

I gulped at the hard lump that had formed my throat. Suddenly, it became real. I'm going to have some arseholes eye implanted somewhere on my body.

“I thought we were going to check in with Shilo.” They were the only words I could come up with. I needed to know if Jenny was alright. I needed to urgently speak with her. I needed to . . .

Nathan responded by words that were way too loud. “You can if you want. It’s a bit noisy, though. You might like to wait until we get on the ground.”

I nodded my agreement but I didn’t like it.

“When was the last time you guys ate something?” Nathan asked.

“Roughly eighteen hours.”

“That’s good. In that case, we should be able to go straight into surgery!”

CHAPTER TWENTY-THREE

Holiday

THE BLACK HAWK TOUCHED DOWN on the main helipad at Adelaide Repatriation Hospital. We were met there by a team of doctors who were dressed in the white garb all doctors get around in. But also, as we left the Black Hawke, we were all treated as though we were all high-profile patients. After being whisked away on wheelchairs which was quite odd considering our legs were capable of taking us anywhere we needed to go, we then found ourselves on gurneys, then taken down corridors, elevators, and more corridors, until we arrived at a darkened and empty ward.

Finally, an army officer bearing a peaked cap with the insignia of the snake going up a pole, stepped into the ward. He quickly introducing himself as Captain Bryan Holiday. Then, he stepped back slightly and appeared to hold his breath. After a few seconds, he relaxed a little.

"Are you okay?" I asked Doc Holiday.

"Yes I'm fine thank you. Let's begin, shall we?"

There were the normal formalities and paperwork to sign, then we were off to pre-op. By the time we reached the operating theatre, I really couldn't have cared less about anything. The lights were so bright. Doc Holiday's face faded from my memory. Then came the dream.

* * *

I found myself drifting to another place. A place where I'd never been before.

Where am I?

While on my back, I looked up at a solid circle of bright orange light. The light pierced my skull and made my brain throb, forcing me to squint and to look away. I was forced to try and cover my eyes, but my arms . . . they didn't work. I tried again. My arms were . . . tunas that were floppy and dead. There was no feeling. They were just there.

Where am I?

I squinted, gazing into a cloudless deep blue sky. Deep blue, like nothing I'd seen before. Deep blue like the deepest oceans on Earth. I lifted my head. I managed only a couple of centimetres. I was just able to see the tops of my toes. I relaxed, knowing my body was all there. But the tunas! I still couldn't move those tunas. They were floppy, motionless, dead about my sides, heavy and lifeless.

What is this place?

The ground. Red. Dusty. Dry. Hot. The light beat down from a disk too bright to see. It hurt. I winced again. It wasn't enough. Then wind. Slight at first. A cooling breeze pushed up against my face. Then, the sound of something in the distance, racing up toward me. The galloping sound of hooves pounding the ground. With the sound, the laughter of a child echoed through the valley, as the hooves pounded closer. Suddenly, the sound stopped. I looked up with a squint. It was a horse, but no, it couldn't be. I focussed my eyes on the beast which was supported by one leg at the front; one leg at back.

"Mummy! Get up, Mummy. Poppet wants to play."

I tried to speak.

"Mummy. C'mon," the little girl with bright red flowing hair said, looking cheerful sitting on her strange beast thing. I tried again.

"Ada . . . Adakol."

It didn't make any sense.

"I know, Mummy. You gave me my Adakol. C'mon. Poppet wants to play!"

My arms . . . tunas hurt trying to move them.

Then, an eagle cried in the distance. The sound of it drilled through the sky. Instantly, the girl who called me Mummy galloped away. She giggled, riding off to the sound of belting twin hooves.

This place. Where am I?

The land, deep red in contrast to the dark blue at the far horizon. I managed to move. I got up on an… elbow. A fish spine. The fish spine bent. It hurt all over again with sharp spears of electricity that went straight through my left eye socket. The eagle cried and hovered and soared high above towering red craggy peaks—the shape of upturned cones. Then there were seven. Seven eagles, one of which all white.

Where did I see those eagles before?

Then, the first white-hot shot of pain drilled deep into my forearm. White-hot an unbearable. The pain drilled. The tuna's head. Or was it tail? I lay back down, wincing away from that bright yellow glow beating down. The music started to play in my head. The whooshing. The beating. A helicopter's blades in slow motion, whooshing high above me. I'd heard that sound before.

The Movie. Apocalypse Now . . .

Whooshing in slow motion like a ghost helicopter flying over. The sound of a Fender electric guitar sprang to life. A sound, all to of its own—unmistakable. Someone was looking down at me. A face, all I could see. I saw the outline of an old man with deep facial wrinkles. Black and white feathers dangled from the end of interwoven braids. Another white-hot spear of pain drilled into my tuna. The tuna alive, looked up and started to sing.

. . . this is the end . . . Beautiful friend . . .

* * *

I awoke with a serious feeling of vertigo, and with a big, puffy, white pad wrapped on my forearm. Nausea. Oh no. I placed a hand up over my mouth, fighting and uncontrollable sickness. My eyes were foggy and everything swam. As I gained focus, a nurse stood beside me swabbing my sickness away. Then, wordless, she stepped away and was gone.

A few hours into the day, with a small packet of Panadol Fort and repeat prescriptions of antibiotic, I finally met up with Nathan and Bosco, who were both wearing the same big white pads over their forearms. They also appeared groggy and suffered the same symptoms. I wondered oddly if I looked as bad as they did. The dark circles around their eyes. I stood there with Nathan and Bosco, bandages over our forearms, pondering what might be lurking beneath.

"No time to waste. Are we all good to go?" Nathan asked.

Bosco gave thumbs up. I went to acknowledge Nathan, but the nausea was intense and relentless. I was horrified and struggled for composure. Then I projectile vomited.

It was the 'oh no' look Nathan's gave me that sent me into a panic. I needed to sit down and get things under control. Taking a seat, I held my hands up to my mouth in the hope of keeping things down.

"I feel terrible. I'm sick all the time."

Nathan grabbed a napkin from a hospital chest of drawers behind him and offered it. "Angel, I think you need this."

"Oh shit! You know, I rue the day you talked me into all this. What a mess I'm in right now."

I did my best cleaning myself up. A few moments later, Doc Holiday arrived in the ward. The doctor leaned forward looking down at me. He checked my pupil dilation and I wasn't sure why he did that. Then, he slightly lifted the bandage on my forearm and quickly glanced under. Grinning wide, Doc Holiday took a step back in time to avoid another sudden violent wave of nausea.

"Doc," Nathan said, "What's this all about?"

"It'll pass. It's a reaction to the anaesthesia. Nothing major."

If things weren't bad enough, a hypodermic needle into my shoulder was just what the doctor ordered.

"How long, Doc?" Nathan asked him. "How long will this go on for?"

I wanted to say something but I couldn't. I did the universal sign language for pen and paper. Nurse somebody understood and quickly got me something to write on. I took it and started scrawling. After I finished writing down what needed to be said, I held it up. "I want this fucking eyeball off me!"

Nathan ignored my message and cut me off. "Doc, how long?"

"Could be a couple of hours. A day at the most. It'll pass. I don't think there's cause for alarm. But it'd be different if she was pregnant."

I fainted.

* * *

I woke up again and found myself back in the ward, just as Nurse Somebody was speaking with Nathan. "I'm guessing by the nature of this operation you guys are in urgent need of being elsewhere?"

Nathan nodded his reply to Nurse Somebody. "Time is luxury and something we don't have."

"Take the pads off in the morning, not before. We don't want any bumps. And . . . you'll need to prepare before you see what you have on your arms. It's a medical miracle, if you want my opinion." Then she turned and disappeared from the ward.

* * *

"Nathan Masters, you might want to come and take a look."

We were in the C-130 Hercules transport out from RAAF Base Edinburgh, heading for Darwin when Nathan was given the message. He disappeared for several moments before returning to his seat, opposite Bosco and me. I knew something was wrong. I could see it in his complexion that had drained of colour. Bosco must've felt it as well. He immediately spun his baseball hat backward. Then, Bosco began jiggling his left leg up and down.

Nathan looked down at the floor and rubbed his hands together. Something had him rattled. If Nathan got rattled, it was serious. Now I wondered what in the heck was wrong.

Just as I was about to ask, Nathan spoke without any prompting. "The US Ambassador to Japan is dead. He and his family were executed this morning."

". . . Fuck!" Bosco shouted. He took his hat off and threw it to the floor. I felt glued to my seat, knowing what it all meant.

"And so, it begins." Nathan got up again and walked away before turning back. "Project Amber. We need to get there. We need to destroy this goes critical mass."

"Can we please check in with Shilo?" I shouted. By now, the pain in my arm was throbbing with every beat of my heart.

Nathan nodded and stepped toward the front of the aircraft, returning with Xe's tactical laptop. He sat down in between Bosco and me and flipped the lid open. After a few seconds, Christina answered the call. "Guten tag."

"Jenny," was my first word. Christina nodded and disappeared from the screen. Maggie appeared momentarily after. "I don't know if destroying Project Amber is going to make any difference with what's just happened."

"It's still worthwhile," Nathan replied. "In my opinion, we should proceed as planned."

"After you get back here, we'll discuss it. And Angel, I know what you're about to ask. I'm sorry, Jenny's gone."

"GONE. How? Why?"

"We don't know. She left a note. That's all I can say."

I was left reeling as Maggie expertly changed the subject and continued. "We need to regroup and discuss our options. The game has changed. This plays out differently with the Americans' imminent retaliation. How it plays out *now,* is the question. If we had our backs up against it before, consider yourself on borrowed time from this moment on." Maggie's expression hardened further before she disconnected from the server.

Nathan closed the lid and carried the laptop back to his bergen. He went over to the door and looked out of the window. I knew what he was doing. I knew he was contemplating. Then he turned slowly and made his way back. "How bad do you guys want Project Amber?" Nathan asked. "It seems the only way we're going to get a chance at destroying it is if we go outside Shilo's request."

"You're thinking of a HALO?" Bosco began to rub his hands together.

Nathan nodded with a wink. "I've already checked. There's enough gear down the back."

"HALO?" I asked. "What's HALO?"

"High altitude, low open," Bosco answered. "You've never jumped before, have ya?"

Nathan butted in. "Yeah but there won't be a low open this time, Bosco. Angel and I will jump tandem."

I was all of a sudden on the edge of freaking out. "Not happening!"

"Nothing to worry about," Nathan assured me.

"I say we do it." Bosco agreed. "I haven't had a good HALO in years."

"Roger that." Nathan got up and walked to the front.

As he came back to his chair, the aircraft yawed slightly left and straightened out again. "We'll be over Alice Springs in about thirty minutes. We should prepare and be ready for my go."

"Why can't we just land in Alice Springs?" I asked. "Its much easier if you want my opinion."

"Because, Angel, we're gonna drop right into Pine Gap. The lights are on but no-one's home."

CHAPTER TWENTY-FOUR

Jump

I FELT NATHAN PRESSED up behind me. I felt his lungs fill, then compress. I felt his heartbeat pumping in a steady rhythm. In the tandem harness, facing forward, I could only see his gloved hands pass my peripheral vision. Vulnerability washed over me as Nathan gave thumbs up to the Jump Master.

The rear door of the Hercules was locked down in the open position. Nothing beyond that, just the bitter cold I felt trying to invade my HALO jumpsuit. I had all the right gear for the job. My hastily modified jumpsuit, altered to allow for the new addition on my arm, consisting of a big plastic bag to cover the grotesqueness I hadn't yet seen. The breathing apparatus, the helmet and goggles. I felt Nathan behind me. His heartbeat pick up as he waddled, fully laden, closer to the ledge. I felt him hard up against me. Nathan had the life-saving parachute. Bergens attached to a line. SA-80s attached the bergens. Beyond that, luck. Nothing else. Just rabbit's feet, four-leaf clovers and rusty old horseshoes that were nailed to a fence.

Bosco stepped forward and faced the outside, then stepped further to the wide-open aperture. His form became silhouetted against the light. Nathan followed awkwardly with his attached human cargo at his front. He reached out and placed his hand on Bosco's shoulder. Bosco looked back and gave thumbs up again. Nathan's gloved hand passed my vision. Another thumbs up and maybe for the last time. Bosco waited for the Jump Master's hand signals. He stood motionless, poised and ready to go on command.

The Jump Master signalled 'jump ready.'

Bosco moved a little closer to the edge of the opening and looked down. I couldn't see, but I imagined the view from where Bosco was standing. There'd be no clouds. There'd be nothing but the wind and the cold. And the hard ground far below that would rush up and instantly kill. My heart rate picked up. Nathan's increased—I could feel him. I'd placed my life into his hands.

The Jump Master held up a hand. Fingers out. Four, then three, then two. Then the signal, and Bosco was gone, just like that. No second thought. No hesitation. Just gone, out into the never-never. Nathan pushed forward. I lifted my feet off the floor. Nathan now had my full weight in his harness. He waddled to the edge. I peered down then closed my eyes. The Jump Master must've signalled him off, and Nathan must've stepped out into mid-air. The tumble. My eyes still shut tight; I held my breath. I clenched my teeth. I was on my way to the ground. If I could scream, I would have. I was now head down as Nathan tilted forward and became a bullet, head first to catch up with Bosco.

At last, I dug up the courage to open my eyes. Bosco did something with his arms to slow himself down. He stretched them out like a bat. When Nathan caught up to Bosco, he did the same thing. The mad rushing wind pushed past my ears to the point of real pain shooting somewhere inside my head—we slowed down into a controlled free-fall.

It was mere moments of gliding and soaring. It seemed like forever. I was surprised with my loving it. I felt like an eagle. It was Charlotte's view on the world and it was awe-inspiring, breath-taking, wonderful.

Bosco repositioned himself and came in closer. I could almost reach out and grab him. He gave thumbs up again. This time, I answered him with my own gloved hand. He moved away far enough to perform a few manoeuvres in mid-air, just to show off. Bosco was doing the 'woo-hoos,' I just knew it. What a blast. If it were possible for Nathan to join in, perhaps he might have. But Nathan was a mid-air pack mule. He had no business with the manoeuvres Bosco was doing.

Nathan positioned his tight arm to view his altimeter. The ground was rushing up fast. He swooped in toward Bosco and signalled to deploy chutes. They pulled on their ripcords almost in complete synchronicity. The parachutes blew out and opened, fluttered and arranged without effort. Then, a sharp jolt and an immense tug and we began to float.

Bosco pointed down below to a squarish patch of land the size of a postage stamp. If it was Pine Gap, I could only just make out the all-white radomes. In the next second, the circling and spiralling began. I wasn't sure why both Nathan and Bosco leaned into their cords, steering their chutes into a controlled spiral. We drifted down, spiralling, circling as we went. Then, it was perfectly clear why.

The first few projectiles zipped and cracked past, missing us by only centimetres. "They're shooting at us!" I screamed into my facemask, and I was horrified to realised that no one could hear me scream.

I felt Nathan's chest compress. He put a hand on my shoulder, pulling me in. More bullets cracked past. It was no longer fun. I felt panic and bile rise to my throat.

More shots cracked past. This time there were tracer rounds. I screamed again but this time with no words. My heart was in my throat and I could taste my own blood.

Down, we drifted and the spiralling intensified. I glanced at Bosco as a burst of shots cracked past us again. Bosco's helmet flicked back. A cloud of red vapour ejected into the atmosphere and Bosco's spiralling ceased.

Nathan immediately screamed from behind his mask; I felt his lungs compress and another scream to Bosco. Nathan pulled on the control cords and changed direction, following Bosco as he drifted out of control. All the while, I felt Nathan's lungs inflate and compress. Inflate and compress again.

We drifted down and away, somewhere to the east. Somewhere over the MacDonnell Ranges, where the tops of trees and sharp rocks rose up and craggy creek beds that were the colour of deep red earth. The ground was rushing up fast, getting close, almost close enough to my touch toes.

Bosco hit the ground first, narrowly missing a clump of ghost gums and the jagged edges of sandstone rocks. As he hit the ground, his legs collapsed from under him. I watched as the wind on the ground his dragged his lifeless body along for a short distance. Finally, Bosco came to rest wedged between two large sandstone boulders.

"Legs up, Angel." Nathan yelled, then he pulled the control lines of his rig hard down. After we were steady on the ground, Nathan ripped off his helmet and tossed it away..

"BOSCO!" Nathan screamed out. "NO. BOSCO NO!"

Nathan desperately and frantically wrenched the parachute cords and harness away from his body. "GOD! NO! BOSCO!"

Nathan wept openly as he cradled Bosco in his arms. It broke my heart to see it. I got down beside them and comforted Nathan as best as I could.

* * *

It was well into the evening before Nathan could finally let go of Bosco's body. I'd already tried several times to coax him away. But it was dangerous out in the open in the desert during the blackness of night; and we needed get back to home base. The question was how?

"Nathan, listen to me. No one knows we're here. How do we get out of this place? We have to think. I know it's hard. We have to think about getting out."

Nathan pointed to his bergen. "There's an emergency GPS beacon in the side pocket. Activate it, and we're out of here."

CHAPTER TWENTY-FIVE

War . . . War never changes.

—Ulysses S. Grant, 18th US President, 1869-77

THE DOOR OPENED, AND CHRISTINA stared back through her watery eyes. She stepped aside slowly. Nathan walked through. I followed, expecting to see Maggie somewhere—if only to start with the dressing down. But Maggie was nowhere in sight, not even in earshot. Christina had explained the circumstances of Maggie becoming ill. It happened so quickly, Christina explained in her best English, then Christina explained that Maggie's demeanour had totally changed. The light had gone out in her eyes, and it was as though Maggie had lost her will to endure.

We stepped past Christina. I wasn't prepared to see Maggie so different. It seemed only hours ago Maggie was the same hard, steadfast individual I'd always known. This Maggie was reduced to something I'd not at all expected. As Nathan and I approached Maggie in the ops room, she was seated at the head of the meeting table, staring vacantly, clutching at a bunch of old photographs. She looked up at me and smiled as I sat down next to her. The photos she was holding in her hands, I noticed, were photographs of a much younger Maggie with her husband, Theo. Maggie's smile then fell away after her eyes met Nathan. At first, it was as if Maggie wanted to say something. Her mouth opened slightly, and then closed.

"Maggie?" Nathan said as he approached her

Maggie then came back from where she'd gone. "What—may I ask—were you thinking, Nathan? Everything we've worked for. Did I *not* instruct you to return here? Look where we are now. We had a solid plan. We had options. We had a chance. Not anymore, Nathan. None. Thanks to what you've done."

"Maggie . . . I'm sorry. Our intelligence suggested Pine Gap was empty. You know that. I had the opportunity on Project Amber, and I took it."

"You're sorry." Maggie's top lip curled slightly. "Is that it, Nathan? You're sorry?"

Maggie then coughed into her hand. She reached and grabbed some medication from the top drawer of the credenza to her rear. Before taking a tablet from the blister pack, she held it up. "Heart medication. I'm only alive because of these damn tablets. I've considered not taking them at all. Why bother?" She sighed then swallowed a handful of tablets, chasing them down with a long drink of water. "It's pointless now, Nathan." Maggie coughed again then pointed to the LCD on the wall. Christina stepped over and switched it on. Maggie sunk in her chair and became quiet as Christina replayed the live and breaking CNN broadcast from the streets of Tokyo.

I watched on as the video showed The Democratic People's Republic of Korea push the entire globe to the point of no return. Random shelling had begun on the city. I then understood this was less about war and more about mass murder on the citizens of Japan. People ran panic stricken in the streets. The camera moved down on a group of civilians who were hunkered down behind concrete road barriers. A flash, and an almighty explosion. They were instantly erased as though they were never there at all.

The shelling was relentless, causing collateral damage on a scale not seen since World War II.

From his high-rise apartment window, a CNN broadcaster's voice broke with sadness and dismay through the audio while attempting to cover the shelling from his view over the city. Below him was anarchy, bloodshed, rioting, and looting. Another flash, then a massive thud. Glass and debris were sent flying into the air, mixed with body parts, and only God knew what else.

"That was an hour ago, Nathan. These were the first shots fired in anger by the North Koreans," Maggie said. "Unfortunately, there has been no other forthcoming news broadcast from Tokyo. We don't know what's happening over there as of this moment. It seems all communications, in or out, have been cut off"

"And the *Steinbeck*?"

"*Steinbeck* is in the Sea of Japan, with *Minnesota* and *Dallas*. They were on the way to the South China Sea but diverted. China started amassing her forces, threatening the island of Taiwan. Now that the US Ambassador to Japan has been executed, things have escalated out of control."

"China is in on this?"

"Thick into it," Maggie replied. "Who would've thought? Diplomacy goes out the door backward, now everything's dark. But bet your arse, China is in cahoots with the bloody North Koreans. Our secured communication network back to Langley and the United States has been severed. I imagine the US President and his Joint Chiefs are already in the air, formulating joint war strategy from Airforce One and the E-4B. Had we managed to destroy the Project Amber in time, this mightn't have started. But now, there's no way back. It's a matter of time before North Korea ramps things up with their bloody Peacemaker. And Milestone? Nathan, our worst nightmare is unfolding before our very eyes."

"It's not over." I immediatley produced the microwave emitter from my thigh pocket. "I bet this is what'll get us to Project Amber. And I know where to start looking."

"It's no good, Angel," Maggie chuckled lightly. "That thing you've got. *And* your Plan B, I might add, won't change anything now. Pine Gap isn't deserted, as our intelligence had us believe. Getting into Pine Gap would require nothing short of a full-frontal invasion. Even then, the Guardianship would be well dug in. And even if we *did* succeed, it'd make no difference now."

I described to Maggie what I'd seen from the window at the airport terminal. The door that led to somewhere. The door that required a certain security to pass through. I turned to Nathan. "The message sent to my phone. You said it came from Alice Springs Airport and the IP was via Airport Wi-Fi. My gut tells me it came from behind that door. I bet my life on it. We need to investigate, and I think this microwave emitter is our ticket to wherever that door leads."

My words got Nathan's attention. He placed a hand to his beard and rubbed it vigorously, at the same time I noticed Maggie's sparkle. She sat up straight in her chair. Her body language changed. It was as though new purpose brought Maggie back to the here and now.

"What do you think, Maggie?" Nathan put in. "One last shot at this? No one's nuking yet. Maybe we stand a chance after all."

"Better get your arses into gear then," Maggie said, then turned to Christina. "Get us a government charter, Christina. Top priority, if you please."

Christina nodded and stepped out of the room.

* * *

Before getting ready for the trip south, I slowly opened the door to the bunk-room where I'd spent my last night with Jenny. I stood at the door momentarily before stepping through. The night lamp was left on. The bed had been neatly made. On the pillow where Jenny rested her head was my rock crystal figurine I'd given the name Charlotte. A note lay underneath it. And also, Bosco's red bandana. I couldn't help but wonder if Bosco would still be alive if he'd had it on him. His lucky charm.

I moved forward and placed a hand on Jenny's pillow. My chest felt tight, and my heart started to break. I sat on the edge of the bunk, knowing the note was still there, unopened. I didn't want to read it. I wanted a moment, and knowing what was in front of me, I decided a moment to remember Jenny wasn't too much to ask.

I picked up my figurine which Jenny surprised me with on my birthday and held it in my hands. I felt the weight, and smoothness which was cold to the touch. The note from Jenny had been infused with perfume, the kind Jenny knew I loved. Finally, I picked up the envelope and opened it. The paper inside was a matching pink. Jenny loved pink. I opened the letter.

Always remember who I am.

* * *

The government-staffed RAAF Challenger 604 left Darwin the day the United States airstrikes began on strategic targets around the city of Pyongyang. Nathan and I watched on from an overhead LCD as CNN covered the United States' answer to the shelling of

Tokyo—the destruction of five Democratic People's Republic of Korea Warships which were in the Sea of Japan. During the flight out of Darwin, bound for Alice Springs, a secured feed via ASIO HQ showed live video that was earmarked *'not for general release.'* Live from the hard decks of the *Steinbeck*, among the flurry of activity, several F-117 Nighthawk stealth fighters shot across and up, with afterburners blasting them aloft. The United States flexing its muscles from the decks of the *Steinbeck* was a sobering sight. No sooner did the F-117s disappear into the distance, they were followed up with the deafening turbofan engine scream of F-16 Fighting Falcons and F-14 Tomcats, all of which dispersed into the distance under the parade of afterburners, armed to the max, ready to rain hell.

I pointed to the overhead display from my seat. Something got my attention. Several fighters stood parked at the rear of the *Steinbeck*'s flight deck. They were poised, but it wasn't clear which way they were facing. Of all things, they looked similar from the rear as they appeared from the front.

"Nathan, what are those things?"

After holding his breath a little, Nathan began to explain. "Remember you asked me about what else I knew about the *Steinbeck*?"

"Yeah, you knew about something, and you weren't going tell me."

"No. I couldn't at the time. But you're about to see," Nathan pointed. "These are the craft the Americans were testing at Roswell all those years ago. Now you know everything, Angel."

"You must be joking. Spaceships?"

"No. Not exactly. But Oudarretian technology nonetheless."

"Now I know why there was such an uproar when the *Steinbeck* was in Melbourne. Now I know why the Americans shunned nuke patrol. I can imagine the backlash if any of this stuff was leaked. So, I'm assuming these crafts are nuclear powered?"

"Not nuclear powered. Force Generational Antimatter-Electromagnetism. F-GAE." Then it was as though the nerd in Nathan *really* started to shine. "The LHC in Geneva. Heard of it?"

"The Large Hadron Collider? Sure. I think everyone knows about that."

"Without the LHC, there'd be no fuel for the F-GAEs. Why do you think there was so much money thrown at it? F-GAE technology warps space and time into an envelope. The crafts travel within the envelope through gravity. Mind-blazingly fast. They can stop and change direction instantly. There's no G-force inside them because they generate their own force of gravity, free from any other external force."

I paused, then said, "My head hurts thinking about all this."

"Don't think about it. We have other things to worry about. And only a handful of hours to get it done. I hope your gut feelings are right. This is our final push. If it doesn't work out, I hate to think . . ."

Five F-GAEs were standing line abreast at the rear of the *Steinbeck's* flight deck. Aerodynamically shaped, matt black, the same colour as the F-117 Nighthawks. One by one, they came to life, glowing blue. The same glow as the point of condensed universe Xe created. Nathan pointed to the overhead screen. "Look. The show's about to begin." He grinned at the sight of human/advanced human hybrid technology. The F-GAEs lifted off the flight deck vertically, and then suddenly shot away as if they'd never been there.

Whoever was behind the camera on deck followed the F-GAEs out to the horizon, where all five craft instantly burst into flames and exploded into fireballs.

"That wasn't supposed to happen!"

"I reckon!" Nathan said.

The video shook wildly, and voices of horror were heard in the background. The camera shifted up high. Another F-GAE, huge, much larger than the first five, hovered above the *Steinbeck.*

I was about to ask. The video suddenly went blank.

"NATHAN!"

"I know!"

"Did we just lose the connection?"

"Beats me. I hope it's as simple as that." Nathan got out of his seat and bobbed down slightly while pacing to the front of the aircraft. He was away for several moments. All the while the LCD above showed nothing but grain. Returning to his seat with a couple of bottles of water, he sat slowly down, devoid of emotion.

"Brace yourself," Nathan said, clasping his seat-belt. "Airborne early warning control reports the *Steinbeck* is lost."

"How?"

"We don't know yet. AWAC hailed all frequencies while I was up front. There's no response. Over five and a half thousand souls on board. They're also reporting *Air Force One* has turned back to Washington. The E-4B stays airborne and is now in the control of the Joint Chiefs. They're gonna lock down the Whitehouse. They're going to ground."

"What does that mean?"

"DEFCON One, Angel. 'Cocked pistol.' As soon as the President is safely below Andrews Air Force Base, he will authorise EMERGCON. We won't hear from him again. No one will. He'll emerge during peace; whatever that means. We're in unchartered waters from here."

"Jeeeesus Christ!" I was truly shocked. "Is this really happening?"

"I'm afraid so."

"Can we patch in with Shilo? Maybe she's is up to date."

"I'm already on it. The ASIO guys up front will let us know if they can get a patch. The problem is with the internet. It's dark. Maybe it's temporary. Maybe there's too much traffic. We just don't know. I hope America hasn't been hit. If it has, it's more likely dark because of EMP."

"Electromagnetic pulse attack?"

"Yeah. It knocks out everything electronic. Computers, devices, you name it. Everything that uses a computer chip is dead. Even the computer management in car engines. You can imagine the result of . . ."

"Oh no, Nathan. All those people, driving on the highways. Their cars just stop?"

"Yeah. A catastrophe just in itself."

"Who would do this? How?"

"It only takes one high altitude nuke. The resulting EMP does the damage."

A man in a black suit appeared from the front of the aircraft. He leaned forward and whispered something into Nathan's ear. Nathan nodded, and the man stepped away in a hurry.

"They've managed to get Charlotte Station on the 5G network. They'll bring a handset down in a moment. It appears Australia isn't safe from EMP either. As a precaution, our national airspace is on lockdown, and our nation's airports are being evacuated as we speak. After we land at Alice Springs, there'll be no flights in or out until further notice. Until the EMP threat is over."

I suddenly realised. "Nathan. Aircraft in the sky?"

"I'd hate to think what America is going through at this moment."

"And *Air Force One*?"

"The US President's aircraft is shielded from EMP. Exactly for that reason. Civilian and commercial aircraft, on the other hand, is another story."

I paused for a second. "This aircraft?"

"I'd say so. Or we'd have been told to land by now."

As I had that horrible thought in my mind, the ASIO guy from up front brought the handset down the aisle, I guessed, with Maggie already on the other end. Nathan took the handset from him without any acknowledgment. The ASIO guy stepped away with a nod. Nathan then switched the handset to hands-free.

"Angel? Nathan?"

"We're here, Maggie."

"Oh, thank god. News from Canberra. The Prime Minister and his Chiefs of Staff have locked down Parliament House. They're in the War Room discussing strategy at this time. We have our entire available navy on its way to the conflict zone in the Sea of Japan."

"It'll be over before they get there."

"Sadly, I agree." Maggie sighed heavily. "But there is also a coalition of special forces on the ground in South Korea. The South Korean Army is preparing for an invasion to the north. They're going after the Peacemaker, Nathan. If anything, the ground invasion may get us a bit of time."

"Time—yes. Maybe. But they're . . ."

"Remember your objective. Just get to Project Amber and destroy it. I want us all to get through this madness. Do you hear me?"

CHAPTER TWENTY-SIX

Project Amber

REMEMBER, AS LONG AS IT'S DARK, we have the advantage. Let's keep things dark, Nathan told me, at the exact time he pushed his NVG over his forehead. I did the same. I got the device from my bergen and positioned it so I could flip the NVG down as soon as the lights went out. We stood at the door and prepared to move. I got the microwave emitter out and was about to place it up to the security device. "Wait," Nathan said. "Weapons check."

"I already did it."

"Do it again just to be sure."

I rechecked and re-cocked my suppressed nine-millimetre Beretta. I eyed Nathan with intense resolve, "Good to go." I held up the emitter again. Nathan put a hand on my sleeve. I stopped.

"Our first priority is to shoot out any light switches. If there are cameras in there, they'll go dark."

I nodded and held the emitter up again. This time there was an audible click. The door opened, and we stepped through. I crouched down and shot out four ceiling lights one after the other. The place went black. My NVG lit up the stairwell again, under a green monochrome glow.

Down the flight of stairs we tabbed. Our footfalls echoed around concrete walls. Another flight of stairs down to another door. Still dark. Now, it was starting to get cold. The scent of cold concrete hung in the air. The scent reminded me of was exiting Coles through the back entrance. I held up the emitter. Another click and the door unlocked. I pulled the lever. Nathan reached out and placed a hand on my sleeve. "Slow," he whispered. "Slow and quiet." I opened the door very slightly and peered through. Then closed it again.

"What is it?" Nathan whispered.

"Fluorescent lights. Lots of them."

"Can you see a switch?"

I peered through again. I nodded.

"Lift your NVG and take out the light switch," he whispered.

I opened the door enough for the Beretta to poke through. I squeezed off a volley of shots, and the place went dark. Under NVG again, we walked through. A small corridor ran away. Another corridor shot off to the left and one to the right. More fluorescent lights went dead after we destroyed more switches.

"This place is already a rabbit hole, Nathan. Which way will we go?"

"Go straight on. We'll come back here if we get to a dead end."

The corridor led to another door marked N412. Another security device was attached to the side. I brought up the emitter. Immediately, electronic servos disengaged the locks with a series of loud clunks.

"Look, but don't go through. Tell me what you see."

"Why don't *you* bloody do it this time?"

Nathan said nothing. He gave me a small push from behind.

I opened the door slightly and peered through a tiny slit. I closed the door again. "More lights. Another corridor. I think an elevator at the end."

“Shit. We don’t do elevators yet. We won’t know what we’re dropping in on. We’ll go back and try the other corridors.”

I double tapped Nathan’s arm and retreated under NVG green.

We took a right turn and arrived at a door marked N526.

“Go ahead, your turn this time,” I said, passing Nathan the emitter.

Nathan held it up to the security lock. Nothing happened. “Shit! Not to worry. We’ll try the other way.”

We about-faced and headed down the corridor past the entry door we’d trundled through, and into another corridor, arriving at a steel door marked N577.

“Retina scanner, this one,” Nathan said reaching up touching the security device with two gloved fingers. “You need to place your eye implant up and press the sensor button at the same time.”

I sighed, unfolding the flap of artificial skin on my arm. Someone else’s dead eye looked up at me. I was about to hold it up to the locking device.

“Wait just a second.” Nathan got something out of his breast pocket that looked like a suction cup attached to a wire. He placed the suction cup to the door and then placed an earplug into his ear. He listened for a few seconds before taking the device, winding it back up and putting it back in his pocket. “Ready for this?”

“Yeah. I hope it works.”

I held up the implant to the sensor and pressed the button. A red laser started to scan across the surface of the eye and then, electronic servos gave way within the door’s internal locking mechanism.

“Open it. Take a peek,” Nathan whispered.

I double tapped him and peeked through. I closed the door again.

“Large open area. Incandescent lighting. A large amount of electronic equipment.”

"Good. Don't destroy the light switch. Look for cameras and take them out first. We need to know what the equipment is used for. Take another peek and see if there are cameras around. Look at the ceilings for black domes or other obvious signs."

I peeked through. I scanned the area. I closed the door again.

"I can't see any cameras."

"Are you're sure?"

I peeked through again, then closed the door.

"No cameras."

"I don't like it," Nathan whispered. "There'd be some kind of security at least."

Nathan paused for a while then said, "Looks like we take the elevator after all."

"Too risky. What if we land well and truly in the shit? I think there must be an electronic control actuator for the other wing somewhere in there. It makes sense, don't you think?"

Nathan paused a beat then slowly nodded. "Okay. Make it quick. Look for security measures first."

I opened the door slightly again and peered through. A little further for a better view. A bit more, and it was open enough for a body roll to the desk in the centre of the room. We hunkered down behind the desk. I flipped up my NVG and looked around at the four corners of the ceiling, then back to above the door. "Nothing in here," I whispered. "No cameras."

"That's too ridiculous for words," Nathan replied.

We both stood up and stepped back to the door with our backs hard up to it. I looked around. There was an array of steel filing cabinets to the left. A steel locker stood next to the filing cabinets. A small desk was next to the locker with a computer terminal, switched off. Another computer to the right, also switched off. A desk in the centre with a laptop and other stationery items scattered around on the desktop. A large LCD monitor was mounted on the wall opposite and shut down. A rack roughly two metres high, full of electronics, all switched off and shut down.

"Looks like this place has been abandoned," I whispered.

"Okay. I think it's clear. Have a look around and see what you can find."

Then, the sound of an electric motor from down the end of the main corridor.

"What's that noise?" I whispered.

"It's the elevator. Someone's coming up."

"Shit!"

"Behind the door, quick."

We both snuck back behind the door and waited. The elevator arrived, and voices were heard.

"Hey . . . what happened to the lights?" someone said.

"Dunno. The light switch is broken. It looks like someone went to it with a hammer."

"Power surge?"

"Yeah. Maybe."

"I hate this place off the grid. Everything blows up, breaks down or goes to shit one way or another."

"I know . . ."

Voices and footfalls were coming closer. My heart leaped into my throat.

"Angel," Nathan whispered so lightly I struggled to hear, even though I was right next to him. "Stealth kill only. No weapons. Got it? We don't want any blood. Not yet."

I double tapped his arm, while trying to remember the silent, unarmed method I'd learned back at Swan Island.

The door swung open. Two men stepped through. Nathan lunged at the first guy, taking him to the floor. I struggled with the second guy who managed to spin around as I attempted to squeeze him up. He pushed me away, the same moment I heard a loud crack coming from the first guy's neck. The second guy swung a punch, connecting, sending me backward. Nathan was up behind him with the pit of his elbow pushed hard up to his throat. Nathan grunted, lifting the guy's chin to the ceiling.

CRACK!

His lifeless body, like a bag of fish, slumped to the floor.

"You good?" Nathan asked.

"Yeah. Sorry about that."

He shook his head. "No need. Let's get into their uniforms."

"That's not a good idea. We won't have our gear."

"Yeah, I know. The element of surprise, Angel. If we need to use the elevator, it might buy us a bit of time. Every second in our favour is crucial."

We dressed in the American desert fatigues and a baseball style cap. I rolled up the sleeves and adjusted the length of my trousers. "I'm a freaking beacon in this."

Nathan smiled. "It'll do. Don't forget your knife and sidearm," he said while putting a couple of flash-bangs in his pocket. "Before we go, let's have a look at the computers. Maybe there's something we can use."

"What about our Semtex?"

"Leave it. We'll improvise, depending on what we find."

Nathan lifted the lid of the laptop and appeared surprised when the screen came to life without any security login. He smiled and rubbed his hands together. I turned and went for the filing cabinets. I rifled through them, unsure of what I was looking for.

I opened and closed drawers, moving quickly to the next. And the next.

"I have something," Nathan said. "Finally." He lifted the laptop off the desk and brought it over to the filing cabinets.

"Look at this." He pointed to the screen.

I saw what he was seeing. An accessed Excel document revealed a list of archive numbers he ascertained to be relevant, corresponding to the filing cabinets in the room.

"A list of reference numbers. This one popped out at me," he said, smiling as he rubbed his beard. 'N526 Amber Sanctuary.'

"What's N526?"

"The door that wouldn't open. But there's more. Look. 10324-269. It's a reference to a file. I reckon a hard copy. We're getting close. Are there numbers on the cabinets somewhere?"

I looked. "They have a Dymo label on the top drawers. One to ten."

"Good. It's in the cabinet number ten, third drawer, twenty-fourth file. Dunno what 269 is yet, but we'll know soon enough. I can feel it."

"How'd you cross-reference that?"

"Old school, Angel. Sometimes you need to think old school."

I moved straight to the cabinet, to the third drawer, and grabbed out the documents from the numbered file. I brought the bundle of documents across to the desk and sprawled it all out. In among the pages were progress reports, but some pages that didn't make any sense. The pages that didn't make any sense, Nathan pored over. And a handful of colour photos. I held up the photos one by one and studied them.

"Oh fuck, Nathan!"

"What did you find?"

"This photo. It's my uncle Scotty-Blue."

Nathan took the photo, then looked at it. He then appeared to turn into stone.

"Yeah," I said. "I thought you might do that."

"Blue is part of this?"

"Seems so. This is so hard to believe, Nathan."

"And guess what else? I've found Project Amber," Nathan said. "Here."

The Excel document Nathan opened led to another, which led to more references to the cabinets behind us. On inspection, we found more photos in full colour of people. Records of people, of varying ages, ranging from young to old, both male and female. Records of births. Records of deaths. Records of health and medical status. Records of physical strengths and weaknesses. Records of marriages. Records of mental capabilities and IQ assessments. The more we dug, the more we found. It was never-ending. It was almost as if these people were the product of some scientific experiment. And they were all here, living somewhere in this rabbit warren. But there was something else we found that couldn't be ignored. Everyone—every single one of them had white skin with a decent sprinkling of freckles, and, everyone had auburn hair. Hair the colour of red. The colour of . . . Amber?

After reading through the dozens of dossier pages, the horror of Project Amber suddenly dawned. We both stood agog for a few moments. Nathan finally broke the silence. "We have ourselves a job kicking this one in the arse."

I stood back almost in shock. "Nathan, how do we do this? We were looking for something tangible. We were looking for a device of some description. Something we could pick up and hold in our hands. Something we could take away from this place and destroy. Now, this? Every one of them? Who knows how many. Hundreds? Thousands? They all have it? Project Amber is—are *them?* They're all down here somewhere. Somewhere among these walls. They're all genetically modified to resist radiation. And melanoma. This is seriously insane. And then, one has to think—if this is one bunker, are there any more? Then, how many bunkers?"

"It's been going on for decades," Nathan responded. "They've found a cure for cancer and are using it for their own purposes. To prepare for Milestone. Now it all falls into place. The DNA, or gene-ark we've been looking for is not a device as such. They're all *living* DNA. Modified over time. And Scotty-Blue? Many years ago, Scotty-Blue told me that under no circumstances was I to acknowledge him. In his words, 'you don't know me, and I don't know you.'"

"Now, where are we?" I said. "To destroy Project Amber means . . ."

"To kill them all," Nathan finished my sentence.

I stood back shaking my head, thinking it over. "I've only killed once and that guy needed to be dealt with. But this? This is mass murder, Nathan. This is genocide."

"N526 will give us a clue. We need to access that wing and find out how to get this done. 269. It's a clue. Look around."

I went back to the photos again. Some were old—some weren't. But they all had that one thing in common. I cast a quick glance at the dead guys on the floor. "They *ALL* have red hair."

"Amber. Project Amber. Now it's making sense."

"Red-headed, fair-skinned people who're normally more susceptible to melanoma?"

"Ordinarily, that would be case. Not with these Ambers. Their immunity has been specifically engineered. This is part of the exit strategy and the new world order."

"It's seriously fubar. So, there'd be breeders no doubt, women who do the breeding? Somewhere behind the door marked N526?"

"Maybe. But maybe not. What I do know is this. They've engineered an entire new community. Maybe the Ambers pair off, then have babies as do ordinary people. They'd keep their genetic code in a controlled closed circle."

I picked up the photo of Scotty-Blue and studied it more closely. I put it back on the desk, then picked it up again. I flipped it over. On the back, written in blue ink were some numbers at the very lower right edge. 14/2/69.

I remembered Scotty-Blue being the same age as my father. Now I knew about the 269 part of the equation. I took the information to Nathan and showed him. "That's the 269 you were looking for. It's a birth date. Maybe the computer terminal over there can tell us more."

"I've booted it but . . . it's old—It's Windows XP and requires a passcode."

"I think I know what the passcode might be. Try typing 'Scotty-Blue.'"

Nathan stepped back to the terminal. At the flashing cursor on the screen, he typed the passcode.

Access denied.

"No good."

"Try again. All lower case. XP is case sensitive."

Nathan retyped the passcode with a few repeated taps of the backspace key, then hit enter. The computer terminal came to life showing a graphical menu.

"How'd you know how to do that?"

"Old school, Nathan. Sometimes you gotta think old school. Is there a button there that will let us into Amber Sanctuary N526?"

"There is. But there's also another that says CCTV feed." Before I had the chance to stop him, Nathan moved the cursor over to CCTV feed and clicked. The screen flickered then split into several camera views.

"Holy crap! We've got a view of everything from here."

We hovered over the terminal trying to make out what everything meant. I pointed to the thumbnail that said, *'MCOC.'*

"Any ideas what that might be for?"

"Let's take a wild stab. Milestone Control Operations Centre?"

"Jesus, Nathan. You don't think . . ."

Too late. Nathan immediately clicked on the thumbnail. A full screen appeared complete with real time audio feed. We both stood back and watched the mad flurry of activity, with people running back and forth from computers screens and workstations. They spoke loudly and shouted to each other in a language I thought could be Chinese.

"It's not Chinese." Nathan said as though reading my mind. "It's Korean. But check out what they're doing! Can you see what's on their terminal screen?"

I saw it. I didn't want to believe it. But as it began to register, I knew, now, there was no turning back. "Shit Nathan. That's the *Peacemaker*?"

"Yeah."

"How are we getting a real time feed if there's no internet?"

"Satellite. That's not important right now. Look."

The Atlas Five rocket stood tall as explosions and fire raged in the background around the city of Pyongyang. People screamed in panic, racing around aimlessly, trying to hide and shelter from the shelling and bombing from US lead air strikes.

"You're about to witness the destruction of the *Peacemaker*, Angel. It looks like we got there in time after all."

"Destruction my arse. Even I can see it's being cycled for launch."

"They're almost on top of it . . ."

Just as Nathan said it, the real time video feed from *MCOC* showed the rocket's service gantries and beams collapse. Then the engines ignited and burst into billows of white-hot flames. Slowly, *Peacemaker* lifted from the ground.

Nathan screamed his fury at the sight of the rocket lifting into the sky. He thumped fists hard down on the table. "They're supposed to blow the fucker up, not let it escape!"

For the first time in my life, I had become genuinely lost for anything to say. The consequences of what I'd seen took its time to hit home. Then finally, I realised it. I thought about this unfolding scenario as the line in the sand which early humans once dragged across the beach. The line that one tribe had dared an enemy to come across and make war. The North Koreans had just stepped over that line. Now, the notion of a world living in the tranquillity of peace and harmony had just been tossed into the nearest rubbish bin. Peace . . . Peace will now become the stuff of legend handed down to the few who might survive the devastation of this approaching apocalypse.

We both stood there glued in horror at the sight of the 1.1 gigaton thermonuclear hybrid ICBM lifting higher into the sky, heading downrange, on its way to the designated target, complete with the audible applause from those in *MCOC.*

A metallic click from behind made me instantly spin around. The man stood there in the doorway with a handgun pointed directly at me. "Nathan!" I called out, and he instantly rotated to see what I was seeing.

"Don't fucken move," the man said. "Get on ya fucken knees. Put ya hands up there on ya 'eads." He stood there momentarily. He took a step closer, then stopped. His hand began to shake slightly. I could see him waver as his angry facial expression immediately faded. "Angelique?"

His eyes went to Nathan. I saw him, scrutinising Nathan up and down.

"Canter? Fuck-me, Canter is that you? Well, Jesus H bloody Christ, mate. You took ya time getting here, eh?"

CHAPTER TWENTY-SEVEN

Death from Above

I INSTANTLY RECOGNISED HIS BLUE EYES, which were the colour of glacial ice. His face was the same as I remembered, although now, his facial lines were much deeper. His hair was no longer the rich shade of red. Scotty-Blue's once bright carrot top was now replaced with the grey-whiteness of age. Through his smile and through his eyes, I could tell he was still my Uncle Scotty. I couldn't have help it if I tried. I launched myself into his arms.

Scotty-Blue dropped his weapon with a 'clack' on the floor. I felt his arms squeeze me in. "Angelique. 'ow I've missed ya all these years, eh?"

After I was done, Scotty-Blue turned and vigorously took Nathan's hand and shook. "I still can't believe you're 'ere. Looks like what I did worked after all, eh?"

"You sent the message to my phone?"

"Ah, T'was I. Tadaah! Now, let's git our backsides out of 'ere, eh? Times a wasting."

"Wait, Blue. I think it's high time for an explanation. Wouldn't you agree?"

"Too bloody right, Canter. But now there's a shit storm you've never imagined comin' down on us. Now's not exactly the time to 'ang around gasbaggin'. Walk and talk, mate. Let's git to the tunnel. We gotta get there before they leave without us."

Nathan reached and grabbed Scotty-Blue, spinning him around. "No walk and talk! You owe me!"

"You wanna hear it? Okay here it is. You already know most of it so let's skip a few details. You already know that Project Amber is the preparation for a new world order after we all come back to this place. But this is what you don't know.

"We're Bunker N. And Bunker N Ambers are a resistance mob set up by the CIA. Partisans, if ya like. We call ourselves 'The Breakers.' We aim to fuck the Os over in another future. Stuff 'em up really bad, y'know? Remember them Chinooks you were looking for, Angelique? The ones from the *Steinbeck*?"

I nodded my response even though I was trying hard to close my ears. This was turning out to be much too hard for me to swallow for one day's work.

"Those Chinooks are all 'ere. They're waiting for us now. And as much as ya try to come to terms with it, the fact remains you're with us. It was always planned that way."

"The Americans are party to this? Everything that's here?"

"More than ya know, Angelique. When you broke that story on live telly, I thought more than twenty years of prep just got shit canned. It doesn't matter now. None of it matters any more. What matters now is you. It's time to realise your destiny."

"Destiny? What destiny?"

Scotty-Blue took a step closer toward me. "Bunjil. You're our Angel of Bunjil. You're the one who gets to lead the fight and take it back to the Os."

Before I had words, Nathan butted in. "No. This stops. We need to make it so."

Scotty-Blue laughed. “Stop it? ICBMs are rising up from American airspace right now. They’ve already answered the North Korean’s launch of the *Peacemaker*. Not only that, mate, the Russians cycled their ICBMs. A few moments from now, they’ll be risin’ up too. A shit storm. It’s all comin’ down.”

“What’s the designated target for *Peacemake*r? Do you know?”

“Well, it was supposed to be DC. The North Koreans had the heart of the yanks pegged right from the get-go. But there were some technical things that went wrong. Guidance system stuff-ups. Stuff they couldn’t control. So, them Nork arsholes went for the secondary.”

“Which is?”

“Frisco, mate. San Fran-bloody-cisco. They going for the soft target.”

Nathan put his head down and began to pace around in circles with a hand to his beard. “The President is in his bunker. Maybe he’ll ride out the storm.”

“You gotta be fucken kiddin’, mate. A 1.1-gigaton thermonuclear super-bomb is a worldwide catastrophe. No-one survives.”

“There has to be a way,” Nathan said. “There has to be a way to put an end to this madness!”

“Mate, there ain’t nothin’ short of the ‘and of God ‘imself that can change anythin’.”

“There must be a way to hack *Peacemaker’s* guidance control system!”

“Ya can’t stop it. Ya don’t seem to be ‘earing me. It’s like you got some kind mushroom growin’ in ya ears. Those up top are done and dusted. Why even think about it?”

“How much time have we got before *Peacemaker* goes critical mass?”

“A couple of hours at the most. Then . . . fucken boom, mate.”

“I have an idea, Blue. Satellite phone. Have you got one?”

“Yeah. There’s one in me drawer. Why?”

“We can use the satellite phone hooked up to the laptop and ping *Peacemaker’s* override systems. We can at least disarm the warhead.”

“You’ve got a slim chance at best, I reckon. Okay, if that’s what ya want, let’s get up top and get this shit done. Like the old days again, eh Canter?”

“Up top?” I said. “Have you two lost your minds?”

“We have to try, Angel It’s worth it, don’t you think?”

“ ‘ang on a sec, mate. Since we’ve decided, an’ there’s not a bloody thing I can do about it, there’s something else you need to know first. The Russians. I know of at least one of their ICBMs, targeted ‘ere. They’ve targeted Pine Gap. We need to move fast. Right bloody now.”

* * *

I wasn’t sure why I did it., but before heading up top, I reached into my bergen and retrieved my rock crystal figurine. I ran my eyes over it for a second before I thrust it down into my thigh pocket. The three of us bolted through doors, up flights of stairs, and finally reached the outside.

Nathan found a place out in the open and knelt down just outside the ghostly silent airport hangar. A strange orange glow hung in the air to the north, and the wind blew past, bringing with it the scent of something that smelt like a bushfire. The sound of the wind eerily sung as it pushed past the abandoned aircraft that sat silent and empty on the tarmac.

Nathan opened Scotty-Blue's laptop. I passed Nathan the satellite phone. "Nathan. I have a bad feeling about this. Please hurry."

Nathan didn't acknowledge and I went ignored as he grabbed the satellite phone and unfolded the large antenna. He held it up and waited for a connection . . .

"It's not happening!"

"Go out further, mate," Scotty-Blue said. "The buildin's are blockin' the signal."

I grabbed the laptop and followed Nathan as he moved away, holding the phone up for a signal as he strode. We came to rest on a small rise away from the main runway. "Here. We got reception. Blue! Get your arse over and give us a hand!"

Nathan connected the phone to the laptop and waited for the signal to transfer.

"Good stuff, mate" Scotty-Blue said. "Now we need to login. Get outta me way."

Scotty-Blue went at the keyboard and punched in strings of commands. The screen suddenly went blank. He clenched his fists and stood up. "Fuck-it!"

"What?"

"The laptop battery's dead!"

"You're kidding!"

"Nah, mate. Fucken serious! The bunker power supply is off the grid. Chargin' the laptop was one of the things we 'ad to do without, since we mainly used the terminals down there."

"Calm down and think, Blue. How do we get a charge on the laptop?"

Scotty-Blue pranced around like a spooked racehorse, then suddenly stopped as though an idea abruptly struck him.

"C'mon, Blue! Think!" Nathan yelled.

Without any warning, Scotty-Blue turned on his heel, and sprinted away.

"Where're ya going, Blue? BLUE!"

I watched as Scotty-Blue disappeared behind a parked aircraft. A few moments later, I heard a truck engine rev up and black smoke billowed from twin stacks. Scotty-Blue was behind the wheel of an airport support vehicle, and was driving it flat out, diesel engine screaming, chugging out black smoke. He screeched the vehicle to a halt just where we stood.

"Get in yous two!"

* * *

The airport support vehicle bounced and veered as Scotty-Blue drove it north along the Stuart Highway as fast as it could go.

"Blue? Where're we going?"

"We need a battery. I know where to get one," Scotty-Blue shouted over the diesel engine. "The old Camera Shop. It's still there."

As we drove, for most of the way into Alice Springs, there was silence. But Nathan cut the silence, "Tell me it's not true, Blue."

"It'd be good to know what you're on about first, mate." Scotty-Blue shouted over the diesel engine.

"*The Blue Enquiry*. Was that you!"

"Ah, that Cobalt Blue thing. You've had that in you head all this time and couldn't work it out? That's surprises me, Canter. Yeah that was me who leaked to the agencies. It was also me who flew the drone. Any more bloody questions? As if we have the time for this right now. The Camera Shop. That's our objective."

"I thought ASIO shut it down," I offered.

"Nah, Angelique. ASIO sold it to someone. They didn't have the heart to burn it, like you blokes were gonna do. So, they just sold it off and probly at a discount rate, knowin' ASIO."

As we drove north, billows of smoke from the direction of Alice Springs blew up high into the atmosphere. As the support vehicle cut through The Gap, I saw almost the entire township was engulfed in fire. Crowds were rioting and looting on the streets. People were shooting and killing each other. Bodies were strewn all over the ground. Cars had stopped on the sides of the roads, their hoods up, some of them ablaze.

Closer into town, our momentum slowed to a crawl as more and more people gathered on the streets, shouting and screaming, killing with weapons ranging from sticks to automatic assault weapons. There wasn't a shop on the main street with a window intact. Fire was everywhere. The whole place was overwhelmed in upheaval and devastation.

"Why don't they just get in their cars and go?" I asked.

"They probably would, if they could. Notice all the cars on the sides of the roads? They're all late model. That says one thing. Their computer management systems are all dead. That says something else. An EMP attack."

Scotty-Blue put in, "Hence the need for this vehicle. No turbo and no engine management, mate! And we're also lucky, we were in the Faraday shelter when the EMP struck. Otherwise, no bloody laptop neither, eh?"

We finally stopped in front of the old photo shop that looked as though someone had thrown a grenade through the front door. Broken glass was everywhere. Not a spec of anything inside was left untouched. Debris was strewn all over and spewed out into the street.

Nathan got out of the vehicle, Scotty-Blue followed behind him. I was also about to step out.

"No," Nathan called out to me. "Stay with the damn vehicle. Get behind the wheel. Lock the doors. We'll be back in a few moments." Nathan and Scotty-Blue stepped away with the sound of crunching debris under their feet.

Then, people appeared at my window in the numbers, all begging me to take them away from the calamity. They stood at the door and screamed. Someone stepped up behind a woman that was wailing, screaming to please, please, let her in. Then her head exploded, sending blood and brain all over my window. The man who pulled the trigger pointed the shotgun directly at me. "Open the fucken door!" he screamed. "Open the fucken . . ."

CRUNCH!

Someone stepped up behind the man with the shotgun and belt him in the back of the head with a brick. The man with the brick then demanded to be let in, just the same as the dead man with the shotgun, and the woman who lost her head. The man grabbed at the door handle and tried to force it open. He put a boot on the door pillar for leverage. Then, after failing to force the door open, he started pounding on the glass with his fists. By some miracle, the glass didn't break. He kept beating on it. He stepped back, picked up his brick and was poised to throw it. Nathan stepped up behind him and smashed him to the ground.

"Open up, Angel!" Nathan screamed above the noise of the rioting.

My shaking hand went for the door lock and I unlatched it. Nathan and Scotty-Blue flew into the back. "Go! Go! Go!"

I stepped on the accelerator, and the airport support vehicle lurched away.

* * *

Back at Alice Springs airport, Nathan flipped the laptop open, then connected the laptop to the satellite. Scotty-Blue went at the keyboard again. “We’re in,” Scotty-Blue announced. “Just need to log in . . .”

Then.

It happened!

A blinding white flash—brighter than the sun—lit up the sky and everything was turned pure white. I screwed up my face, raised my hands and tried to hide from the heat. Radiant heat! It was all over my body. I felt the burn collapse over my skin. After the white blinding flash faded away, the ever-familiar, forever-threatening mushroom cloud from a nuclear explosion towered up high through the clouds in the distance.

“JESUS!” Nathan screamed. “Not good! Not good! We gotta run!”

“We’re already dead, mate! Look!” Scotty-Blue pointed.

Out there on the horizon, the shockwave rolled across the desert plane. I could see the top of the shockwave mushrooming, pushing over trees as though they were mere toothpicks, picking up dust and debris, racing across the desert at a furious rate. Somehow, I knew, just behind the shockwave was the ear-splitting low roll of the blast that was coming toward us at three hundred and forty-three metres per second.

“NO! NATHAN!”

I ran to Nathan as he put his arms around me and pulled me in. “Angel . . . I’m sorry!” Nathan yelled out over an increasing low rumble that seemed to move my feet sideways in the dirt. I looked up. Already a wind had Nathan’s hair dancing around as though a freight train had rushed past.

“Don’t look!” Nathan yelled over the wind storm. The low rumble intensified. The earth then wanted to kick me over.

Then.

Another blinding white light fell down, once again drowning out all of my vision . . .

I scrunched up my face while trying to see through the pure whiteness. I saw her. How could I not notice her face. The outline of Jenny's face looked down at me.

"JENNY!"

"Get down," Jenny said.

Jenny pushed me onto the ground. The heavy pushing sensation over my body wasn't at all gentle.

In the next split second, the shockwave rolled in, carrying with it the ferocious energy of a thermonuclear blast. I didn't feel anything. I didn't hear anything. And yet, debris of everything, humanmade and natural, flew ferociously past me. It went on for minutes. In went on forever.

When it was over, the entire landscape had changed. Once there was an airport with large buildings and hangars. It all was gone, replaced by a blackened wasteland of debris and carnage. Once there were aircraft parked on the tarmac. They were all gone, replaced by upturned and shredded metal and aluminium. Everything that was once there had disintegrated. Fire had erupted and the radiant heat was intense.

I managed to get up on my feet. Jenny's smiling face was staring down at me. What was I seeing? Jenny appeared to float. Her feet were inches above the ground.

"Jenny?"

"Remember who I am," Jenny said softly. "Remember who I am, Angel."

I remembered the words she'd written on the note she left me. But what did it all mean?

Then, right in front of my eyes, Jenny was no longer Jenny. Jenny shifted her shape into and became as eagle. She lifted into the sky with her wings stretched out. "Remember who I am," she said again as I felt the bursts of air pressure from under her enormous wings. "I am your Angel . . . I am, Azrael."

The archangel Azrael lifted further up under her immense eagle wings, then she became one of seven eagles which were circling as though waiting for her; one of which I couldn't help but notice, was all white.

Nathan finally broke the silence.

"Need to get to cover. Now!"

Before running, I caught sight of Nathan's face. His complexion was burned. His face was a fiery red.

CHAPTER TWENTY-EIGHT

Hard Farewells

AFTER SPRINTING THROUGH SMOKE, FIRE and debris to get to a door that was no longer there, we stepped into the hole in the ground that was once a stairwell. The door at the bottom of the stairwell was lightly damaged, and after clearing a passage through minor rubble, it was easy to pass through.

Nathan placed his hand on Scotty-Blue's shoulder and I place mine of Nathan's as we traversed the total blackness below.

"Blue, what now?" Nathan asked in the stale air of total darkness. "Get us outta here?"

"Mate, follow me. Destiny. All Ambers are at Pine Gap at this point."

"What do you mean, Scotty?" I said. "Pine Gap is gone. It doesn't exist."

"The surface has been wiped away—that's all. The connecting tunnel to the Pine Gap bunker is down 'ere. C'mon. No time to waste," Scotty-Blue said as he somehow managed to find the elevator call button and pressed it. The electric motor kicked over and whirred. The elevator was on the way up, then suddenly, it went dead. Scotty-Blue tapped the button a few more times. "I reckon the power for this wing just got shut down. Not to worry.

We'll 'ave ta take the stairs down. This way, you two. Follow me—an' please don't take ya 'and off me shoulder, eh?"

Scotty-Blue put his eye up to the device and opened the door marked N526—the door that earlier eluded us. Down the flight of stairs we stepped, then another, and another.

"I thought there was no power," Nathan said.

"The doors and scanners are on a different circuit. Just in the case of blackout situations."

We stepped through into a large open space, filled with the glow of amber light. It was good to be able to see again.

"What's this place?" Nathan looked around in obvious amazement, then coughed lightly into his hand.

"Welcome to the lab. Twenty years ago, this was the place where us Ambers got assigned our genetic code. Now, it's used for medical research. I reckon this was the place you blokes were gonna put an axe to, eh? I'd love to stay and chat a while, but youse can see we don't 'ave the time right now." Scotty-Blue paced off again immediately headed down another corridor that was lit up with fluorescent lights. "C'mon people. Keep up, will ya? Sheesh! Times gettin' away."

Nathan reached out and grabbed Scotty-Blue's shoulder, stopping him in his tracks. He again coughed in his hand and cleared his voice.

"Are you okay, Nathan?" I reached up and placed a hand on his face. "My god, you're burning up."

"Was afraid of that," Scotty-Blue said. "You got some heat goin' on inside 'ave ya?"

Nathan nodded. "It's nothing but a cold coming. Nothing I can't handle." As soon as he finished his sentence, Nathan threw up. "Jesus!"

"Nah, mate, you're red as a fire truck. It's more than a cold."

It was as though Nathan knew what Scotty-Blue was talking about. “How much time do I have?”

“Mate, you’ve been kicked in the arse with more than a few thousand rems a second.”

“That didn’t answer my question, Blue.”

I was dumbstruck. Nathan coughed again into his hand. As he pulled his hand away, he tried desperately to hide the blood. “Jesus!”

I raced to Nathan and took both of his hands.

“Not now, Angel. We don’t have the time. You’ll get another chance at the end of where we’re going.”

“You’re not going to die from this. I’ll make sure of it.”

Nathan smiled, looking down at me. He had a certain look in his eyes that I didn’t recognise. It was as though . . .

“C’mon people, we ‘ave to keep movin’. You think this is over? It’s only just started. Feel the tremors at your feet? That’s Melbourne or Sydney or Brisbane going up like a firestorm you’ve never imagined. Maybe they’ve all been hit at the same time. These bunkers are blast-proof, but they’re not waterproof. That’s the real danger we’re lookin’ at.”

“What do you mean water? We’re in the middle of a desert.”

Scotty-Blue stopped and stepped up closer with an urgent expression on his face. “Angelique. *Peacemaker* just carved a crater the size of a half-moon into the ground. Worse than that, the entire Pacific Ocean has been disrupted and a wave you’ve never imagined is heading this way. Frisco is gone. The catastrophe after that is what we’re all trying to avoid. That, combined with all the other nukes going off, what do ya think’s gonna ‘appen? Roughly twenty-three hours. That’s what our pre-modelling ‘as foretold. That’s all we’ve got till up top goes under the waters. Now, we gotta get goin’, because the Gadget is our only chance to escape this hell hole.”

"Go with him, Angel," Nathan said. "Leave me here. I'm just holding you two up.

"Nah, mate. You're comin' too. Our doc can do something for ya. Now, I ain't sayin' he can save ya, but he might be able to stem it long enough to get through to the other side."

"Other side? What other side?"

"Oudarret. That's where the Gadget's gonna take us. But time, people. We have to keep moving."

Nathan coughed again. "I've had a lethal dose, Blue, just like you say. This is it for me. Get going will you."

"Jesus, mate. Stop ya bloody whining. I'm not gonna tell ya you're sounding like a little school girl. If we get ya through the Gadget, who knows what medicine will be available for ya. Maybe the Oudarretians can get ya better. So, stop with the martyr shit, and let's get a fucken move on, eh?"

I relaxed a little and placed a hand on Scotty-Blue's back, urging him on. Nathan coughed again in a fit, before picking up the pace.

Down more flights of stairs we traversed, then it levelled out through more corridors and small passageways. We walked on at route-march pace. Nathan fell behind and began limping badly. I ran back to him and raised his arm around my shoulder.

"I can fix you now, Nathan. Let me help you. Please."

"No time right now. You'll have your chance later. I promise."

As I helped him along, Nathan gripped his chest as though he was in pain. Lesions had already started to appear on his face, and the whites of his eyes yellowed to a dark shade, with the redness of burst capillaries.

I'd had enough. "No. Stop. We do this now."

As I stopped and helped Nathan balance, Scotty-Blue raced back toward us. "C'mon! They'll leave without us. Can't risk being left behind."

We trudged on but I was more worried than ever. Nathan was getting worse as every second went past. We needed a moment for me to tune in to my healing powers. I could fix him, right here and now. But it was precious moments we didn't have. We had to keep moving.

At last, we came to a large double door that was labelled J.D.F.P.G. We went through to an underground rail car network that sprawled out into the distance. The air was musty and smelled like coal. Scotty-Blue reached out and pressed a button that was raised on a steel post just short of the doorway. We waited a few moments. A few moments more. "Looks like the powers been cut down 'ere too," Scotty-Blue said. "Damn it. We'll need to walk down the line. I reckon our mob are already in the process of leaving for the Gadget. Gotta make this quick, people!"

I sucked back breath as I strutted along, angry at myself only because the moments we waited could have been used helping Nathan. I fumed from under my skin. Why didn't I do anything? It was an opportunity that was missed.

Scotty-Blue turned and got under Nathan's other arm.

"It's no good, Angel," Nathan grunted. His stride slowed to almost a crawl. "I'm just holding you up. Please. Get going. The both of you."

"Nah, mate. Not havin' it. Stop ya girlie shit and move your arse."

"Thanks, Scotty," I said. "He's a bit of a pain in the backside at times."

Nathan coughed again. Blood trailed from the corners of his mouth. He placed his hand to his mouth, and when he pulled it away, some of his teeth had come loose and fell out, landing in the palm of his hand. He flicked them away in disgust and they scattered against the tunnel wall, clicking and echoing as they fell. We trudged on.

Finally, under floodlight at the far distant end of the tunnel, I saw the silhouettes of figures walking around. "Hello!" I called out. "We need help!"

"Who's there?" a voice instantly demanded.

"Calm down," Scotty-Blue shouted back. "Amber N526-269, Scott Thomson, and company of two. And yeah, we need some bloody help down 'ere, mate."

The figure in the distance relaxed his weapon to his side and jogged down the tunnel toward us. Two other figures at his rear, ran to the sound of booted feet echoing around the tunnel. They held up their weapons again as they got closer, looking at us from down their sights.

"I said company of two! That means they're with me, you fucken dope."

One figure stepped a little closer and scanned us. The man was Oudarretian. There was doubt in my mind. "Not authorised," he said. "Scott Thompson, this way. You two . . . this is as far as you go."

"As I said, they're with me. The lady 'appens to be the daughter of Franco 269. That's authority enough, don't ya reckon?"

"Bunjil?" the man sounded genuinely surprised. He moved in a little closer, peering at me. "Are you're sure?"

Scotty-Blue gestured for me to tuck my hair around my ear. "Go on. Show the man, Angelique."

As I sighed and flicked my hair around my ear, another tremor hit. It was enough to make me wonder if mother nature had begun her fightback. It was strong enough to loosen the dust from the tunnel walls, and a cloud of white powder sprinkled down on us.

At the same time, I was surprised by the Oudarretian stepping back in pure amazement. Then he stepped up closer squinting his eyes. He lifted a hand to my left ear and I instantly smacked it away.

As if reading my thoughts, Scotty-Blue intervened. “Don’t worry. We have other Os on our side. Such are the ways of human nature,” Scotty-Blue chuckled. “But now we ‘ave our Angel of Bunjil—it’s gonna lift the spirits of many a thousand.”

“What makes you think I’m this so-called Angel of Bunjil? And what makes you think I even *want* to be this person?”

“It’s destiny, Angelique. Destiny. C’mon then, there’s not much time.”

* * *

By the time Nathan found a gurney in the medical ward, I was at his side, gripping his fiery hand. A young Amber doctor by the name of Lang administered morphine to take the pain from his internal blaze. Nathan’s once flowing hair was patchy, and most had fallen away. His eyes were seriously bloodshot and sunken. His face was covered in burns and lesions that oozed a strange orange/red sticky liquid. His lips were cracked, and most teeth were already missing. The sores had spread from his face to his body and limbs. Large boils had developed at the base of his neck and chest. I was incredibly sad, looking down at him. He tried to speak as soon as it appeared he found the strength. I don’t know what I must’ve looked like to him. I did my level best to keep that in check. I knew he didn’t need to know my sorrow.

It was only a moment before, Nathan objected to my helping him. He refused me of any healing I could give him. Sadly, he pushed me away with just one word that escaped him. The word, Teresa. And as soon as he said, it I understood completely.

As he tried to speak again, I placed my hand softly on his lips. “Shhh. Don’t speak.” I passed him a glass of water and helped him to drink. He took a sip and coughed. The fit lasted much longer this time. He winced, as blood appeared, and I wiped it away. He looked up at me again through the eyes of someone who was at the very edge of his life.

"Angel," Nathan said hoarsely, as though trying to stem another fit of coughing.

I leaned slightly forward and peered down at him through my watery eyes. "Please don't speak," I whispered gently. "Save your strength, Nathan."

"I see her. I see my Teresa. She . . ."

Nathan smiled for a second, then he coughed again. More blood. I again dabbed at it with a moistened hand towel.

"Angel . . . We've had a wild ride, you and me."

It was as though he fought for every letter in the words he'd just told me. He smiled as though more for his success, than at getting the words out. He coughed hard again but this time there was a rattle in his chest I couldn't ignore. It made my tears flow in a stream. "Yeah. We did . . . didn't we."

Nathan's breathing heaved and the rattling sounds of liquid in his lungs got louder. I placed my hands on my face and tried desperately not to bawl like a baby.

Nathan raised a hand, reached up and placed the back of his blood engorged fingers on my cheek. "Don't be sad, Angel. One day, the entire world will step aside for you. And you'll be with me again. You'll be with me and Teresa."

I was surprised by his words. I wanted to show strength for Nathan. Somehow, I knew I'd not manage it much longer. But my internal desire wanted only for Nathan to be at peace, and without pain. I looked up to the doctor and nodded.

More morphine was delivered into Nathan's central line, and Nurse Rosemary Keane nodded and stepped away without a word. The beeps and chirps of equipment began to slow in the background. Nathan, I knew, was only moments away from his last breath.

I looked down at him lying there, his chest rising and falling. He went to say something again, but I relaxed him from his words with a soft touch to his lips. “It’s okay. I’ll be fine. You may go and find peace, my good friend.”

Nathan’s lips curled into a smile, and I recognised his grin. It took me back to happier times. Only Nathan could smile in that way. All of my memories with Nathan flooded back to my senses. All of the memories of those years together flashed past as I sat looking down at him. The battle had begun to keep my sadness in check. Another tear came. It sat at the edge of my eyelid and lingered. I blinked, and it fell away, landing on Nathan’s fiery red and boiled skin. “It’s okay. I’ll be fine,” I said again smiling down at him for the last time.

Nathan closed his eyes. His chest raised and fell slightly before his life quietly left him through a last rush of air.

Nathan, my lifelong friend, was gone.

CHAPTER TWENTY-NINE

Mother Nature Always Wins

DOCTOR LANG STOOD BEHIND me in the underground medical clinic. Behind the doctor, Rosemary Keane placed her hand on my shoulder and comforted me, I already knew, as best she could as I wailed openly for Nathan. The doctor had done all he could do, bringing comfort and taking pain away from Nathan, and I was thankful for his efforts. However, already, the sense of urgency in the air and was something I tried hard to push aside.

"A few more moments, please," I asked, Rosemary Keane. She leaned forward over the body of Nathan and positioned his hands across his chest, in the same way an Egyptian pharaoh might be laid down to rest in his sarcophagus. She glanced respectfully at her wristwatch. "Take as long as you need," Rosemary said. I placed my crystal eagle figurine down on Nathan's chest. I leaned over and kissed him lightly on his forehead before my sobs erupted all over again.

I made a silent promise before I left him. I promised that some day I will return. And when I do, I will find Nathan's remains and give him the burial he deserves. This was my vow. And it was written in stone.

* * *

I followed Scotty-Blue down the tunnel to another huge open space that was lit up under large florescent lighting. Ambers—both men and women, some with children—crowded around the base of six Chinook helicopters that were parked side by side. It all became clear at that moment. In big letters, down the sides of each Chinook were the letters, '*USS John Steinbeck.*' I realised I was standing among friends and a well thought out plan by the Americans that will come in to play many years from now.

The Chinooks stood in silence as the human cargo began to load from the rears. Oddly, escaping from this place was the last thing on my mind. If things were different, I wouldn't even consider it. But what was left for me now? The entire surface of the planet was under siege. The death of billions was at hand. Millions upon millions of lives had already passed. And my thoughts returned to Maggie and Christina. What had become of them? Were they alive or not? And after I gave it some thought, I knew without question they had to be among the dead.

There was no longer a reason for me to hang on to anything I used to be. I'm no longer Angel, the kick arse journalist. I'm no longer the girl who lives in Melbourne. As I got my head around it, I realised the importance of Breakers. Could I be the one to lead them all to their destiny? Am I the one who they should follow willingly into battle? No, there was no longer a reason to hang on to my past any longer. From this moment on, The Angel I once was . . . is gone.

As I stood among the hundreds of orange-haired humans making a queue to get on the Chinooks, already murmurs filled the space around the immense underground hangar. People turned and faced me as I walked to my calling. One by one, they placed their hands on their hearts. One by one, they stepped back a few paces, and space opened up for me to walk through.

Scotty-Blue gave me a sideways glance and smiled. "Destiny, Angelique. They're all realising your presence as you walk among us."

Suddenly, another earthquake hit that was much stronger than before. The Chinook helicopters danced sideways on their suspension. Dust came down in a cloud, and orange-headed people coughed as it sprinkled on top of them.

I took a few paces forward, and the crowd of Ambers responded by making a path clear, all the while holding hands on their hearts.

"What's the sign they're making?" I whispered. "Surely that's not because of me."

"It is," Scotty-Blue smiled. "It's their mark of respect, and honour for Bunjil."

"You make me sound like I'm some kind of chosen one. What if I'm not?"

"You'll know yourself soon enough. But we already know about The Angel of Bunjil. Now, they've made way for you. The least you can do now is respect their honour. Go Angelique. Walk through your followers."

Another earthquake hit the bunker which was strong enough to toss people off their feet. The scent of kerosene thickened in the air as the Chinooks were being fuelled. I walked the small distance to the first Chinook arriving at the rear door. People with bright orange hair reached out and touched me as I walked among them. "Bunjil . . . Bunjil . . ." they chanted softly to themselves.

Just before stepping aboard, I heard an urgent voice.

"Dad!"

After I spun around and saw the woman running up behind us, I immediately recognised her face. There was no doubt in my mind. It was the air hostess I'd met on the aircraft up from Melbourne.

"Angel. This is my daughter, Natalie-Jade," Scotty-Blue said.

I put my hand out and shook hers. Natalie-Jade smiled at me as though she knew me, intimately. "Glad you could make it along with us, Angel. I'm sorry about what went down after you left the Melbourne. We did try to warn you. If it wasn't for the turbulence, we might've got you and Nathan out of harm's way. But I heard you had that sorted without too much trouble."

"You said you were from Nebraska."

"A throwaway line. I couldn't tell you the truth, could I? And If I told you I lived in a hole in the ground at Pine Gap, *what* would you have thought then?"

I thought about it and she was right. There wasn't anything in my mind that could've registered had she told me the truth.

"Nat," Scotty-Blue cut in. "I thought you've got up top sorted out."

"Sorry, Dad. The blast-proof roof. It won't open."

"You've gotta to be kidding me, love. Why?"

"I think there's debris stopping the roof from sliding open. We've disengaged the clamps. Everything's jammed."

"Cripes!" Scotty-Blue shouted out loud and people stopped boarding the Chinooks. "And I'm guessin' by ya expression the escape shafts are also blocked?"

Natalie-Jade nodded. "There's no way up there to see what the problem is. The cameras up top have been knocked out, so there's just no way of knowing one way or another."

Scotty-Blue began to pace around. His white complexion drained even further. After everything that went on, now it's a real threat that everyone might drown.

I tapped Scotty-Blue on the shoulder. "I'll go up there and see what the problem is."

"How, Angelique? There's no way up. If the roof won't open, we're all trapped down 'ere."

"The airport end of the tunnel," I said. "Nathan and I brought explosives with us. It's in our bergens back at the other end. I can use it to clear the debris from up top."

"But there's no time."

"There *is* time if you divert power back to the rail car. I can take it back down there and get the Semtex."

Scotty-Blue stood there and thought it over. "Even if you could get to the Semtex, ya still can't go up top because the shafts are blocked."

"It's not blocked at the other end, Scotty. We'll walk cross-country to Pine Gap."

"That's ten bloody Ks."

"What choice do we have? I need to try." I turned to Natalie-Jade. "Open the blast-proof roof after I clear the debris away. You can pick me up from up there."

* * *

Scotty-Blue me, as we raced toward the Pine Gap bunker entrance. Stepping out in front of us was nurse Rosemary Keane. I called out to her as she ducked out of sight. She didn't look back.

"Where in the heck is she going?"

"I dunno, love. But we need to keep focused. Time is getting away."

Leaping from the entrance door, we emerged into a darkened underground rail car tunnel. The car was waiting for us with its internal red lamps glowing. We jumped aboard. Scotty-Blue went for the controls, pressed a few buttons, and wrenched at a lever. The car lurched forward, slowly at first, then picked up speed as the wheels clacked and squealed on long steel rails.

"You'll need ya HAZMAT, Angelique," Scotty-Blue said, handing me a parcel from under the seat. "We'll be at the other end before you know it."

"I won't need it. I didn't need it before. Why would I need it now?"

"It's gonna be crazy hot up there. The HAZMAT will give ya some insulation."

I took it and opened up the package. "Can I ask you something, Scotty?"

"Yeah, what is it?"

"Can you please stop calling me that name? I'm Angel, not Angelique."

Scotty-Blue looked back at me with a half-smile. "Yeah. Okay then . . . Angel. It's kinda ironic, isn't it?"

"What is?"

"What 'appened up there? What we saw before."

"You're talking about Jenny?"

Scotty-Blue nodded. "Y'know, I wouldn't 'ave believed it if I didn't see it with me own eyes. Do ya think . . . Nah, forget it. That's for another time."

"Why Jenny didn't save Nathan from the radiation? Jenny saved us all from the nuclear blast. I think it was my job to heal Nathan from radiation sickness but he didn't let me do it."

"Yeah I know love. I reckon Nathan already knew he was a goner. So that being what it is, I reckon 'e was lookin' forward to peace with Teresa. That's why 'e never let you heal 'im."

"He spent his entire life alone. I'm just now learning why? I thought it was because of me."

"Oh? Nathan never talked about Teresa with ya?"

"Not even once. I don't know who she is. All I know is that she must've been part of Nathan's life somehow."

"That's a shame 'e never shared it with ya, Angel. Nathan and Teresa were very much in love with each other."

"What happened to her?"

"She died. Nathan shot her in the 'ead."

"WHAT?"

"It's a story for another time, love. But the fact Nathan spent the rest of 'is life alone tells of 'is love for her. It also tells of 'is guilt with the way 'e 'ad ta end 'er life. Shockin' as the truth is."

"I think perhaps Nathan's story isn't over," I added. "Don't ask me how I know. Intuition maybe. But I can't believe he could just end this way. It doesn't seem right." Then I thought about the figurine I left him. The figurine that was given to me by Jenny. By Azrael. It's not the end. He might be deceased in body. Something told me, Nathan's spirit will never die.

The car arrived at the end of the tunnel, coming to an abrupt halt. After we dressed in our HAZMAT suits, and under the green glow of NVGs with our trusty SA-80s, we travelled through the adjoining corridor and upstairs, until finally, we were at the location where Nathan and I had left our bergens. I was relieved to find the Semtex and detonators still there. On my travel down the tunnel, the horrible thought of someone coming into the airport bunker and stealing the explosives had played on my mind. We left the darkened room and began the journey to the surface.

CHAPTER THIRTY

Nuclear Winter, Acid Rain

WE STEPPED OUT OF THE BUNKER AND made our way up a flight of stairs, out into smouldering wasteland that smelled thickly of death and destruction.

"Hey. I thought you said it was gonna be hot up here. It's snowing."

"Not snow," Scotty-Blue said as he held out his hand. I did the same. The flakes floated down into my open palm. I closed my hand and the flakes fell away in fine particles of dust.

"Is it ash?"

"Yeah," Scotty-Blue said. "It's ash comin' down. And it's a lot cooler than I first thought. Probly a good thing. We've got a bit of a hike in front of us. We can't stay out here too long, though. The nuclear winter is comin'. The temperature will drop below zero before too long."

"Which way is it?" I asked. "I can't see more than thirty metres out. It's like a blizzard."

"It *is* a blizzard in a sense. Instead of snowflakes, ash flakes. Boggles the mind, eh? C'mon. Let's get going. I reckon we'll head directly west of 'ere, and reach the road going into Pine Gap. Then it's just a matter of followin' the road in."

We trudged along the scorched earth that was absolutely littered with debris. We passed trees that were no longer trees, but blackened trucks that stuck out of the ground—some still smouldered, and smoke billowed straight up in the strange stillness. Some trees were still well alight with fire and crackled as we stepped past into the grey.

Finally, we found the road to Pine Gap. We followed the dirt track that disappeared into more ash fall. We walked on, following the edge of the track into the distance. Then another earthquake hit and was strong enough to knock me off my feet. The ground rolled and bumped and went sideways beneath me as I sat dazed from the force that had planted me square on my backside.

"You okay?" I yelled out Scotty-Blue. He responded with thumbs up as the earth beneath me settled again.

"We have to move," Scotty-Blue muffled back. "We're most definitely running out of time."

I got to my feet just in time to see a pack of angry, snarling dingoes racing towards us. "Watch out!" I yelled. I aimed my weapon and squeezing off shots that silenced the dingo's rushing attack.

"Jesus, Angel!" Scotty-Blue hopped backward, as a dead dingo skidded to a halt just short of where he stood.

I stepped toward the dead dingoes and looked down at them. They were severely burned. Their skin was covered in open red sores, and radiation burns. I kneeled down and placed a hand on each of them, stopping momentarily to show my dismay. "It's sad that wildlife has to suffer like this," I said before moving on again.

"Time, Angel," Scotty-Blue said.

Overhead in the distance, the thumping sounds of helicopters cut through the silence. I suffered an incredible sinking feeling. The feeling that they'd succeeded getting the blast-proof roof open, and now they were headed away. I stopped and looked up toward the thumping rotor noises as they trailed off into the distance. Scotty-Blue raced back and gripped my arm, pulling me forward. “C’mon Angel. We have to move.”

“They’re leaving!”

“No. That’s another bunker heading for the Gadget.”

“There’s another bunker around here?”

“Not here. Nurrungar. How I’d love to shoot those mongrels out of the sky. Now c’mon,” Scotty-Blue muffled, grabbing me by the arm and pulling me forward.

The track ended at the entrance to Pine Gap. It was a sobering site. The ground at my feet crunched as I walked toward the debris field. I looked down and noticed the dirt was no longer dirt, but glass. It crunched as though walking in snow. However, there was no crater, as I was half-expecting to see. I wondered where the impact crater was. Then I realised, if the impact crater was at Pine Gap, there’d probably be no sign of any bunker below. And most likely, no debris field to deal with.

As we got closer, the debris thickened with steel girder work twisted up like plasticine scattered around. Large sheets of iron and glass fragments littered the place. Military vehicles, large and small, were tossed around and upended on their roofs. All of them smouldering, with black smoke rising up. Then, there were the body parts that was horrifying to see. It made me baulk in my place, only to be edged forward again by Scotty-Blue’s tugging at my HAZMAT suit.

Another earthquake hit, and this time the ground cracked and opened. One part rose while the other part fell away. Dirt and dust went flying off as I once again was left planted on my rear.

“I don’t like this,” I muffled out after the ground settled once again.

"That's why we 'ave to get this done quickly, Angel. Gawdsake!"

We arrived at the blast-proof roof just as it started to rain. The rain fell with the cracking of overhead thunderclaps. Strange thick globs of black grossness fell on my yellow HAZMAT. Black liquid stuff that looked more like crude oil. The noise of the rainfall on my suit seemed to drown my voice short of yelling. At last, I could see what was preventing the roof from opening. The debris was heaped in a pile—almost as if it were purposefully placed there by some God of wrath. Steel pylons twisted and distorted, mixed with materials that were once large buildings, sat on top of a burned-out and wrecked semitrailer, all heaped in a pile of calamity and destruction. Somewhere below the rubble was the blast proof roof, and under that, a new chance at making things right in some distant future. It all had to be somehow cleared away with all but a few small slabs of Semtex.

We set about placing the charges under a grey sky that spat gritty black globs of ugliness back down.

"One chance at this," Scotty-Blue muffled over the increasing sound of the deadly black rain. "We have to make sure the charges are laid, so it pushes the debris clear. Not up in the air and straight back down."

The charges were laid strategically enough. Sufficiently for the job. We strutted awkwardly away, far enough away to seek protection from when it all goes bang.

Holding the detonation device in my grip, I wondered if it would do the job. "Get down," I yelled out to Scotty-Blue. As soon as I saw he was down, I twisted the knob.

An almighty explosion drilled through the ground and caused me to fall over backwards. Dust leaped up into the air and blocked out my vision. But with the sound of debris landing somewhere out there, it was welcoming to my ears.

Momentarily after everything settled, Scotty-Blue and I returned to the blast proof roof and waited.

* * *

The roof gave way and began to retract with metallic screeches ringing out as it slid. The first sign of success was the sound of applause erupting from way down there. The next sign was the sound of turbofan engines spooling up. But there was another sound not so welcoming. The sound of water. The sound of the sea. Out in the distance, it was rushing toward us.

CHAPTER THIRTY-ONE

The Plan

I LOOKED OUT TO HORIZON THE MOMENT the first Chinook lifted up through the blast proof roof, with its enormous twin props thumping. I could see to the north-east where the crest of a wave had formed and as I focused, I knew it would only be moments before this place is swamped; probably forever. It was coming just as Scotty-Blue predicted, raging along the desert plane. From my view, the wave seemed small. But somehow I knew, it was anything but.

"C'mon Angel," Scotty-Blue yelled with his HAZMAT undone from the top and now dangled from waist. "This way."

The Chinook promptly landed not far from where we stood waiting. The rear door opened slowly and I willed it on hoping to speed things along. After we were finally aboard, we had barely found a seat before I heard the engines scream and then I felt the Chinook virtually leap into the sky from a standing position. The twin rotors thumping hard and I was jostled as the aircraft rolled hard left.

As we climbed, all I could think about was all those people who'd died. For the first time in all of this, I began to feel a sense of anger. It wasn't fair at all that the human race had to end in such a way. In my mind, I saw myself for the very first time as a leader and I would indeed lead my people back to their right to have their redemption. If this was my calling, so be it. If this was the way to return our species to Earth in the distant future? Then *I* will be the one to lead them. This is my oath. This is my vow and I will make this happen, or I will die with my enemy on the field of battle.

Rotating to the south-west, the nose of the Chinook dipped before accelerating and climbing higher. As we tracked, the vision of the ocean rushing in was replaced by smoke fire and debris. Destruction was everywhere and I just couldn't believe the carnage. As the Chinook reached higher altitudes, so did my wanting for revenge. The anger inside me, I knew, I had to channel into a positive energy and save it all for another day. But even so, rattles and vibrations with the scent of jet fumes filled the cabin space and invaded my thoughts of seeking retribution.

Scotty-Blue took his seat before grabbing a headset, while gesturing to me to grab for an identical pair. After I plugged it in and placed it over my ears, I was on the same channel as all the other voices on board.

Scotty-Blue reached and twisted a knob then did the same with mine. "It'll be a while," he said. "Let's 'ope we make it to the Gadget on time."

"What happens if we don't?"

After appearing to be away in his thoughts momentarily, he said, "In that case, we go due south."

"South? where? Everything will go under the water, won't it?"

"Yep. But there's another place that's been set up for just in case. Somethin' that was worked out if in the case the Gadget gets to be out of the question. Kangaroo Island. The Breakers built a bunker system down there. It's big enough for all of us should things turn out shit. It's a fully decked out back-up plan with life support ready to take us on if the Gadget is compromised."

"But it'll be underwater for God knows how long."

"That's the thing, Angel. Pre-modelling didn't show any sign of water going up to it. That's why it was considered. Also, there's somethin' else."

"What?"

"Ambers are to settle there, on Kangaroo Island when we get back. We start there. It's set up, but the passin' of time is the problem. No one knows if the bunker system will still be viable after so many years. As it is now, it's fully decked out and ready, but nobody knows what'll 'appen over the next one 'undred and fifty years. The Earth will most likely start to reclaim everythin'. Also, there's the threat that it might become overrun by survivors. And it doesn't matter what anybody thinks. I still reckon that there might be people who've survived all of this shit. Y'know?"

I remembered Nathan's drawing and what he'd told me all that time ago. It came back slowly.

"Nathan told me, Oudarret is ten thousand light years away."

"Ya spot on, love."

"And yet humans will return in only one hundred and fifty years? That's not making any sense."

"Well, Angel. It depends on who's technology ya using. If using our technology, ya lookin' at a twenty thousand year return trip. And that's at the speed of light."

"I knew that already. What I cant understand is the one hundred and fifty year return trip."

"That's because we're using the Os technology. The Gadget is a neutrino particle acceleration cannon. Or, N-PAC. It converts matter into subatomic particles and then shoots the particle stream into deep space way beyond the speed of light. That way, we get to span vast distances." Scotty-Blue went on, "But never forget,

Angel. The Os are our enemy. The Os, the As, and the Gs. We'll live among them because that's the plan with the Breakers. But there'll be the day when we bring the fuckers down. Every last one of the bastards."

"So, when we get to where we're going, we're all operating undercover?"

"We're already *are* undercover. How do ya reckon we're passin' through the Gadget? We're all dinky-die Ambers to those blokes. Won't they get a big fucken surprise, eh?"

"But what about me? I don't look like an Amber."

Scotty-Blue nodded to his daughter, Natalie-Jade who was a few seats away and gave her a wink. It seemed Scotty-Blue had worked this problem out a long time ago. Natalie-Jade reached into her bag and got out a set of battery-powered clippers. I knew then, my hair would have to go.

"Dun worry, Angel. It'll grow back, and we'll make sure it's coloured proper. In the meantime, we've got ya sorted with a wig. It's bloody real 'uman hair too. Natalie-Jade went to so much trouble, y'know?" Scotty-Blue smiled.

CHAPTER THIRTY-TWO

The Gadget

THE PLACE JUST NORTH OF MUNDRABILLA, in Western Australia, came into view after several hours of travelling in a steady south-westerly direction.

By the time we arrived, my ears were ringing from the noise inside the cabin. I was feeling very giddy from the ever present scent of jet fumes. My backside was numb from the hard, uncomfortable seats. But even so, I'd made several new friends along the journey, all of whom were adorned with the shiny red, glowing hair, and white skin almost the colour of milk, dotted with an abstract pattern of freckles.

Scotty-Blue had introduced me to a handful of his associates who were senior members of the Partisan group known as The Breakers. Those souls were all hardened to the task of seeking revenge for the collapse of the Earth's human race. All through my introductions and conversations with these people, I felt our cause become was more and more justified. I listened to their conversations through my headset, with an ever growing enthusiasm and an ever increasing will to do battle and put to them to death once and for all.

* * *

Out of all the people I met while traveling on the Chinook, one who interested me the most was an Amber woman. Natalie-Jade introduced me to Ruby Cross. Ruby was a science officer, and she was helpful giving me a heads-up as to what to expect when I finally make my way through the N-PAC, and into another world, another future, and another time that was so far away.

“How do you know it to be so?” I asked, after grabbing Ruby on a private channel. “Have you been through it?”

“No,” Ruby said. “Of course not. But my position in science, and from what I’ve learned about Oudarretian technology, I’m more than sure that I’m spot on.”

“So, it’s the pulling sensation you feel? Nothing more than that?”

Ruby smiled. “Yep. Just a slight tug and that’s it. Then you’re spewed out the other end.”

“Do you know what’s on the other side?”

“Yes. I’ve been given detailed info.”

“Let me guess, you’re not gonna tell me, are you?”

“Nope. It’s a surprise. And I’m not going to spoil your adventure.”

Then, it was the laugh that immediately attracted me to Ruby. The laugh was exactly the same as Jenny’s laugh.

“Tell me about you?” Ruby asked me, smiling in the way I just happened to adore. “Tell me about who Angel is, and where she grew up. All that stuff.”

I was about to answer Ruby’s personal inquiry when I happened to look out of the window and noticed so many Chinook helicopters advancing toward the N-PAC, down there at Mundrabilla. “There’s so many of them. I had no idea.”

“Oh yes, you’ll see how many when we arrive.”

"Arrive down there?"

Ruby laughed and shook her head. "No, silly. I mean after we arrive at Perseus. At Oudarret."

"East Kandesh?"

Ruby's eyes widened. "You knew?"

"Scotty-Blue told me."

I didn't know why I asked it, let alone thought it, but when it came out, it surprised us both equally. "It won't . . . hurt, will it?"

Ruby smiled and placed a comforting hand on my knee. "No, Angel. It won't hurt a bit. I promise." Ruby then launched into her logical scientific tone. "The particle separation is exactly what it means. You'll have no memory of the event. So, there's no pain. And it'll seem instant just like a dream." She took her hand away from my knee. Something inside me gave me the willies. That feeling of butterflies. I felt giddy and sweaty. Exactly the same way I felt after Jenny . . . No, this is too soon. Way too soon.

But I couldn't ignore it. Could this be another first time? Could this be the start of something again? Out of all the sadness, and death, and destruction; something nice? Maybe it was something to feel happy about all over again. A new beginning. A new life, and a new adventure just over the edge of the horizon. All the options are just waiting, just over there. I could almost reach out and touch it. Then, I thought about the Ambers who considered me as their chosen one. The Bunjil. The Breakers wanted nothing short of vengeance for the global death and destruction of humankind. I was now convinced I could lead them and become part of their vengeance. But now? when it appeared a happier life might be just dawning?

"Penny for your thoughts?" Ruby asked, eyeing me inquiringly.

"There's so much to do."

"What're you saying, Angel?"

"Being Bunjil. The responsibility of it all. Everything is happening so fast. I'm so exhausted. I . . ."

"It's okay," Ruby cut in. "Rest. You deserve the rest. There's a brand-new world for you. Welcome it into your heart and rest. Our people will understand."

As the Chinook began to descend, my breath began to shorten, and my heart rate picked up. The palms of my hands became clammy and sticky, my mouth suddenly went dry. I looked out the window again, and I saw for the first time what I'd heard about from Scotty-Blue. The N-PAC everybody talked about was down there.

Two towering radomes rose from the ground—the same radomes that once existed around a place that was once called Pine Gap. And between them was a steady, pulsing, glow of blue light. Below the radomes were a series of lights that lit up the twilight sky. Chinooks in the dozens had already arrived and landed— and their passengers with their shiny red hair and pale milky skin had already stepped through for the new world.

After our Chinook had landed in what I supposed was a predetermined position away from the N-PAC, the rear door opened and everyone stood. Some groaned audibly, as they stood for the first time in several hours. I stood and I realised my leg muscles refused to cooperate.

I left the Chinook in the same way as I left my home Earth. Ruby took me by my hand. We both stepped through the N-PAC together without looking back.

CHAPTER THIRTY-THREE

Greater Things

UNDER THE SHADE OF A TOWERING tree we all referred to as a Hadgitol, I sat among the thorny rough grasses on a hill overlooking the East Kandesh Citadel. I looked out across the thickly vegetated valley, to the snow-covered peaks in the distance. Just above the horizon, the huge fireball hung low and would stay there—not rise, nor fall.

On Oudarret, to see the stars, travel was required. To feel the cold, or the heat, or to see the numerous galaxies at night, travelling to other locations was the only way. Soon after I came to the place, I learned the rotation of Oudarret was locked in a dance where the same face of the planet faced the sun at all times. It was difficult to get used to in the beginning. Sleeping at night and waking in the morning was an Earth human biorhythm that wasn't easily changed.

But I *did* change.

Nadine was down at the bottom of the hill, about a hundred metres away. Nadine, my daughter, with her face the mirror of her father, Andrew, played and laughed with her pet Adakol she'd named Poppet. It warmed my heart to see her so happy. I smiled contentedly while smelling the sweet air as it drifted in from the mountains behind.

One day, Poppet will carry my daughter away. From where I sat viewing, Poppet was a creature resembling an old-Earth animal known as a dog. That will change. With one leg in front and one in back, it will grow to the size of a living being once known as a horse. Nadine will share most of her life with her Adakol. And, there'll be a time soon for Poppet to be trained in the way old-Earth humans once trained their beasts to carry them.

"Nadine's growing up, isn't she," Ruby said.

"Yeah, she is. Too fast. It's much too fast, Rubes. It seems like only yesterday when she was born."

"Eighty wind cycles. Where did that time go?"

"Nadine! Don't tease your Adakol! Play nice!" I shouted down the hill.

A young voice answered, "I'm not teasing her, Mummy. Poppet's not playing nice with me. That's all."

"You know we've got to get her into school soon," Ruby interrupted me. I glanced sideways to Ruby. "I thought we've discussed this already."

"We did, but you seem to keep dodging the subject whenever I bring it up. There's no certain answer, yes, no or otherwise."

I said nothing. I realised I *was* dodging the subject. Living among our enemy wasn't too hard so long as I kept the colour in my hair. It seemed I was accepted and melted into the crowds of Non-Breakers easy enough. But if Nadine went to school, it would mean only one thing. I'd lose her for the rest of my life.

Then, my thoughts drifted back to Nathan and the oath I made. I knew I'd find him again but how? When all that land is now under the ocean.

"See? Your silence is deafening," Ruby said.

"I know. It's just . . ."

"What?"

"I made a promise. To Nathan. And to the Breakers. Ruby going to school seems to complicate things."

"I see. But you realise school isn't forever and your commitment with the Breakers doesn't have to be right away."

"I never wanted to be settled here, Rubes. Not in the beginning at least. I always thought going back was the priority with The Breakers. I thought you'd be with me on going back. I know you've changed your mind, being happy here and all. But Nadine going into school . . .? I'll miss her. If I go, I'll never see her again."

"Whatever gave you that idea? Of course, I'll go with you. *We'll* go with you. We're a family. I haven't talked about it as openly as you. And you're right. I do love it here. But I'll be glad to go back home again. Nadine will come with us."

"She can't, Rubes. You know she can't. We both know as soon as she steps onto the surface, she'll get radiation sickness."

"There's a way," Ruby said. "Even though Nadine isn't an Amber, we'll find a way. What was it that Nathan told you once?"

I nodded, then smiled. "Yeah. One day, the entire world will step aside for me."

ABOUT THE AUTHOR

Carl Lakeland lives with his wife in the sleepy town of Snake Valley, 36 kilometres south west of Ballarat in Australia.

Lakeland grew up during the early seventies western suburbs of Sydney. Having enlisted into the military at the age of seventeen, he draws on his experience to create powerful and engaging speculative fiction

"Sometimes, I can't let things be," says Lakeland. "I write stories with passion that others might see as being obsessive. I live and breathe it. I dream it when I sleep. But I never write down my dreams. If I can't remember those things I've dreamt, they're not important enough."

Carl Lakeland's stories revolve around the element of 'what if?' He pushes the boundaries of his stories to the edge of the *Official Secrets Act,* which will have the reader wondering about the aspect of creative licence, or the possibility of fact in his writing. Either way, the reader will be left to make up their own mind. His books are fast paced, edge of your seat thrillers which are distinctively written in a way that will have the reader guessing which way the story is about to head.

"As a writer, unpredictability is key essence. If I write something that can be foreseen in coming chapters, it's not good enough. I will scrap it. My goal is to keep the reader wondering, even sometimes to the detriment of my good guys!"

www.ingramcontent.com/pod-product-compliance
Lightning Source LLC
Chambersburg PA
CBHW030826310726
48980CB00006B/648/J

* 9 7 8 0 9 8 7 6 1 9 8 9 1 *